PENGUIN ESSENTIALS

COLD COMFORT FARM

Stella Gibbons was born in London in 1902. She went to North London Collegiate School and studied journalism at University College, London. She then worked for ten years on various papers, including the *Evening Standard*. Her first publication was a book of poems, *The Mountain Beast* (1930), and her first novel, *Cold Comfort Farm* (1932), won the Femina Vie Heureuse Prize. Amongst her other novels are *Miss Linsey and Pa* (1936), *Nightingale Wood* (1938), *Westwood* (1946), *Conference at Cold Comfort Farm* (1949) and *Beside the Pearly Water* (1954). Stella Gibbons died in 1989.

Mark Hearld was born in York in 1974. He studied illustration at Glasgow College of Art and then completed a master's degree in natural history illustration at the Royal College of Art. He works across a number of mediums, producing limited edition lithographic and linocut prints, unique paintings, collages and hand-painted ceramics.

Cold Comfort Farm

STELLA GIBBONS

PENGUIN BOOKS

PENGUIN ESSENTIALS

Published by the Penguin Group
Penguin Books Ltd, 80 Strand, London WC2R ORL, England
Penguin Group (USA) Inc., 375 Hudson Street, New York, New York 10014, USA
Penguin Group (Canada), 90 Eglinton Avenue East, Suite 700, Toronto, Ontario, Canada M4P 2Y3
(a division of Pearson Penguin Canada Inc.)
Penguin Ireland, 25 St Stephen's Green, Dublin 2, Ireland (a division of Penguin Books Ltd)
Penguin Group (Australia), 250 Camberwell Road, Camberwell, Victoria 3124, Australia
(a division of Pearson Australia Group Pty Ltd)
Penguin Books India Pvt Ltd, 11 Community Centre, Panchsheel Park,
New Delhi – 110 017, India
Penguin Group (NZ), 67 Apollo Drive, Rosedale, Auckland 0632, New Zealand
(a division of Pearson New Zealand Ltd)
Penguin Books (South Africa) (Pty) Ltd, 24 Sturdee Avenue, Rosebank,
Johannesburg 2196, South Africa

Penguin Books Ltd, Registered Offices: 80 Strand, London WC2R ORL, England

www.penguin.com

First published 1932
First published in Penguin Books 1938
This Penguin Essentials edition published 2011

009

Printed in England by Clays Ltd, Elcograf S.p.A

ISBN: 978-0-241-95151-4

www.greenpenguin.co.uk

MIX
Paper from
responsible sources
FSC™ C018179
www.fsc.org

Penguin Books is committed to a sustainable
future for our business, our readers and our planet.
This book is made from Forest Stewardship
Council™ certified paper.

NOTE

The action of the story takes
place in the near future.

FOREWORD

TO ANTHONY POOKWORTHY, ESQ.,
A.B.S., L.L.R.

My dear Tony,

It is with something more than the natural deference of a tyro at the loveliest, most arduous and perverse of the arts in the presence of a master-craftsman that I lay this book before you. You know (none better) the joys of the clean hearth and the rigour of the game. But perhaps I may be permitted to take this opportunity of explaining to you, a little more fully than I have hitherto hinted, something of the disabilities under which I had laboured to produce the pages now open beneath your hand.

As you know, I have spent some ten years of my creative life in the meaningless and vulgar bustle of newspaper offices. God alone knows what the effect has been on my output of pure literature. I dare not think too much about it – even now. There are some things (like first love and one's reviews) at which a woman in her middle years does not care to look too closely.

The effect of these locust years on my style (if I may lay claim to that lovely quality in the presence of a writer whose grave and lucid prose has permanently enriched our literature) has been perhaps even more serious.

The life of the journalist is poor, nasty, brutish and short. So is his style. You, who are so adept at the lovely polishing of every grave and lucent phrase, will realize the magnitude of the task which confronted me when I found, after spending ten years as a journalist, learning to say exactly what I meant in short sentences, that I must learn, if I was to achieve literature and favourable reviews, to write as though I were not quite sure about what I meant but was jolly well going to say something all the same in sentences as long as possible.

Far be it from me to pretend that the following pages achieve what first burned in my mind with pure lambency ten years ago. Which of us does? But the thing's done! Ecco! E finito! And such as it is, and for what it is worth, it is yours.

You see, Tony, I have a debt to pay. Your books have been something more to me, in the last ten years, than books. They have been springs of refreshment, loafings for the soul, eyes in the dark. They have given me (in the midst of the vulgar and meaningless bustle of newspaper offices) joy. It is just possible that it was not quite the kind of joy you intended them to give, for which of us is infallible? But it was joy all right.

I must confess, too, that I have more than once hesitated before the thought of trying to repay some fraction of my debt to you by offering you a book that was meant to be ... funny.

For your own books are not ... funny. They are records of intense spiritual struggles, staged in the wild setting of mere, berg or fen. Your characters are ageless and elemental things, tossed like straws on the seas of passion. You paint Nature at her rawest, in man and in landscapes. The only beauty that lights your pages is the grave peace of fulfilled passion, and the ripe humour that lies over your minor characters like a mellow light. You can paint everyday domestic tragedies (are not the entire first hundred pages of The Fulfilment of Martin Hoare *a masterly analysis of a bilious attack?) as vividly as you paint soul cataclysms. Shall I ever forget Mattie Elginbrod? I shall not. Your books are more like thunderstorms than books. I can only say, in all simplicity, 'Thank you, Tony.'*

But funny ... No.

However, I am sure you are big enough, in every sense of the word, to forgive my book its imperfections.

And it is only because I have in mind all those thousands of persons, not unlike myself, who work in the vulgar and meaningless bustle of offices, shops and homes, and who are not always sure whether a sentence is Literature or whether

8

it is just sheer flapdoodle, that I have adopted the method perfected by the late Herr Baedeker, and firmly marked what I consider the finer passages with one, two or three stars. In such a manner did the good man deal with cathedrals, hotels and paintings by men of genius. There seems no reason why it should not be applied to passages in novels.

It ought to help the reviewers, too.

Talking of men of genius, what a constellation burns in our midst at the moment! Even to a tyro as unpractised as myself, who has spent the best creative years of her life in the vulgar and meaningless bustle of newspaper offices, there is some consolation, some sudden exaltation into a serener and more ardent air, in subscribing herself,

Ever, my dear Tony,

Your grateful debtor,

Stella Gibbons

Watford.
Lyons' Corner House.
Boulogne-sur-Mer.
January 1931–February 1932.

CHAPTER I

THE education bestowed on Flora Poste by her parents had been expensive, athletic and prolonged; and when they died within a few weeks of one another during the annual epidemic of the influenza or Spanish Plague which occurred in her twentieth year, she was discovered to possess every art and grace save that of earning her own living.

Her father had always been spoken of as a wealthy man, but on his death his executors were disconcerted to find him a poor one. After death duties had been paid and the demands of creditors satisfied, his child was left with an income of one hundred pounds a year, and no property.

Flora inherited, however, from her father a strong will and from her mother a slender ankle. The one had not been impaired by always having her own way nor the other by the violent athletic sports in which she had been compelled to take part, but she realized that neither was adequate as an equipment for earning her keep.

She decided, therefore, to stay with a friend, a Mrs Smiling, at her house in Lambeth until she could decide where to bestow herself and her hundred pounds a year.

The death of her parents did not cause Flora much grief, for she had barely known them. They were addicted to travel, and spent only a month or so of each year in England. Flora, from her tenth year, had passed her school holidays at the house of Mrs Smiling's mother; and when Mrs Smiling married, Flora spent them at her friend's house instead. It was therefore with the feelings of one who returns home that she entered the precincts of Lambeth upon a gloomy afternoon in February, a fortnight after her father's funeral.

Mrs Smiling was fortunate in that she had inherited house property in Lambeth before the rents in that district soared to ludicrous heights, following the tide of fashion as it swung away from Mayfair to the other side of the river, and the stone parapets bordering the Thames became, as a consequence, the sauntering ground of Argentinian women and their bull-terriers. Her husband (she was a widow) had owned three houses in Lambeth which he had bequeathed to her. One, in Mouse Place, was the pleasantest of the three, and faced with its shell fanlight the changing Thames; here Mrs Smiling lived, while of the other two, one had been pulled down and a garage perpetrated upon its site, and the third, which was too small and inconvenient for any other purpose, had been made into the Old Diplomacy Club.

The white porcelain geraniums which hung in baskets from the little iron balconies of 1, Mouse Place, did much to cheer Flora's spirits as her taxi stopped before its door.

Turning from the taxi to the house, she saw that the door had already been opened by Mrs Smiling's butler, Sneller, who was looking down upon her with dim approval. He was, she reflected, almost *rudely* like a tortoise; and she was glad her friend kept none as pets or they might have suspected mockery.

Mrs Smiling was awaiting her in the drawing-room overlooking the river. She was a small Irishwoman of twenty-six years, with a fair complexion, large grey eyes and a little crooked nose. She had two interests in life. One was the imposing of reason and moderation into the bosoms of some fifteen gentlemen of birth and fortune who were madly in love with her, and who had flown to such remote places as Jhonsong La Lake M'Luba-M'Luba and the Kwanhattons because of her refusal to marry them. She wrote to them all once a week, and they (as her friends knew to their cost, for she was ever reading aloud long, boring bits from their letters) wrote to her.

These gentlemen, because of the hard work they did in savage foreign parts and of their devotion to Mrs Smiling, were known collectively as 'Mary's Pioneers-O', a quotation from the spirited poem by Walt Whitman.

Mrs Smiling's second interest was her collection of brassières, and her search for a perfect one. She was reputed to have the largest and finest collection of these garments in the world. It was hoped that on her death it would be left to the nation.

She was an authority on the cut, fit, colour, construction and proper functioning of brassières; and her friends had learned that her interest, even in moments of extreme emotional or physical distress, could be aroused and her composure restored by the hasty utterance of the phrase:

'I saw a brassière to-day, Mary, that would have interested you . . .'

Mrs Smiling's character was firm and her tastes civilized. Her method of dealing with wayward human nature when it insisted on obtruding its grossness upon her scheme of life was short and effective; she pretended things were not so: and usually, after a time, they were not. Christian Science is perhaps a larger organization, but seldom so successful.

'Of *course*, if you *encourage* people to think they're messy, they *will* be messy,' was one of Mrs Smiling's favourite maxims. Another was, '*Nonsense*, Flora. You *imagine* things.'

Yet Mrs Smiling herself was not without the softer graces of imagination.

'Well, darling,' said Mrs Smiling – and Flora, who was tall, bent and kissed her cheek – 'will you have tea or a cocktail?'

Flora said that she would have tea. She folded her gloves and put her coat over the back of a chair, and took the tea and a cinnamon wafer.

'Was the funeral awful?' inquired Mrs Smiling. She knew that Mr Poste, that large man who had been serious about games and contemptuous of the arts, was not regretted by his child. Nor was Mrs Poste, who had wished people to live beautiful lives and yet be ladies and gentlemen.

Flora replied that it had been horrid. She added that she was bound to say all the older relatives seemed to have enjoyed it no end.

'Did any of them ask you to go and live with them? I meant to warn you about that. Relatives are always wanting you to go and live with them,' said Mrs Smiling.

13

'No. Remember, Mary, I have only a hundred pounds a year now; and I cannot play Bridge.'

'Bridge? What is that?' inquired Mrs Smiling, glancing vaguely out of the window at the river. 'What curious ways people have of passing their time, to be sure. I think you are very fortunate, darling, to have got through all those dreadful years at school and college, where you had to play all those games, without getting to like them yourself. How did you manage it?'

Flora considered.

'Well – first of all, I used to stand quite still and stare at the trees and not think about anything. There were usually some trees about, for most games, you know, are played at in the open air, and even in the winter the trees are still there. But I found that people *would* bump into me, so I had to give up standing still, and run like the others. I always ran after the ball because, after all, Mary, the ball *is* important in a game, isn't it? until I found they didn't like me doing that, because I never got near it or hit it or did whatever you are supposed to do to it.

'So then I ran *away* from it instead, but they didn't seem to like that either, because apparently people in the audience wondered what I was doing out on the edge of a field all by myself, and running away from the ball whenever I saw it coming near me.

'And then a whole lot of them got at me one day after one of the games was over, and told me I was *no good*. And the Games Mistress seemed quite worried and asked me if I really didn't *care* about lacrosse (that was the name of the game), and I said no, I was afraid I didn't, really; and she said it was a pity, because my father was so "keen", and what *did* I care about?

'So I said, well, I was not quite sure, but on the whole I thought I liked having everything very tidy and calm all round me, and not being bothered to do things, and laughing at the kind of joke other people didn't think at all funny, and going for country walks, and not being asked to express *opinions* about things (like love, and isn't so-and-so *peculiar*?). So then she said, oh, well, didn't I think I could try to be a little less slack, because of Father, and I said no, I was afraid I couldn't; and after that she left me alone. But all the others still said I was *no good*.'

Mrs Smiling nodded her approval, but she told Flora that she talked too much. She added:

'Now about this going to live with someone. Of course, you can stay here as long as you like, darling; but I suppose you will want to take up some kind of work some time, won't you, and earn enough to have a flat of your own?'

'What kind of work?' asked Flora, sitting upright and graceful in her chair.

'Well – organizing work, like I used to do.' (For Mrs Smiling had been an organizer for the L.C.C. before she married 'Diamond' Tod Smiling, the racketeer.) 'Do not ask me what that is, exactly, for I've forgotten. It is so long since I did any. But I am sure you could do it. Or you might do journalism. Or book-keeping. Or bee-keeping.'

Flora shook her head.

'I'm afraid I couldn't do any of those things, Mary.'

'Well ... what then, darling? Now, Flora, don't be *feeble*. You know perfectly well that you will be *miserable* if you haven't got a job, when all your friends have. Besides, a hundred pounds a year won't even keep you in stockings and fans. What will you live on?'

'My relatives,' replied Flora.

Mrs Smiling gave her a shocked glance of inquiry, for, though civilized in her tastes, she was a strong-minded and moral woman.

'Yes, Mary,' repeated Flora firmly, 'I am only nineteen, but I have already observed that whereas there still lingers some absurd prejudice against living on one's friends, no limits are set, either by society or by one's own conscience, to the amount one may impose upon one's relatives.

'Now I am peculiarly (I think if you could see some of them you would agree that that is the word) rich in relatives, on both sides of the family. There is a bachelor cousin of Father's in Scotland. There is a sister of Mother's at

Worthing (as though that were not enough, she breeds dogs). A female cousin of Mother's lives in Kensington. And there are also some distant cousins, connections of Mother's, I believe, who live in Sussex . . .'

'Sussex . . .' mused Mrs Smiling. 'I don't much like the sound of that. Do they live on a decaying farm?'

'I am afraid they do,' confessed Flora, reluctantly. 'However, I need not try them unless everything else fails. I propose to send a letter to the relatives I have mentioned, explaining the situation and asking them if they are willing to give me a home in exchange for my beautiful eyes and a hundred pounds a year.'

'Flora, how *insane!*' cried Mrs Smiling; 'you must be *mad*. Why, you would *die* after the first week. You know that neither of us have ever been able to *abide* relatives. You must stay here with me, and learn typing and shorthand, and then you can be somebody's secretary and have a nice little flat of your own, and we can have lovely parties . . .'

'Mary, you know I hate parties. My idea of hell is a very large party in a cold room, where everybody has to play hockey properly. But you put me off what I was going to say. When I have found a relative who is willing to have me, I shall take him or her in hand, and alter his or her character and mode of living to suit my own taste. Then, when it pleases me, I shall marry.'

'Who, pray?' demanded Mrs Smiling, rudely; she was much perturbed.

'Somebody whom I shall choose. I have definite ideas about marriage, as you know. I have always liked the sound of the phrase "a marriage has been arranged". And so it should be arranged! Is it not the most important step a mortal creature can take? I prefer the idea of arrangement to that other statement that marriages are made in Heaven.'

Mrs Smiling shuddered at the compelling, the almost Gallic, cynicism of Flora's speech. For Mrs Smiling believed that marriages should arise naturally from the union of two loving natures, and that they should take place in churches, with all the usual paraphernalia and hugaboo; and so had her own marriage arisen and been celebrated.

'But what I wanted to ask you was this,' continued Flora. 'Do you think a circular letter to all these relatives would be a good idea? Would it impress them with my efficiency?'

'No,' returned Mrs Smiling, coldly, 'I do not think it would. It would be *too* putting-off. You must write to them, of course (making it an *entirely* different letter each time, Flora), explaining the situation – that is, if you really are going to be so insane as to go on with the idea.'

'Don't fuss, Mary. I will write the letters to-morrow, before lunch. I would write them to-night, only I think we ought to dine out – don't you? – to celebrate the inauguration of my career as a parasite. I have ten pounds, and I will take you to the New River Club – angelic place!'

'Don't be silly. You know perfectly well we must have some men.'

'Then you can find them. Are any of the Pioneers-O home on leave?'

Mrs Smiling's face assumed that brooding and maternal look which was associated in the minds of her friends with thoughts of the Pioneers-O.

'Bikki is,' she said. (All the Pioneers-O had short, brusque nicknames rather like the cries of strange animals, but this was quite natural, for they all came from places full of strange animals.)

'And your second cousin, Charles Fairford, is in town,' continued Mrs Smiling. 'The tall, serious, dark one.'

'He will do,' said Flora, with approval. 'He has such a funny little nose.'

Accordingly, about twenty minutes to nine that night Mrs Smiling's car drove away from Mouse Place carrying herself and Flora in white dresses, with absurd little wreaths of flowers at the side of their heads; and opposite sat Bikki and Charles, whom Flora had only met half a dozen times before.

Bikki, who had a shocking stammer, talked a great deal, as people with stammers always love to do. He was plain

17

and thirtyish, and home on leave from Kenya. He pleased them by corroborating all the awful rumours they had heard about the place. Charles, who looked well in tails, spoke hardly at all. Occasionally he gave a loud, deep, musical 'Ha Ha!' when amused at anything. He was twenty-three, and was to be a parson. He stared out of the window most of the time, and hardly looked at Flora.

'I don't think Sneller approves of this excursion,' observed Mrs Smiling, as they drove away. 'He looked all dim and concerned. Did you notice?'

'He approves of me, because I look serious,' said Flora. 'A straight nose is a great help if one wishes to look serious.'

'I do not wish to look serious,' said Mrs Smiling, coldly. 'There will be time enough to do that when I have to come and rescue you from some impossible relations living in some ungetatable place because you can't bear it any longer. Have you told Charles about it?'

'Good heavens, no! Charles is a relation. He might think I wanted to go and live with him and Cousin Helen in Hertfordshire, and was angling for an invitation.'

'Well, you could if you liked,' said Charles, turning from his study of the glittering streets gliding past the windows. 'There is a swing in the garden and tobacco flowers in the summer, and probably Mother and I would quite like it if you did.'

'Don't be silly,' said Mrs Smiling. 'Look – here we are. Did you get a table near the river, Bikki?'

Bikki had managed to do that; and when they were seated facing the flowers and lights on their table they could look down through the glass floor at the moving river, and watch it between their slippers, as they danced. Through the glass walls they could see the barges going past, bearing their romantic red and green lights. Outside it had begun to rain, and the glass roof was soon trickling with silver.

In the course of supper Flora told Charles of her plan. He was silent at first; and she thought he was shocked. For though Charles had not a straight nose, it might have been written of him, as Shelley wrote of himself in the Preface to *Julian and Maddalo*, 'Julian is rather serious.'

But at last he said, looking amused:

'Well, if you get very sick of it, wherever you are, phone me and I will come and rescue you in my plane.'

'Have you a plane, Charles? I don't think an embryo parson should have a plane. What breed is it?'

'A Twin Belisha Bat. Its name is Speed Cop II.'

'But, really, Charles, do you think a parson *ought* to have a plane?' continued Flora, who was in a foolish mood.

'What has that to do with it?' said Charles calmly. 'Anyway, you let me know and I will come along.'

Flora promised that she would, for she liked Charles, and then they danced together; and all four sat a long time over coffee; and then it was three o'clock and they thought it time to go home.

Charles put Flora into her green coat, and Bikki put Mrs Smiling into her black one, and soon they were driving home through the rainy streets of Lambeth, where every house had windows alight with rose, orange, or gold, behind which parties were going on, card or musical or merely frivolous; and the lit shop windows displayed a single frock or a Tang horse to the rain.

'There's the Old Diplomacy,' said Mrs Smiling interestedly as they passed that ludicrous box, with baskets of metal flowers tipping off the narrow sills of its windows, and music coming from its upper rooms. 'How glad I am that poor Tod left it to me. It *does* bring in such a lot of money.' For Mrs Smiling, like all people who have been disagreeably poor and have become deliciously rich, had never grown used to her money, and was always mentally turning it over in her hands and positively revelling in the thought of what a lot of it she had. And this delighted all her friends, who looked on with approval, just as they would have looked upon a nice child with a toy.

Charles and Bikki said good night at the door because Mrs Smiling was too afraid of Sneller to ask them in for a last cocktail, and Flora muttered that it was absurd; but all the same she felt rather subdued as the two wandered to bed up the narrow, black-carpeted staircase.

'Tomorrow I will write my letters,' said Flora, yawning, with one hand on the slender white baluster. 'Good night, Mary.'

Mrs Smiling said 'Good night, darling.' She added that to-morrow Flora would have thought better of it.

CHAPTER 2

NEVERTHELESS, Flora wrote her letters the next morning. Mrs Smiling did not help her, because she had gone down into the slums of Mayfair on the track of a new kind of brassière which she had noticed in a Jew-shop while driving past in her car. Besides, she disapproved so heartily of Flora's plan that she would have scorned to assist in the concoction of a single oily sentence.

'I think it's *degrading* of you, Flora,' cried Mrs Smiling at breakfast. 'Do you truly mean that you don't ever want to work at *anything*?'

Her friend replied after some thought:

'Well, when I am fifty-three or so I would like to write a novel as good as *Persuasion*, but with a modern setting, of course. For the next thirty years or so I shall be collecting material for it. If anyone asks me what I work at, I shall say, "Collecting material". No one can object to that. Besides, so I shall be.'

Mrs Smiling drank some coffee in silent disapproval.

'If you ask me,' continued Flora, 'I think I have much in common with Miss Austen. She liked everything to be tidy and pleasant and comfortable about her, and so do I. You see, Mary' – and here Flora began to grow earnest and to wave one finger about – 'unless everything is tidy and pleasant and comfortable all about one, people cannot even begin to enjoy life. I cannot *endure messes*.'

'Oh, neither can I,' cried Mrs Smiling, with fervour. 'If

there is one thing I do detest it is a mess. And I do think *you* are going to be messy, if you go and live with a lot of obscure relations.'

'Well, my mind is made up, so there is no purpose in arguing,' said Flora. 'After all, if I find I cannot abide Scotland or South Kensington or Sussex, I can always come back to London and gracefully give in, and learn to work, as you suggest. But I am not anxious to do that, because I am sure it would be more amusing to go and stay with some of these dire relatives. Besides, there is sure to be a lot of material I can collect for my novel; and perhaps one or two of the relations will have messes or miseries in their domestic circle which I can clear up.'

'You have the most revolting Florence Nightingale complex,' said Mrs Smiling.

'It is not that at all, and well you know it. On the whole I dislike my fellow-beings; I find them so difficult to understand. But I have a tidy mind, and untidy lives irritate me. Also, they are uncivilized.'

The introduction of this word closed, as usual, their argument, for the friends were united in their dislike of what they termed 'uncivilized behaviour': a vague phrase, which was nevertheless defined in their two minds with great precision, to their mutual satisfaction.

Mrs Smiling then went away, her face lit by that remote expression which characterizes the collector when upon the trail of a specimen; and Flora began on her letters.

The oleaginous sentences flowed easily from her pen during the next hour, for she had a great gift of the gab, and took a pride in varying the style in which each letter was written to suit the nature of its recipient.

That addressed to the aunt at Worthing was offensively jolly, yet tempered by a certain inarticulate Public School grief for her bereavement. The one to the bachelor uncle in Scotland was sweetly girlish, and just a wee bit arch; it hinted that she was only a poor little orphan. She wrote to the cousin in South Kensington a distant, dignified epistle, grieved yet business-like.

It was while she was pondering over the best style in which to address the unknown and distant relatives in Sussex that she was struck by the singularity of their address:

Mrs Judith Starkadder,
Cold Comfort Farm,
Howling, Sussex.

But she reminded herself that Sussex, when all was said and done, was not quite like other counties, and that when one observed that these people lived on a *farm* in Sussex, the address was no longer remarkable. For things seemed to go wrong in the country more easily and much more frequently, somehow, than they did in Town, and such a tendency must naturally reflect itself in local nomenclature.

Yet she could not decide in what way to address them, so she ended (for by now it was nearly one o'clock and she was somewhat exhausted) by sending a straightforward letter explaining her position, and requesting an early reply as her plans were so unsettled, and she was anxious to know what would happen to her.

Mrs Smiling returned to Mouse Place at a quarter after the hour, and found her friend sitting back in an arm-chair with her eyes shut and the four letters, ready for the post, lying in her lap. She looked rather green.

'Flora! What is the matter? Do you feel sick? Is it your tummy again?' cried Mrs Smiling, in alarm.

'No. That is, not physically sick. Only rather nauseated by the way I have achieved these letters. Really, Mary' – she sat upright, revived by her own words – 'it is rather frightening to be able to write so revoltingly, yet so success-fully. All these letters are works of art, except, perhaps the last. They are positively *oily*.'

'This afternoon,' observed Mrs Smiling, leading the way to lunch, 'I think we will go to a flick. Give Sneller those; he will post them for you.'

'No ... I think I will post them myself,' said Flora, jealously. 'Did you get the brassière, darling?'

A shadow fell upon Mrs Smiling's face.

'No. It was no use to me. It was just a variation on the "Venus" design made by Waber Brothers in 1938; it had three elastic sections in front, instead of two, as I hoped, and I have it already in my collection. I only saw it from the car as I drove past, you know; I was misled by the way it was folded as it hung in the window. The third section was folded back, so that it looked as though there were only two.'

'And would that have made it more rare?'

'But, *naturally*, Flora. Two-section brassières are *extremely* rare: I intended to buy it – but, of course, it was useless.'

'Never mind, my dove. Look – nice hock. Drink it up and you'll feel more cheerful.'

That afternoon, before they went to the Rhodopis, the great cinema in Westminster, Flora posted her letters.

When the morning of the second day brought no reply to any of the letters, Mrs Smiling expressed the hope that none of the relatives were going to answer. She said:

'And I only pray that if any of them *do* answer, it won't be those people in Sussex. I think the names are awful: *too ageing* and putting-off.'

Flora agreed that the names were certainly not propitious.

'I think if I find that I have any third cousins living at Cold Comfort Farm (young ones, you know, children of Cousin Judith) who are named Seth, or Reuben, I shall decide not to go.'

'Why?'

'Oh, because highly sexed young men living on farms are always called Seth or Reuben, and it would be such a nuisance. And my cousin's name, remember, is Judith. That in itself is most ominous. Her husband is almost certain to be called Amos; and if he *is*, it will be a typical farm, and you know what *they* are like.'

Mrs Smiling said sombrely:

'I hope there will be a bathroom.'

'Nonsense, Mary!' cried Flora, paling. 'Of course there will be a bathroom. Even in Sussex – it would be too much . . .

23

'Well, we shall see,' said her friend. 'And mind you wire me (if you do hear from them and do decide to go there) if either of your cousins is called Seth or Reuben, or if you want any extra boots or anything. There are sure to be masses of mud.'

Flora said that she would.

Mrs Smiling's hopes were dashed. On the third morning, which was a Friday, four letters came to Mouse Place for Flora, including one in the cheapest kind of yellow envelope, addressed in so barbed and illiterate a hand that the postman had some difficulty in deciphering it. The envelope was also dirty. The postmark was 'Howling'.

'There you are, you see!' said Mrs Smiling, when Flora showed her this treasure at breakfast. 'How revolting!'

'Well, wait now while I read the others and we will save this one till the last. Do be quiet. I want to see what Aunt Gwen has to say.'

Aunt Gwen, after sympathizing with Flora in her sorrow, and reminding her that we must keep a stiff upper lip and play the game ('Always these games!' muttered Flora), said that she would be delighted to have her niece. Flora would be coming into a real 'homey' atmosphere, with plenty of fun. She would not mind giving a hand with the dogs sometimes? The air of Worthing was bracing, and there were some jolly young people living next door. 'Rosedale' was always full of people, and Flora would never have time to be lonely. Peggy, who was so keen on her Guiding, would love to share her bedroom with Flora.

Shuddering slightly, Flora passed the letter to Mrs Smiling; but that upright woman failed her by saying stoutly, after reading it, 'Well, I think it's a very kind letter. You couldn't *ask* for anything kinder. After all, you didn't think any of these people would offer you the kind of home you *want* to live in, did you?'

'I cannot share a bedroom,' said Flora, 'so that disposes of Aunt Gwen. This one is from Mr McKnag, Father's cousin in Perthshire.'

Mr McKnag had been shocked by Flora's letter: so shocked that his old trouble had returned, and he had been in bed with it for the last two days. This explained, and he trusted that it excused, his delay, in replying to her suggestion. He would, of course, be delighted to shelter Flora under his roof for as long as she cared to fold the white wings of her girlhood there ('The old *lamb*!' crowed Flora and Mrs Smiling), but he feared it would be a little dull for Flora, with no company save that of himself – and he was often in bed with his old trouble – his man, Hoots, and the housekeeper, who was elderly and somewhat deaf. The house was seven miles from the nearest village; that, also, might be a disadvantage. On the other hand, if Flora was fond of birds, there was some most interesting bird-life to be observed in the marshes which surrounded the house on three sides. He must end his letter now, he feared, as he felt his old trouble coming on again, and he was hers affectionately.

Flora and Mrs Smiling looked at one another, and shook their heads.

'There you are, you see,' said Mrs Smiling, once more. 'They are all quite hopeless. You had much better stay here with me and learn how to work.'

But Flora was reading the third letter. Her mother's cousin in South Kensington said that she would be very pleased to have Flora, only there was a little difficulty about the *bedroom*. Perhaps Flora would not mind using the large attic, which was now used as a meeting-room for the Orient-Star-in-the-West Society on Tuesdays, and for the Spiritist Investigators' League on Fridays. She hoped that Flora was not a *sceptic*, for manifestations sometimes occurred in the attic, and even a trace of scepticism in the atmosphere of the room spoiled the conditions, and prevented phenomena, the observations of which provided the Society with such valuable evidence in favour of Survival. Would Flora mind if the parrot kept his corner of the attic? He had grown up in it, and at his age the shock of removal to another room might well prove fatal.

'Again, you see, it means sharing a bedroom,' said Flora. 'I do not object to the phenomena, but I do object to the parrot.'

'*Do* open the Howling one,' begged Mrs Smiling, coming round to Flora's side of the table.

The last letter was writen upon cheap lined paper, in a bold but illiterate hand:

Dear Niece,

So you are after your rights at last. Well, I have expected to hear from Robert Poste's child these last twenty years.

Child, my man once did your father a great wrong. If you will come to us I will do my best to atone, but you must never ask me what for. My lips are sealed.

We are not like other folk, maybe, but there have always been Starkadders at Cold Comfort, and we will do our best to welcome Robert Poste's child.

Child, child, if you come to this doomed house, what is to save you? Perhaps you may be able to help us when our hour comes.

Yr. affec. Aunt,

J. STARKADDER

Flora and Mrs Smiling were much excited by this unusual epistle. They agreed that at least it had the negative merit of keeping silence upon the subject of sleeping arrangements.

'And there is nothing about spying on birds in marshes or anything of that kind,' said Mrs Smiling. 'Oh, I do wonder what it was her man did to your father. Did you ever hear him say anything about a Mr Starkadder?'

'Never. The Starkadders are only connected with us by marriage. This Judith is a daughter of Mother's eldest sister, Ada Doom. So, you see, Judith is really my cousin, not my aunt. (I suppose she got muddled, and I'm sure I'm not surprised. The conditions under which she seems to live are probably conducive to muddle.) Well, Aunt Ada Doom was always rather a misery, and Mother couldn't abide her because she really loved the country and wore artistic hats. She ended by marrying a Sussex farmer. I suppose his name was Starkadder. Perhaps the farm belongs to Judith now, and her man was carried off in a tribal raid from a neighbouring village, and he had to take her name. Or perhaps she married a Starkadder. I wonder what has happened to Aunt Ada? She would be quite old now; she was fifteen years or so older than Mother.'

'Did you ever meet her?'

'No, I am happy to say. I have never met any of them. I found their address in a list in Mother's diary; she used to send them cards every Christmas.'

'Well,' said Mrs Smiling, 'it sounds an appalling place, but in a different way from all the others. I mean, it does sound *interesting* and appalling, while the others just sound appalling. If you have really made up your mind to go, and if you will not stay here with me, I think you had best go to Sussex. You will soon grow tired of it, anyhow, and then, when you have tried it out and seen what it is really like to live with relatives, you will be all ready to come sensibly back here and learn how to work.'

Flora thought it wiser to ignore the last part of this speech.

'Yes, I think I will go to Sussex, Mary. I am anxious to see what Cousin Judith means by "rights". Oh, do you think she means some money? Or perhaps a little house? I should like that even better. Anyway, I shall find out when I get there. And when do you think I had better go? To-day is Friday. Suppose I go down on Tuesday, after lunch?'

'Well, surely you needn't go quite so soon. After all, there is no hurry. Probably you will not be there for longer than three days, so what does it matter when you go? You're all eager about it, aren't you?'

'I want my rights,' said Flora. 'Probably they are something too useless, like a lot of used-up mortgages; but if they are mine I am going to have them. Now you go away, Mary, because I am going to write to all these good souls, and that will take time.'

Flora had never been able to understand how railway time-tables worked, and she was too conceited to ask Mrs Smiling or Sneller about trains to Howling. So in her letter

27

she asked her cousin Judith if she would just mention a few trains to Howling, and what time they got in, and who would meet her, and how.

It was true that in novels dealing with agricultural life no one ever did anything so courteous as to meet a train, unless it was with the object of cutting-in under the noses of the other members of the family with some sordid or passionate end in view; but that was no reason why the Starkadders, at least, should not begin to form civilized habits. So she wrote firmly: 'Do let me know what trains there are to Howling, and which ones you will meet,' and sealed her letter with a feeling of satisfaction. Sneller posted it in time for the country collection that evening.

Mrs Smiling and Flora passed their time pleasantly during the next two days.

In the morning they went ice-skating at the Rover Park Ice Club with Charles and Bikki and another of the Pioneers-O whose nickname was Swooth and who came from Tanganyika. Though he and Bikki were extremely jealous of one another, and in consequence suffered horrid torments, Mrs Smiling had them both so well in hand that they did not dare to look miserable, but listened seriously while she told them, each in his turn, as they glided round the rink holding her hands, how distressed she was about yet a third of the Pioneers-O named Goofi, who was on his way to China and from whom she had not heard for ten days.

'I'm afraid the poor child may be worrying,' Mrs Smiling would say, vaguely, which was her way of indicating that Goofi had probably committed suicide, out of the depths of unrequited passion. And Bikki or Swooth, knowing from their own experience that this was indeed probably the case, would respond cheerfully, 'Oh, I shouldn't fret, if I were you, Mary,' and feel happier at the thought of Goofi's sufferings.

In the afternoons the five went flying or to the Zoo or to hear music; and in the evenings they went to parties; that is, Mrs Smiling and the two Pioneers-O went to the parties, where yet more young men fell in love with Mrs Smiling, and Flora, who, as we know, loathed parties, dined quietly with intelligent men: a way of passing the evening which she adored, because then she could show-off a lot and talk about herself.

No letter had come by Monday evening at tea-time; and Flora had thought that her departure would probably have to be postponed until Wednesday. But the last post brought her a limp postcard; and she was reading it at half past ten on her return from one of the showing-off dinners when Mrs Smiling came in, having wearied of a nasty party she had been attending.

'Does it give the times of the trains, my dove?' asked Mrs Smiling. 'It *is* dirty, isn't it? I can't help rather wishing it were possible for the Starkadders to send a clean letter.'

'It says nothing about trains,' replied Flora with reserve. 'So far as I can make out, it appears to be some verses, with which I must confess I am not familiar, from the Old Testament. There is also a repetition of the assurance that there have always been Starkadders at Cold Comfort, though why it should be necessary to impress this upon me I am at a loss to imagine.'

'Oh, do not say it is signed Seth or Reuben,' cried Mrs Smiling, fearfully.

'It is not signed at all. I gather that it is from some member of the family who does not welcome the prospect of my visit. I can distinguish a reference, among other things, to vipers. I must say that I think it would have been more to the point to give a list of the trains; but I suppose it is a little illogical to expect such attention to petty details from a doomed family living in Sussex. Well, Mary, I shall go down to-morrow, after lunch, as I planned. I will wire them in the morning to say I am coming.'

'Shall you fly?'

'No. There is no landing-stage nearer than Brighton. Besides, I must save money. You and Sneller can work out a route for me; you will enjoy fussing over that.'

'Of course, darling,' said Mrs Smiling, who was by now

beginning to feel a little unhappy at the prospect of losing her friend. 'But I wish you would not go.'

Flora put the post card in the fire; her determination remained unmoved.

The next morning Mrs Smiling looked up trains to Howling, while Flora superintended the packing of her trunks by Riante, Mrs Smiling's maid.

Even Mrs Smiling could not find much comfort in the time-table. It seemed to her even more confused than usual. Indeed, since the aerial routes and the well-organized road routes had appropriated three-quarters of the passengers who used to make their journeys by train, the remaining railway companies had fallen into a settled melancholy; an idle and repining despair invaded their literature, and its influence was noticeable even in their time-tables.

There was a train which left London Bridge at half past one for Howling. It was a slow train. It reached Godmere at three o'clock. At Godmere the traveller changed into another train. It was a slow train. It reached Beershorn at six o'clock. At Beershorn this train stopped; and there was no more idle chatter of the arrival and departure of trains. Only the simple sentence 'Howling (see Beershorn)' mocked, in its self-sufficing entity, the traveller.

So Flora decided to go to Beershorn, and try her luck.

'I expect Seth will meet you in a jaunting-car,' said Mrs Smiling, as they sat at an early lunch.

Their spirits were rather low by this time; and to look out of the window at Lambeth, where the gay little houses were washed by pale sunshine, and to think that she was to exchange the company of Mrs Smiling, and flying and showing-off dinners, for the rigours of Cold Comfort and the grossnesses of the Starkadders did not make Flora more cheerful.

She snapped at poor Mrs Smiling.

'One does not have jaunting-cars in England, Mary. Do you never read *anything* but "Haussman-Haffnitz on Brassières"? Jaunting-cars are indigenous to Ireland. If Seth meets me at all, it will be in a wagon or a buggy.'

'Well, I do hope he won't be called Seth,' said Mrs Smiling, earnestly. 'If he *is*, Flora, mind you wire me at once, and about gum-boots, too.'

Flora had risen, for the car was at the door, and was adjusting her hat upon her dark gold hair. 'I will wire, but do not see what good it will do,' she said.

She was feeling downright morbid, and her sensations were unpleasingly complicated by the knowledge that it was entirely due to her own obstinacy that she was setting out at all upon this absurd and disagreeable pilgrimage.

'Oh, but it will, because then I can send things.'

'What things?'

'Oh, proper clothes and cheerful fashion papers.'

'Is Charles coming to the station?' asked Flora, as they took their seats in the car.

'He said he might. Why?'

'Oh – I don't know. He rather amuses me, and I quite like him.'

The journey through Lambeth was unmarked by any incident, save that Flora pointed out to Mrs Smiling that a flower-shop named Orchidaceous, Ltd, had been opened upon the site of the old police-station in Caroline Place.

Then the car drew into London Bridge Yard; and there was Flora's train, and Charles carrying a bunch of flowers and Bikki and Swooth looking pleased because Flora was going away and Mrs Smiling (so they feverishly hoped) would have more time to spend in their company.

'Curious how Love destroys every vestige of that politeness which the human race, in its years of evolution, has so painfully acquired,' reflected Flora, as she leaned out of the carriage window and observed the faces of Bikki and Swooth. 'Shall I tell them that Mig is expected home from Ontario to-morrow? No, I think not. It would be downright sadistic.'

'Good-bye, darling!' cried Mrs Smiling, as the train began to move.

'Good-bye,' said Charles, putting his daffodils, which he had forgotten until that moment, into Flora's hands. 'Don't forget to phone me if it gets too much for you, and I will come and take you away in Speed Cop II.'

'I won't forget, Charles dear. Thank you very much — though I am quite sure I shall find it very amusing and not at all too much for me.'

'Good-bye,' cried Bikki and Swooth, falsely composing their faces into some semblance of regret.

'Good-bye. Don't forget to feed the parrot!' shrieked Flora, who disliked this prolongation of the ceremony of saying farewell, as every civilized traveller must.

'What parrot?' they all shrieked back from the fast-receding platform, just as they were meant to do.

But it was too much trouble to reply. Flora contented herself with muttering, 'Oh, any parrot, bless you all,' and with a final affectionate wave of her hand to Mrs Smiling, she drew back into the carriage and, opening a fashion journal, composed herself for the journey.

CHAPTER 3

DAWN crept over the Downs like a sinister white animal, followed by the snarling cries of a wind eating its way between the black boughs of the thorns. The wind was the furious voice of this sluggish animal light that was baring the dormers and mullions and scullions of Cold Comfort Farm.

The farm was crouched on a bleak hill-side, whence its fields, fanged with flints, dropped steeply to the village of Howling a mile away. Its stables and out-houses were built in the shape of a rough octangle surrounding the farm-house itself, which was built in the shape of a rough triangle. The left point of the triangle abutted on the farthest point of the octangle, which was formed by the cowsheds, which lay parallel with the big barn. The out-houses were built of rough-cast stone, with thatched roofs, while the farm itself was partly built of local flint, set in cement, and partly of some stone brought at great trouble and enormous expense from Perthshire.

The farm-house was a long, low building, two-storied in parts. Other parts of it were three-storied. Edward the Sixth had originally owned it in the form of a shed in which he housed his swineherds, but he had grown tired of it, and had it rebuilt in Sussex clay. Then he pulled it down. Elizabeth had rebuilt it, with a good many chimneys in one way and another. The Charleses had let it alone; but William and Mary had pulled it down again, and George the First had rebuilt it. George the Second, however, burned it down. George the Third added another wing. George the Fourth pulled it down again.

By the time England began to develop that magnificent blossoming of trade and imperial expansion which fell to her lot under Victoria, there was not much of the original building left, save the tradition that it had always been there. It crouched, like a beast about to spring, under the bulk of Mockuncle Hill. Like ghosts embedded in brick and stone, the architectural variations of each period through which it had passed were mute history. It was known locally as 'The King's Whim'.

The front door of the farm faced a perfectly inaccessible ploughed field at the back of the house; it had been the whim of Red Raleigh Starkadder, in 1835, to have it so; and so the family always used to come in by the back door, which abutted on the general yard facing the cowsheds. A long corridor ran half-way through the house on the second story and then stopped. One could not get into the attics at all. It was all very awkward.

. . . Growing with the viscous light that was invading the sky, there came the solemn, tortured-snake voice of the sea, two miles away, falling in sharp folds upon the mirror-expanses of the beach.

Under the ominous bowl of the sky a man was ploughing the sloping field immediately below the farm, where the flints shone bone-sharp and white in the growing light. The ice-cascade of the wind leaped over him, as he guided the plough over the flinty runnels. Now and again he called roughly to his team:

'Upidee, Travail! Ho, there, Arsenic! Jug-jug!' But for the most part he worked in silence, and silent were his team. The light showed no more of his face than a grey expanse of flesh, expressionless as the land he ploughed, from which looked out two sluggish eyes.

Every now and again, when he came to the corner of the field and was forced to tilt the scranlet of his plough almost on to its axle to make the turn, he glanced up at the farm where it squatted on the gaunt shoulder of the hill, and something like a possessive gleam shone in his dull eyes. But he only turned his team again, watching the crooked passage of the scranlet through the yeasty earth, and muttered: 'Hola, Arsenic! Belay there, Travail!' while the bitter light waned into full day.

Because of the peculiar formation of the out-houses surrounding the farm, the light was always longer in reaching the yard than the rest of the house. Long after the sunlight was shining through the cobwebs on the uppermost windows of the old house the yard was in damp blue shadow.

It was in shadow now, but sharp gleams sprang from the ranged milk-buckets along the ford-piece outside the cowshed.

Leaving the house by the back door, you came up sharply against a stone wall running right across the yard, and turning abruptly, at right angles, just before it reached the shed where the bull was housed, and running down to the gate leading out into the ragged garden where mallows, dog's-body, and wild turnip were running riot. The bull's shed abutted upon the right corner of the dairy, which faced the cowsheds. The cowsheds faced the house, but the back-door faced the bull's shed. From here a long-roofed barn extended the whole length of the octangle until it reached the front door of the house. Here it took a quick turn, and ended. The dairy was awkwardly placed; it had been a thorn in the side of old Fig Starkadder, the last owner of the farm, who had died three years ago. The dairy over-looked the front door, in face of the extreme point of its triangle which formed the ancient buildings of the farm-house.

From the dairy a wall extended which formed the right-hand boundary of the octangle, joining the bull's shed and the pig-pens at the extreme end of the right point of the triangle. A staircase, put in to make it more difficult, ran parallel with the octangle, half-way round the yard, against the wall which led down to the garden gate.

The spurt and regular ping! of milk against metal came from the reeking interior of the sheds. The bucket was pressed between Adam Lambsbreath's knees, and his head was pressed deep into the flank of Feckless, the big Jersey. His gnarled hands mechanically stroked the teat, while a low crooning, mindless as the Down wind itself, came from his lips.

He was asleep. He had been awake all night, wandering in thought over the indifferent bare shoulders of the Downs after his wild bird, his little flower ...

Elfine. The name, unspoken but sharply musical as a glittering bead shaken from a fountain's tossing necklace, hovered audibly in the rancid air of the shed.

The beasts stood with heads lowered dejectedly against the wooden hoot-pieces of their stalls. Graceless, Pointless, Feckless, and Aimless awaited their turn to be milked. Some-times Aimless ran her dry tongue, with a rasping sound sharp as a file through silk, awkwardly across the bony flank of Feckless, which was still moist with the rain that had fallen upon it through the roof during the night, or Pointless turned her large dull eyes sideways as she swung her head upwards to tear down a mouthful of cobwebs from the wooden runnet above her head. A lowering, moist, steamy light, almost like that which gleams below the eyelids of a man in fever, filled the cowshed.

Suddenly a tortured bellow, a blaring welter of sound that shattered the quiescence of the morning, tore its way across the yard and died away in a croak that was almost a sob. It was Big Business, the bull, wakening to another day, in the clammy darkness of his cell.

The sound woke Adam. He lifted his head from the flank of Feckless and looked around him in bewilderment for a moment; then slowly his eyes, which looked small and wet and lifeless in his primitive face, lost their terror as he realized that he was in the cowshed, that it was half-past six on a winter morning, and that his gnarled fingers were about the task which they had performed at this hour and in this place for the past eighty years or more.

He stood up, sighing, and crossed over to Pointless, who was eating Graceless's tail. Adam, who was linked to all dumb brutes by a chain forged in soil and sweat, took it out of her mouth and put into it, instead, his neckerchief – the last he had. She mumbled it, while he milked her, but stealthily spat it out as soon as he passed on to Aimless, and concealed it under the reeking straw with her hoof. She did not want to hurt the old man's feelings by declining to eat his gift. There was a close bond: a slow, deep, primitive, silent down-dragging link between Adam and all living beasts; they knew each other's simple needs. They lay close to the earth, and something of earth's old fierce simplicities had seeped into their beings.

Suddenly a shadow fell athwart the wooden stanchions of the door. It was no more than a darkening of the pallid paws of the day which were now embracing the shed, but all the cows instinctively stiffened, and Adam's eyes, as he stood up to face the new-comer, were again piteously full of twisted fear.

'Adam,' uttered the woman who stood in the doorway, 'how many pails of milk will there be this morning?'

'I dunnamany,' responded Adam, cringingly; ''tes hard to tell. If so be as our Pointless has got over her indigestion, maybe 'twill be four. If so be as she hain't, maybe three.'

Judith Starkadder made an impatient movement. Her large hands had a quality which made them seem to sketch vast horizons with their slightest gesture. She looked a

woman without boundaries as she stood wrapped in a
crimson shawl to protect her bitter, magnificent shoulders
from the splintery cold of the early air. She seemed fitted
for any stage, however enormous.

'Well, get as many buckets as you can,' she said, lifelessly,
half-turning away. 'Mrs Starkadder questioned me about
the milk yesterday. She has been comparing our output
with that from other farms in the district, and she says we
are five-sixteenths of a bucket below what our rate should
be, considering how many cows we have.'

A strange film passed over Adam's eyes, giving him the
lifeless primeval look that a lizard has, basking in the swooning Southern heat. But he said nothing.

'And another thing,' continued Judith, 'you will probably have to drive down into Beershorn to-night to meet a
train. Robert Poste's child is coming to stay with us for a
while. I expect to hear some time this morning what time
she is arriving. I will tell you later about it.'

Adam shrank back against the gangrened flank of Pointless.

'Mun I?' he asked piteously. 'Mun I, Miss Judith? Oh,
dunna send me. How can I look into her liddle flower-face,
and me knowin' what I know? Oh, Miss Judith, I beg of
'ee not to send me. Besides,' he added, more practically,
' 'tes close on sixty-five years since I put hands to a pair of
reins, and I might upset the maidy.'

Judith, who had slowly turned from him while he was
speaking, was now half-way across the yard. She turned her
head to reply to him with a slow, graceful movement. Her
deep voice clanged like a bell in the frosty air:

'No, you must go, Adam. You must forget what you know
– as we all must, while she is here. As for the driving, you
had best harness Viper to the trap, and drive down into
Howling and back six times this afternoon, to get your hand
in again.'

'Could not Master Seth go instead o' me?'

Emotion shook the frozen grief of her face. She said low
and sharp:

37

'You remember what happened when he went to meet the new kitchenmaid . . . No. You must go.'

Adam's eyes, like blind pools of water in his primitive face, suddenly grew cunning. He turned back to Aimless and resumed his mechanical stroking of the teat, saying in a sing-song rhythm:

'Ay, then I'll go, Miss Judith. I dunnamany times I've thought as how this day might come . . . And now I mun go to bring Robert Poste's child back to Cold Comfort. Aye, 'tes strange. The seed to the flower, the flower to the fruit, the fruit to the belly. Aye, so 'twill go.'

Judith had crossed the muck and rabble of the yard, and now entered the house by the back door.

In the large kitchen, which occupied most of the middle of the house, a sullen fire burned, the smoke of which wavered up the blackened walls and over the deal table, darkened by age and dirt, which was roughly set for a meal. A snood full of coarse porridge hung over the fire, and standing with one arm resting upon the high mantel, looking moodily down into the heaving contents of the snood, was a tall young man whose riding-boots were splashed with mud to the thigh, and whose coarse linen shirt was open to his waist. The firelight lit up his diaphragm muscles as they heaved slowly in rough rhythm with the porridge.

He looked up as Judith entered, and gave a short, defiant laugh, but said nothing. Judith crossed slowly over until she stood by his side. She was as tall as he. They stood in silence, she staring at him, and he down into the secret crevasses of the porridge.

'Well, mother mine,' he said at last, 'here I am, you see. I said I would be in time for breakfast, and I have kept my word.'

His voice had a low, throaty, animal quality, a sneering warmth that wound a velvet ribbon of sexuality over the outward coarseness of the man.

Judith's breath came in long shudders. She thrust her arms deeper into her shawl. The porridge gave an ominous leering heave; it might almost have been endowed with life, so uncannily did its movements keep pace with the human passions that throbbed above it.

'Cur,' said Judith, levelly, at last. 'Coward! Liar! Libertine! Who were you with last night? Moll at the mill or Violet at the vicarage? Or Ivy, perhaps, at the ironmongery? Seth – my son . . .' Her deep, dry voice quivered, but she whipped it back, and her next words flew out at him like a lash.

'Do you want to break my heart?'

'Yes,' said Seth, with an elemental simplicity.

The porridge boiled over.

Judith knelt, and hastily and absently ladled it off the floor back into the snood, biting back her tears. While she was thus engaged, there was a confused blur of voices and boots in the yard outside. The men were coming in to breakfast.

The meal for the men was set on a long trestle at the farther end of the kitchen, as far away from the fire as possible. They came into the room in awkward little clumps, eleven of them. Five were distant cousins of the Starkadders, and two others were half-brothers of Amos, Judith's husband. This left only four men who were not in some way connected with the family; so it will readily be understood that the general feeling among the farm-hands was not exactly one of hilarity. Mark Dolour, one of the four, had been heard to remark: 'Happen it had been another kind o' eleven, us might ha' had a cricket team, wi' me for umpire. As ut is, 'twould be more befittin' if we was to hire oursen out for carrying coffins at sixpence a mile.'

The five half-cousins and the two half-brothers came over to the table, for they took their meals with the family. Amos liked to have his kith about him, though, of course, he never said so or cheered up when they were.

A strong family likeness wavered in and out of the fierce, earth-reddened faces of the seven, like a capricious light. Micah Starkadder, mightiest of the cousins, was a ruined giant of a man, paralysed in one knee and wrist. His nephew, Urk, was a little, red, hard-bitten man with foxy ears. Urk's brother, Ezra, was of the same physical type, but horsy

39

where Urk was foxy. Caraway, a silent man, wind-shaven and lean, with long wandering fingers, had some of Seth's animal grace, and this had been passed on to his son, Harkaway, a young, silent, nervous man given to bursts of fury about very little, when you came to sift matters.

Amos's half-brothers, Luke and Mark, were thickly built and high-featured; gross, silent men with an eye to the bed and the board.

When all were seated two shadows darkened the sharp, cold light pouring in through the door. They were no more than a growing imminence of humanity, but the porridge boiled over again.

Amos Starkadder and his eldest son, Reuben, came into the kitchen.

Amos, who was even larger and more of a wreck than Micah, silently put his pruning-snoot and reaping-hook in a corner by the fender, while Reuben put the scranlet with which he had been ploughing down beside them.

The two men took their places in silence, and after Amos had muttered a long and fervent grace, the meal was eaten in silence. Seth sat moodily tying and untying a green scarf round the magnificent throat he had inherited from Judith; he did not touch his porridge, and Judith only made a pretence of eating hers, playing with her spoon, patting the porridge up and down and idly building castles with the burnt bits. Her eyes burned under their penthouses, sometimes straying towards Seth as he sat sprawling in the lusty pride of casual manhood, with a good many buttons and tapes undone. Then those same eyes, dark as prisoned king-cobras, would slide round until they rested upon the bitter white head and raddled red neck of Amos, her husband, and then, like praying mantises, they would retreat between their lids. Secrecy pouted her full mouth.

Suddenly Amos, looking up from his food, asked abruptly: 'Where's Elfine?'

'She is not up yet. I did not wake her. She hinders more than she helps o' mornings,' replied Judith.

Amos grunted.

''Tes a godless habit to lie abed of a working day, and the reeking red pits of the Lord's eternal wrathy fires lie in wait for them as do so. Aye' – his blue blazing eyes swivelled round and rested upon Seth, who was stealthily looking at a packet of Parisian art pictures under the table – 'aye, and for those who break the seventh commandment, too. And for those' – the eye rested on Reuben, who was hopefully studying his parent's apoplectic countenance – 'for those as waits for dead men's shoes.'

'Nay, Amos, lad – ' remonstrated Micah, heavily.

'Hold your peace,' thundered Amos; and Micah, though a fierce tremor rushed through his mighty form, held it.

When the meal was done the hands trooped out to get on with the day's work of harvesting the swedes. This harvest was now in full swing; it took a long time and was very difficult to do. The Starkadders, too, rose and went out into the thin rain which had begun to fall. They were engaged in digging a well beside the dairy; it had been started a year ago, but it was taking a long time to do because things kept on going wrong. Once – a terrible day, when Nature seemed to hold her breath, and release it again in a furious gale of wind – Harkaway had fallen into it. Once Urk had pushed Caraway down it. Still, it was nearly finished; and everybody felt that it would not be long now.

In the middle of the morning a wire came from London announcing that the expected visitor would arrive by the six o'clock train.

Judith received it alone. Long after she had read it she stood motionless, the rain driving through the open door against her crimson shawl. Then slowly, with dragging steps, she mounted the staircase which led to the upper part of the house. Over her shoulder she said to old Adam, who had come into the room to do the washing up:

'Robert Poste's child will be here by the six o'clock train at Beershorn. You must leave to meet it at five. I am going up to tell Mrs Starkadder that she is coming to-day.'

Adam did not reply, and Seth, sitting by the fire, was growing tired of looking at his postcards, which were a three-year-old gift from the vicar's son, with whom he occasionally went poaching. He knew them all by now. Meriam, the hired girl, would not be in until after dinner. When she came, she would avoid his eyes, and tremble and weep.

He laughed insolently, triumphantly. Undoing another button of his shirt, he lounged out across the yard to the shed where Big Business, the bull, was imprisoned in darkness.

Laughing softly, Seth struck the door of the shed.

And as though answering the deep call of male to male, the bull uttered a loud tortured bellow that rose undefeated through the dead sky that brooded over the farm.

Seth undid yet another button, and lounged away.

Adam Lambsbreath, alone in the kitchen, stood looking down unseeingly at the dirtied plates, which it was his task to wash, for the hired girl, Meriam, would not be here until after dinner, and when she came she would be all but useless. Her hour was near at hand, as all Howling knew. Was it not February, and the earth a-teem with newing life? A grin twisted Adam's writhen lips. He gathered up the plates one by one and carried them to the pump, which stood in a corner of the kitchen, above a stone sink. Her hour was nigh. And when April like an over-lustful lover leaped upon the lush flanks of the Downs there would be yet another child in the wretched hut down at Nettle Flitch Field, where Meriam housed the fruits of her shame.

'Aye, dog's-fennel or beard's-crow, by their fruits they shall be betrayed,' muttered Adam, shooting a stream of cold water over the coagulated plates. 'Come cloud, come sun, 'tes ay so.'

While he was listlessly dabbing at the crusted edges of the porridge-plates with a thorn twig, a soft step descended the stairs outside the door which closed off the staircase from the kitchen. Someone paused on the threshold.

The step was light as thistledown. If Adam had not had the rush of the running water in his ears too loudly for him to be able to hear any other noise, he might have thought this delicate, hesitant step was the beating of his own blood.

But, suddenly, something like a kingfisher streaked across the kitchen, in a glimmer of green skirts and flying gold hair and the chime of a laugh was followed a second later by the slam of the gate leading through the starveling garden out on to the Downs.

Adam flung round violently on hearing the sound, dropping his thorn twig and breaking two plates.

'Elfine ... my little bird,' he whispered, starting towards the open door.

A brittle silence mocked his whisper; through it wound the rank odours of rattan and barn.

'My pharisee ... my cowdling ...' he whispered, piteously. His eyes had again that look as of waste grey pools, sightless primeval wastes reflecting the wan evening sky in some lonely marsh, as they wandered about the kitchen.

His hands fell slackly against his sides, and he dropped another plate. It broke.

He sighed, and began to move slowly towards the open door, his task forgotten. His eyes were fixed upon the cowshed.

'Aye, the beasts ...' he muttered, dully; 'the dumb beasts never fail a man. They know. Aye, I'd 'a' done better to cowdle our Feckless in my bosom than liddle Elfine. Aye, wild as a marsh-tigget in May, 'tes. And a will not listen to a word from anyone. Well, so 't must be. Sour or sweet, by barn or bye, so 'twill go. Ah, but if he' – the blind grey pools grew suddenly terrible, as though a storm were blowing in across the marsh from the Atlantic wastes – 'if he but harms a hair o' her little goldy head I'll *kill* un.'

So muttering, he crossed the yard and entered the cowshed, where he untied the beasts from their hoot-pieces and drove them across the yard, down the muddy rutted lane that led to Nettle Flitch Field. He was enmeshed in his grief. He did not notice that Graceless's leg had come off and that she was managing as best she could with three.

Left alone, the kitchen fire went out.

CHAPTER 4

THE timeless leaden day merged imperceptibly towards eve. After the rude midday meal Adam was bid by Judith to put Viper, the vicious gelding, between the shafts of the buggy and drive backwards and forwards to Howling six times to revive his knowledge of the art of managing a horse. His attempt to stave off this event by having a fit during the rude meal was unfortunately robbed of its full effect by the collapse of Meriam, the hired girl, while in the act of passing a dish of greens to Seth.

Her hour had come upon her rather sooner than was anticipated, and in the ensuing scene Adam's fit, which he had staged in the cowshed out of regard for his personal comfort and safety, passed almost unnoticed except as a sort of Greek chorus to the main drama.

Adam was therefore left without any excuse, and spent the afternoon driving backwards and forwards between Howling and the farm, much to the indignation of the Starkadders, who could see him from their position at the side of the well they were supposed to be getting on with; they thought he was an idle old man, and said as much.

'How shall I know the maidy?' pleaded Adam of Judith, as they stood together while he lit the lantern hanging on the side of the buggy. Its dim flame flowered up slowly under the vast, uncaring bowl of the darkening sky, and hung heavily, like a brooding corpse-light, in the windless dusk. 'Robert Poste was ay like a bullock: a great moitherin' man, ay playin' wi' batses and ballses. Do 'ee think his maid will be like him?'

'There are not so many passengers as all that at Beershorn,' replied Judith, impatiently. 'Wait until everybody has left the station. Robert Poste's child will be the last; she will wait to see if there is anyone to meet her. Be off wi' you,' and she struck the gelding upon his hocks.

The great beast bounded forward into the gloom before

Adam could check him. They were gone. Darkness fell, a clouded bell of dark glass, eclipsing the soggy landscape.

By the time the buggy reached Beershorn, which was a good seven miles from Howling, Adam had forgotten what he was going there for. The reins lay between his knotted fingers, and his face, unseeing, was lifted to the dark sky.
***From the stubborn interwoven strata of his subconscious, thought seeped up into his dim conscious; not as an integral part of that consciousness, but more as an impalpable emanation, a crepuscular addition, from the unsleeping life in the restless trees and fields surrounding him. The country for miles, under the blanket of the dark which brought no peace, was in its annual tortured ferment of spring growth; worm jarred with worm and seed with seed. Frond leapt on root and hare on hare. Beetle and finch-fly were not spared. The trout-sperm in the muddy hollow under Nettle Flitch Weir were agitated, and well they might be. The long screams of the hunting owls tore across the night, scarlet lines on black. In the pauses, every ten minutes, they mated. It seemed chaotic, but it was more methodically arranged than you might think. But Adam's deafness and blindness came from within, as well as without; earthly calm seeped up from his subconscious and met descending calm in his conscious. Twice the buggy was pulled out of hedges by a passing farm-hand, and once narrowly shaved the vicar, driving home from tea at the Hall.

'Where are you, my birdling?' Adam's blind lips asked the unanswering darkness and the loutish shapes of the unbudded trees. 'Did I cowdle thee as a mommet for this?'

He knew that Elfine was out on the Downs, striding on her unsteady colt's legs towards the Hall and the bright, sardonic hands of Richard Hawk-Monitor. Adam's mind played uneasily, in bewildered pain, with the vision of his nursling between those casual fingers . . .

But the buggy reached Beershorn at last, and safely: there was only one road, and that led to the station.

Adam pulled Viper up on his haunches just as the great

45

gelding was about to canter through the entrance to the booking-hall, and knotted the reins on the rennet-post near the horse-trough.

Then animation fell from him, a sucked straw. His body sank into the immemorial posture of a man thought-whelmed. He was a tree-trunk; a toad on a stone; a pie-thatched owl on a bough. Humanity left him abruptly.

For some time he brooded, but time conveyed to him nothing of itself. It spun endlessly upon a bright point in space, repeating the names of Elfine and Richard Hawk-Monitor. If time passed (and presumably it did, for a train came in, and its passengers got out, and were driven away) there was no time for Adam.

He was at last roused by an obscure agitation which seemed to be taking place on the floor of the buggy.

The straw which had lain upon the floor for the past twenty-five years was being energetically kicked out into the road by a small foot shod in a stout but shapely shoe. The light of the lantern showed nothing above this save a slender ankle and a green skirt, considerably agitated by the movements of the leg which it covered.

A voice from the darkness above his head was remarking, 'How revolting!'

'Eh . . . eh,' muttered Adam, peering blindly up into the vague air beyond the lantern's rays. 'Nay, niver do that, soul. That straw was good enough for Miss Judith's wedding-trip to Brighton, and it must serve. Straw or chaff, leaf or fruit, we mun all come to't.'

'Not while I can prevent myself,' the voice assured him. 'And I can believe *most* things about Sussex and Cold Comfort, but not that Cousin Judith ever went to Brighton. Now, shall we be getting along, if you have finished brooding? My trunk is coming up to the farm by the carrier's van to-morrow. Not' (the voice went on, with a certain tartness) 'that you would be likely to care if it stayed down here until it seeded.'

'Robert Poste's child,' murmured Adam, staring up at the face he could now dimly see beyond the circle of lantern

46

light. 'Eh, but I was sent here to meet 'ee, and I niver saw 'ee.'

'I know,' said Flora.

'Child, child – ' began Adam, his voice rising to a wail.

But Flora thought otherwise. She checked him by asking him if he would prefer her to drive Viper, and this so affronted his male pride that he unhitched the reins from the rennet-post and the buggy drove off without any more delay.

Flora sat with her fur jacket drawn close round her throat against the chill air, nursing her small case containing her night-gown and toilet articles upon her knees. She had not been able to resist the impulse to slip into this small case, at the last moment, her dearly loved copy of the *Pensées* of the Abbé Fausse-Maigre; her other books would come up in her trunk to-morrow, but she had felt she would find it easier to meet the Starkadders in a proper and civilized state of mind if she had her copy of the *Pensées* (surely the wisest book ever compiled for the guidance of a truly civilized person) close at hand.

The Abbé's other and greater work, *The Higher Common Sense*, which had won for him a Doctorate of the University of Paris at the age of twenty-five, was in her trunk.

She thought of the *Pensées* as the buggy left the lights of Beershorn behind and began to mount the road which led to the invisible Downs. Her spirits were somewhat discomposed. She was chilly, and felt soiled (though indeed she did not look it) by the rigours of her journey. The prospect of what she would find at Cold Comfort was not calculated to cheer her spirits. She thought of the Abbé's warning: 'Never confront an enemy at the end of a journey, unless it happens to be his journey,' and was not consoled.

Adam did not say a word to her during the drive. But that was all right, because she did not want him to; he could be coped with later. The drive did not last so long as she had feared, because Viper seemed to be a pretty good horse and went at a smart pace (Flora supposed that the Starkadders had not owned him for long), and in less than an hour the lights of a village appeared in the distance.

'Is that Howling?' asked Flora.

'Aye, Robert Poste's child.'

There did not seem to be anything more to say. She fell into a slightly more comfortable muse, wondering what her rights were, those rights which her Cousin Judith had mentioned in her letter, and who had sent the postcard with the reference to a generation of vipers, and what was the wrong done by Judith's man to her father, Robert Poste.

The buggy now began to climb a hill, leaving Howling behind.

'Are we nearly there?'

'Aye, Robert Poste's child.'

And in another five minutes Viper stopped, of his own will, at a gate which Flora could just see in the obscurity. Adam struck him with the whip. He did not move.

'I think we must be there,' observed Flora.

'Nay, niver say that.'

'But I do say it. Look – if you drive on we shall go slam into a hedge.'

''Tes all one, Robert Poste's child.'

'It may be all right for you, and all one, but it isn't to me. I shall get down.'

So she did; and found her way slowly, through darkness only lit by faint winter starlight, along a villainous muddy path between hedges, which was too narrow for the buggy to enter.

Adam followed her, carrying the lantern, and leaving Viper at the gate.

The buildings of the farm, a shade darker than the sky, could now be distinguished in the gloom, a little distance on, and as Flora and Adam were slowly approaching them a door suddenly opened and a beam of light shone out. Adam gave a joyful cry.

''Tes the cowshed! 'Tes our Feckless openin' the door fer me!' And Flora saw that it was indeed; the door of the shed, which was lit by a lantern, was being anxiously pushed open by the nose of a gaunt cow.

This was not promising.

But immediately a deep voice was heard: 'Is that you, Adam?' and a woman came out of the cowshed, carrying the lantern, which she lifted high above her head to look at the travellers. Flora dimly discerned an unnecessarily red and voluminous shawl on her shoulders, and a tumbling mass of hair.

'Oh, how do you do?' she called. 'You must be my Cousin Judith. I'm so glad to see you. How nice of you to come out in all this cold. Terribly nice of you to have me, too. Isn't it curious we should never have met before?'.

She put out her hand, but it was not taken at once. The lantern was lifted higher while Judith steadily looked into her face, in silence. The seconds passed. Flora wondered if her lipstick were the wrong shade. It then occurred to her that there was a less frivolous cause for the silence which had fallen and for the steady regard with which her cousin confronted her. So, Flora mused, must Columbus have felt when the poor Indian fixed his solemn, unwavering gaze upon the great sailor's face. For the first time a Starkadder looked upon a civilized being.

But one could weary even of this; and Flora soon did. She asked Judith if Judith would think her terribly rude if she did not meet the rest of the family that evening. Might she, Flora, just have a morsel of food in her own room?

'It is cold there,' said Judith, draggingly, at last.

'Oh, a fire will soon warm it up,' said Flora, firmly. 'Too nice of you, I do think, to take so much care of me.'

'My sons, Seth and Reuben — ' Judith choked on the words, then recovered, and added in a lower voice, 'My sons are waiting to see their cousin.'

This seemed to Flora, in conjunction with their ominous names, *too* like a cattle show, so she smiled vaguely and said it was so nice of them, but she thought, all the same, she would see them in the morning.

Judith's magnificent shoulders rose and fell in a slow, billowy shrug which agitated her breasts.

'As you will. The chimney, perhaps, smokes — '

'I should think it more than probable,' smiled Flora. 'But

we can see to all that to-morrow. Shall we go in now? But first' – she opened her bag and took out a pencil and tore a leaf from a little diary – 'I want Adam to send this wire for me.'

She had her way. Half an hour later she sat beside a smoky fire in her room, pensively eating two boiled eggs. She thought these were safest to ask for; Starkadder bacon, especially if cooked by Adam, might interfere with the long night's rest which she proposed to take, and for which, a short time later, she began to prepare.

She was really too sleepy to notice much of her surroundings, and too bored. She wondered if she had been wise to come. She reflected on the length, the air of neglect and the intricate convolutions of the corridors through which Judith had led her to her bedroom, and decided that if these were typical of the rest of the house, and if Judith and Adam were typical of the people who lived in it, her task would indeed be long and difficult. However, her hand was on the handle of the plough, and she would not turn back, because, if she did, Mrs Smiling would make a particular sort of face, which in another and more old-fashioned woman would have meant: 'I told you so.'

And, indeed, Mrs Smiling, far away in Mouse Place, was at that moment reading with some satisfaction a telegram saying:

'Worst fears realized darling seth and reuben too send gumboots.'

CHAPTER 5

BUT her resolve to sleep late into the next morning was partly frustrated by a shocking row which broke out below her window in what she, muttering sleepily and furiously from her bed, described as the middle of the night.

Male voices were raised in anger, coming up out of the blanket of dead, sullen darkness pierced by the far-off shrilling of cockerels. Flora fancied she knew one of the voices.

'Shame on 'ee, Mus' Reuben, to bite the hand that fed thee as a cowdling. Who should know the wants of the dumb beasts better nor me? 'Tes not for nought I nursed our Pointless when she was three days old and blind as a wren. I know what's in her heart better than I know what's in the heart o' some humans.'

'Be that as it may,' shouted another voice, strange to Flora. 'Graceless has lost a leg! Where is it? Answer me that, ye doithering old man. Who will buy Graceless now when I take her down to Beershorn Market? Who wants a cow wi' only three legs, saving some great old circus man looking round for freakies to put in his show?'

There was a piercing cry of dismay.

'Niver put our Graceless in one o' they circuses! The shame of it would kill me, Mus' Reuben.'

'Aye, and I would, tu, if I could get hold of anyone to buy her, circus or no circus. But no one will. Aye, 'tes all the same. Cold Comfort stock ne'r finds a buyer. Wi' the Queen's Bane blighting our corn, and the King's Evil laying waste the clover, and the Prince's Forfeit bringin' black ruin on the hay, and the sows as barren as come-ask-it – aye, 'tes the same tale iverywhere all over the farm. Wheer's that leg? Answer me that?'

'I don't know, Mus' Reuben. And if I did, I wouldn't tell 'ee. I know what goes on in the hearts of the dumb beasts wi'out spyin' round on them to see where they leaves their legs, from morn till eve. A beast needs solitude, same as a man does. I'd take shame to myself, Mus' Reuben, to watch over them beasts like you do, a-waitin' for dead men's shoes and a-countin' every blade of sporran and mouthful the dumb beasts eat.'

'Aye,' said another voice, meaningly, 'and countin' the very feathers the chickens let fall to see as no one makes off wi' em.'

'Well, and why should I not?' shouted the voice called Mus' Reuben. 'Do I pay 'ee wages, Mark Dolour, to steal the chickens' feathers and carry them off into Beershorn and sell them for good money?'

'I doan't sell the feathers. May I niver set hand to plough again if I do. 'Tes my Nancy. I takes 'em whoam to my Nancy.'

'Oh, ye do, do ye? And for why?'

'Ye know well why,' returned the third voice, sullenly.

'Aye, ye told me a pack o' tales about trimmin' dolls' hats wi' the good chicken feathers. As though there was no other use for them feathers them chickens drop than to trim the hats of a lot of idle, worthless dolls. Now hark ye, Mark Dolour – '

Here Flora found it useless to try to pretend herself back into sleep any longer, so she got crossly out of bed and felt her way across the room to the glimmering grey square which marked the window. She pushed it open a little wider and called down into the darkness:

'I say, *do* you think you would mind not talking quite so loudly, please? I *am* so sleepy, and I should be *so* grateful if you would.'

Silence, emphatic as a thunderclap, followed her request. She felt, half asleep as she was, that it was a flabbergasted silence. She hoped, drowsily, that it would last long enough for her to drift off into sleep again; and it did.

When she again woke it was daylight. She rolled over in bed and dutifully did her morning stretch and looked at her watch. It was half past eight.

Not a sound came up from the yard outside nor from the depths of the old house. Everybody might have died in the night.

'Not a hope of hot water, of course,' thought Flora, wandering round the room in her dressing-gown. However, she rubbed a little of the water in the ewer (yes, there was a ewer) between her palms, and was pleased to find that it was soft water. So she did not mind washing in cold. The regiment of small porcelain jars and pots on her dressing-table would help her to protect her fair skin from any rigours of climate, but it was pleasant to know that the water was her ally.

She dressed in pleasant leisure, studying her room. She decided that she liked it.

It was square, and unusually high, and papered with a bold though faded design of darker red upon crimson. The fireplace was elegant; the grate was basket-shaped, and the mantelpiece was of marble, floridly carved, and yellowed by age and exposure. Upon the mantelpiece itself rested two large shells, whose gentle curves shaded from white to the richest salmon-pink; these were reflected in the large old silvery mirror which hung directly above it.

The other mirror was a long one; it stood in the darkest corner of the room, and was hidden by a cupboard door when the latter was opened. Both mirrors reflected Flora without flattery or malice, and she felt that she could easily learn to rely upon them. Why was it, she wondered, that people seemed to have forgotten how to make mirrors? The old mirrors one found in deserted commercial and family hotels in places like Gravesend, or in the houses of Victorian relatives at Cheltenham, were always superb.

One wall was almost filled by a large mahogany wardrobe. A round table to match stood in the middle of the worn red and yellow carpet, which was covered with a design of big flowers. The bed was high, and made of mahogany; the quilt was a honeycomb, and white.

There were two steel engravings upon the walls, in frames of light yellow wood. One showed the *Grief of Andromache on beholding the Dead Body of Hector*. The other showed the *Captivity of Zenobia, Queen of Palmyra*.

Flora pounced on some books which lay on the broad window-sill: *Macaria, or Altars of Sacrifice*, by A. J. Evans-Wilson; *Home Influence*, by Grace Aguilar; *Did She Love Him?*, by James Grant, and *How She Loved Him*, by Florence Marryat. She put these treasures away in a drawer, promising herself a gloat when she should have time. She liked Victorian novels. They were the only kind of novel you could read while you were eating an apple.

The curtains were magnificent. They were of soiled but regal red brocade, and kept much of the light and air out of the room. Flora looped them back, and decided that to-day they must be washed. Then she went down to breakfast.

She followed a broad corridor, lit by dirty windows hung with soiled lace curtains, until it came to a flight of stairs; and at the foot of the stairs, through an open door, she could see into a room with a stone floor. She paused here for a second, and noticed a tray on which was the remainder of what had obviously been a large breakfast, lying on the floor outside a closed door a little way along the corridor. Good. Someone had breakfasted in their room, and if someone else could, so could she.

A smell of burnt porridge floated up from the depths. This did not seem promising, but she went down the stairs, her low heels clipping firmly on the stone.

At first she thought the kitchen was empty. The fire was almost out, and ash was blowing along the floor, and the table was covered with the intimidating remnants of some kind of a meal in which porridge seemed to have played the chief part. The door leading into the yard was open, and the wind blew sluggishly in. Before she did anything else, Flora went across and crisply shut it.

'Eh!' protested a voice from the back of the kitchen, near the sink. 'Niver do that, Robert Poste's child. I cannot cletter the dishes and watch the dumb beasts in the cowshed both together if ye shut the door. Aye, and there's something else I'm watchin' for, too.'

Flora recognized one of the voices which had disturbed her in the middle of the night. It belonged to old Adam Lambsbreath. He had been listlessly slicing turnips over the sink, and had interrupted his work to make his protest.

'I am sorry,' she replied, firmly, 'but I never could eat breakfast with a draught in the room. You can have it open again as soon as I have finished. *Is* there any breakfast, by the way?'

Adam shuffled forward into the light. His eyes were like

54

slits of primitive flint in their worn sockets. Flora wondered if he ever washed.

'There's porridge, Robert Poste's child.'

'Is there any bread and butter and some tea? I don't much care for porridge. And have you a piece of clean newspaper I could just put on the corner of this table (a half-sheet will be enough) to protect me from the porridge? It seems to have got tossed about a bit this morning, doesn't it?'

'There's tea i' the jar, yonder, and bread and butter i' the crocket. Ye mun find 'em yourself, Robert Poste's child. I have my task to do and my watch to keep, and I cannot run here and run there to fetch newspapers for a capsy wennet. Besides, we've troubles enough at Cold Comfort wi'out bringing in sich a thing as a clamourin' newspaper to upset us and fritten us.'

'Oh, have you? What troubles?' asked Flora, interestedly, as she busily made fresh tea. It occurred to her that this might be a good opportunity to learn something about the other members of the family. 'Haven't you enough money?'

For she knew that this is what is the matter with nearly everybody over twenty-five.

'There's money enough i' the farm, Robert Poste's child, but 'tes all turned to sourness and ruin. I tell ye' – here Adam advanced near to the interested Flora and thrust his lined and wrinkled face, indelibly etched by the corrosive acids of his dim, monotonous years, almost into hers – 'there's a curse on Cold Comfort.'

'Indeed!' said Flora, withdrawing slightly. 'What sort of a curse? Is that why everything looked so gone to seed and what not?'

'There's no seeds, Robert Poste's child. That's what I'm tellin' ye. The seeds wither as they fall into the ground, and the earth will not nourish 'em. The cows are barren and the sows are farren and the King's Evil and the Queen's Bane and the Prince's Heritage ravages our crops. 'Cos why? 'Cos there's a curse on us, Robert Poste's child.'

55

'But, look here, couldn't something be done about it? I mean, surely Cousin Amos could get a man down from London or something – (This bread is really not at all bad, you know. Surely you don't bake it here.) – Or perhaps Cousin Amos could sell the farm and buy another one, without any curse on it, in Berkshire or Devonshire?'

Adam shook his head. A curious veil, like the withdrawing of intelligence from the eyes of a tortoise, flickered across his face.

'Nay. There have always been Starkadders at Cold Comfort. 'Tes impossible for any on us to dream o' leavin' here. There's reasons why we can't. Mrs Starkadder, she's sot on us stayin' here. 'Tes her life, 'tes the life in her veins.'

'Cousin Judith, you mean? Well, she doesn't seem very happy here.'

'Nay, Robert Poste's child. I mean the old lady – old Mrs Starkadder.' His voice sunk to a whisper, so that Flora had to bend her tall head to catch the last words.

He glanced upwards, as though indicating that old Mrs Starkadder was in heaven.

'Is she dead, then?' asked Flora, who was prepared to hear anything at Cold Comfort, even that all the family was kept in order by a domineering ghost.

Adam laughed: a strange sound like the whickering snicker of a teazle in anger.

'Nay. She'm alive, right enough. Her hand lies on us like iron, Robert Poste's child. But she never leaves her room, and she never sees no one but Miss Judith. She's never left the farm this last twenty years.'

He stopped suddenly, as though he had said too much. He began to withdraw to his dark corner of the kitchen.

'I mun cletter the dishes now. Leave me be in peace, Robert Poste's child.'

'Oh, all right. But I do wish you would call me Miss Poste. Or even Miss Flora, if you'd rather be all feudal. I do feel that "Robert Poste's child" every time is rather a mouthful, don't you?'

'Leave me in peace; I mun cletter the dishes.'

56

Seeing that he was really bent on doing some work, Flora let him be, and thoughtfully finished her breakfast.

So that was what it was. Mrs Starkadder was the curse of Cold Comfort. Mrs Starkadder was the Dominant Grandmother Theme, which was found in all typical novels of agricultural life (and sometimes in novels of urban life, too). It was, of course, right and proper that Mrs Starkadder should be in possession at Cold Comfort; Flora should have suspected her existence from the beginning. Probably it was Mrs Starkadder, otherwise Aunt Ada Doom, who had sent the postcard with the reference to generations of vipers. Flora was sure that the old lady was Aunt Ada Doom, and none other. It was a most Aunt Ada-ish thing to do, to send a postcard like that. Flora's mother would have said at once, Flora was sure, 'That's typical of Ada.'

If she intended to tidy up life at Cold Comfort, she would find herself opposed at every turn by the influence of Aunt Ada. Flora was sure that this would be so. Persons of Aunt Ada's temperament were not fond of a tidy life. Storms were what they liked; plenty of rows, and doors being slammed, and jaws sticking out, and faces white with fury, and faces brooding in corners, faces making unnecessary fuss at breakfast, and plenty of opportunities for gorgeous emotional wallowings, and partings for ever, and misunderstandings, and interferings, and spyings, and, above all, managing and intriguing. Oh, they *did* enjoy themselves! They were the sort that went trampling all over your pet stamp collection, or whatever it was, and then spent the rest of their lives atoning for it. But you would rather have had your stamp collection.

Flora thought of *The Higher Common Sense*, by the Abbé Fausse-Maigre. This work had been written as a philosophic treatise; it was an attempt, not to explain the Universe, but to reconcile Man to its inexplicability. But, in spite of its impersonal theme, *The Higher Common Sense* provided a guide for civilized persons when confronted with a dilemma of the Aunt Ada type. Without actually laying down rules of conduct, *The Higher Common Sense* outlined a philosophy for the Civilized Being, and the rules of conduct followed automatically. Where *The Higher Common Sense* was silent, the *Pensées* of the same author often gave guidance.

With such guides to follow, it was not possible to get into a mess.

Flora decided that before she tackled Aunt Ada she would refresh her spirit by re-reading part of *The Higher Common Sense*; the famous chapter on 'Preparing the Mind for the Twin Invasion by Prudence and Daring in Dealing with Substances not Included in the Outline'. Probably she would only have time to study a page or two, for it was not easy to read, and part of it was in German and part in Latin. But she thought that the case was sufficiently serious to justify the use of *The Higher Common Sense*. The *Pensées* were all very well to fortify one's spirit against everyday pricks and scourges; Aunt Ada Doom, the crux of life at Cold Comfort, was another matter.

While she was eating the last piece of bread and butter, Flora was thinking that there might be a difficulty about her food while she was at Cold Comfort, for possibly Adam was cook to the family, and eat food prepared by Adam she could not and would not. She would probably have to approach her Cousin Judith, and have what older people love to call a little talk about it.

On the whole, Cold Comfort was not without its promise of mystery and excitement. She had hopes that Aunt Ada Doom would provide both; and she wished that Charles could have been there to enjoy it all with her. Charles dearly loved a gloomy mystery.

Adam, meanwhile, had finished slicing turnips and had gone out into the yard, where a thorn-tree grew, and returned with a long thorn-spiked twig torn from its branches. Flora watched him with interest while he turned the cold water on to the crusted plates, and began picking at the incrustations of porridge with his twig.

She bore it as long as she could, for she could hardly believe her own eyes, and then she said:

'What on earth are you doing?'

'Cletterin' the dishes, Robert Poste's child.'

'But surely you could do it much more easily with a little mop? A nice little mop with a handle? Cousin Judith ought to get you one. Why don't you ask her? It would get the dishes cleaner, and it would be so much quicker, too.'

'I don't want a liddle mop wi' a handle. I've used a thorn twig these fifty years and more, and what was good enough then is good enough now. And I don't want to cletter the dishes more quickly, neither. It passes the time away, and takes me thoughts off my liddle wild bird.'

'But,' suggested the cunning Flora, remembering the conversation which had roused her that morning at dawn, 'if you had a little mop and could wash the dishes more quickly, you could have more time in the cowshed with the dumb beasts.'

Adam stopped his work. This had evidently struck home. He nodded once or twice, without turning round, as though he were pondering it; and Flora hastily followed up her advantage.

'Anyway, I shall buy one for you when I go into Beershorn to-morrow.'

At this moment there came a soft rap at the closed door which led out into the yard; and a second later it was repeated. Adam shuffled across to the door, muttering 'My liddle wennet!' and flung it wide.

A figure which stood outside, wrapped in a long green cloak, rushed across the room and up the stairs so quickly that Flora only had the merest glimpse of it.

She raised her eyebrows. 'Who was that?' she asked, though she was sure that she knew.

'My cowdling – my liddle Elfine,' said Adam, listlessly picking up his thorn twig, which had fallen into the snood of porridge on the hearth.

'Indeed, and does she always charge about like that?' inquired Flora, coldly; she considered her cousin deficient in manners.

'Aye. She's as wild and shy as a pharisee of the woods.

Days she'll be away from home, wanderin' on the hills, wi' only the wild birds and the liddle rabbits an' the spyin' maggies for company. Aye, and o' night, too...' His face darkened. 'Aye, she's away then, too, wanderin' far from those that loves her and cowdled her in their bosoms when she was a mommet. She'll break my heart into liddle sippets, so she will.'

'Does she go to school?' asked Flora, looking distastefully in a cupboard for a rag with which to dust her shoes. 'How old is she?'

'Seventeen. Nay, niver talk o' school for my wennet. Why, Robert Poste's child, ye might as soon send the white hawthorn or the yellow daffodowndilly to school as my Elfine. She learns from the skies an' the wild marsh-tiggets, not out o' books.'

'How trying,' observed Flora, who was feeling lonely and rather cross. 'Look here, where is everybody this morning? I want to see Miss Judith before I go out for a walk.'

'Mus' Amos, he's down seein' the well drained for Sairy-Lucy's Polly, we think she's fallen into it; Mus' Reuben, he's down Nettle Flitch, ploughin'; Mus' Seth, he's off a-mollocking somewhere in Howling; Miss Judith, she's upstairs a-layin' out the cards.'

'Well, I shall go up and find her. What does mollocking mean?... No, you need not tell me. I can guess. What time is lunch?'

'The men has their dinner at twelve. We has ours an hour later.'

'Then I'll come in at one. Does – do – are – I mean, who cooks it?'

'Miss Judith, she cooks the dinner. Ah, was ye feared I would cook it, Robert Poste's child? Set yer black heart at rest; I wouldn't set me hand to cook even a runnet of bacon for the Starkadders. I cooks for the men, and that's all.'

Flora had the grace to colour at his accurate reading of her thoughts, and was glad to hurry upstairs out of his accusing presence. But it was a relief about the cooking. At least she would not have to starve during her visit to Cold Comfort.

She had no notion where Judith's bedroom might be, but she found a guide to take her there. As she reached the head of the stairs the tall girl in the green cloak, who had just dashed through the kitchen, came running lightly down the corridor towards her. She stopped, as though shot, at the sight of Flora, and stood poised as though for instant flight. 'Doing the startled bird stunt,' thought Flora, giving her a pleasant smile; or rather, smiling at the hood which half concealed her cousin's face.

'What do you want?' whispered Elfine, stonily.

'Cousin Judith's bedroom,' returned Flora. 'Would you be a lamb and show me the way? It's easy to get lost in a large house when everything is strange to one.'

A pair of large blue eyes looked at her steadily above the green hand-woven hood. Flora pensively noted that they were fine eyes, and that the hood was the wrong green.

She said, persuasively, 'Do forgive me saying so, but I would love to see you in blue. Some shades of green are good, of course, but dull greens are *very* trying, I always think. If I were you, I should try blue – something *really* well cut, of course, and very simple – but *definitely* blue. You try it, and see.'

Elfine made a brusque, boyish movement, and said off-handedly, 'This way.'

She strode along the corridor with a long, swinging step, letting the hood fall back so that Flora could see the back of her unbrushed mane of hair; it might have been a good gold if it had been properly dressed and cared for. It all seemed deplorable to Flora.

'Here,' jerked out Elfine, stopping in front of a closed door.

Flora thanked her so much, and Elfine, after another long stare at her, strode away.

'She will have to be taken in hand at once,' thought Flora. 'Another year, and there will be no doing anything with her; for even if she escapes from this place, she will only go and keep a tea-room in Brighton and go all arty-and-crafty about the feet and waist.'

And sighing a little at the greatness of the task which she had set herself to perform, Flora rapped at Judith's bedroom door, and in reply to a muttered 'Come in', entered.

Two hundred photographs of Seth, aged from six weeks to twenty-four years, decorated the walls of Judith's bedroom. She sat by the window in a soiled red dressing-gown with a dirty pack of cards on the table in front of her. The bed was not made. Her hair hung about her face, a nest of lifeless black snakes.

'Good morning,' said Flora. 'I'm so sorry to interrupt you if you are busy writing letters; I just wanted to know if you would like me to amuse myself and make my own arrangements, or would you like me to come in and see you about this time every morning. Personally, I think it's much easier if a guest wanders round and finds her own ways of passing the time. I am sure you are far too busy to want to bother with looking after me.'

Judith, after a long stare at her younger cousin, flung back her head with its load of snakes. The raw air splintered before the harsh onslaught of her laugh.

'Busy! Busy weaving my own shroud, belike. Nay, do what you please, Robert Poste's child, if so be as you don't break in on my loneliness. Give me time, and I will atone for the wrong my man did to your father. Give ... us ... all ... time ...' – the words came draggingly and unwillingly – 'and we will all atone.'

'I suppose,' suggested Flora courteously, 'you would not care to tell me what the wrong was? I do feel it would make matters a little easier ...'

Judith thrust the words aside with a heavy movement of her hand, like the blind outflinging of a tortured beast.

'Haven't I told you my lips are sealed?'

'Just as you like, of course, Cousin Judith. And there is another thing ...'

Then Flora, as delicately as possible, asked her cousin when and how she should pay to her the first instalment of the hundred pounds a year which Flora had anticipated that she would have to hand over to the Starkadders for her keep.

'Keep it – keep it,' said Judith violently. 'We will never touch a halfpenny of Robert Poste's money. While you are here, you are the guest of Cold Comfort. Every middock you eat is paid for with our sweat. 'Tes as it should be, seeing the way things are.'

Flora privately thanked her cousin for her generosity, but she privately resolved that, as soon as it was possible, she would make the acquaintance of Aunt Ada Doom, and find out if the old lady approved of this prodigal arrangement. Flora felt sure that she would not approve; and Flora herself was irritated by Judith's remark. For, if she lived at Cold Comfort as a guest, it would be unpardonable impertinence were she to interfere with the family's mode of living; but if she were paying her way, she could interfere as much as she pleased. She had observed a similar situation in houses where there were both poor relations and paying guests.

But this was a point which could be settled at some other time; just now there was something more important to discuss. She said:

'By the way, I adore my bedroom, but do you think I could have the curtains washed? I believe they are red; and I should so like to make sure.'

Judith had sunk into a reverie.

'Curtains?' she asked, vacantly, lifting her magnificent head. 'Child, child, it is many years since such trifles broke across the web of my solitude.'

'I'm sure it is; but do you think I might have them washed, all the same? Could Adam do them?'

'Adam? His frail arms have not the strength. Meriam, the hired girl, might have done them, but – '

Her gaze strayed again to the window, past whose open casement a fine rain was blowing.

Flora, who was willing to try anything once, gazed too. Judith was looking at a little hut which stood at the far end of Nettle Flitch Field, and almost abutted upon the

63

sag-pieces which railed in the yard. From this hut came distinct cries of distress in a female voice.

Flora looked at her cousin with inquiring eyebrows. Judith nodded, lowering her eyelids while a slow scarlet wave of blood swept over her breasts and cheeks.

' 'Tes the hired girl in labour,' she whispered.

'What – without a doctor or anything?' asked Flora, in alarm. 'Hadn't we better send Adam down into Howling for one? I mean – in that grim-looking hut and everything – '

Judith again made the blind animal gesture of repudiation which seemed to thrust a sodden wall of negation between herself and the world of living things. Her face was grey.

'Leave her in peace ... animals like Meriam are best alone at such times ... 'Tes not the first time.'

'Too bad,' said Flora, sympathetically.

' 'Tes the fourth time,' whispered Judith, thickly. 'Every year, in the fullness o' summer, when the sukebind hangs heavy from the wains ... 'tes the same. 'Tes the hand of Nature, and we women cannot escape it.'

('Oh, can't we?' thought Flora, with spirit, but aloud she only made such noises of tut-tutting regret as she felt were appropriate to the occasion.)

'Well, she's out of the question, anyway,' she said, briskly.

'What question?' asked Judith, after a pause.

She had fallen into a trance-like muse. Her face was grey.

'I mean the curtains. She can't wash them if she's just had a baby, can she?'

'She will be about again to-morrow. Such wenches are like the beasts of the field,' said Judith, indifferently.

She seemed bowed under the gnawing weight of a sorrow that had left her too exhausted for anger; but, as she spoke, an asp-like gleam of contempt darted into her over-lidded eyes. She looked quickly across at a photograph of Seth which stood on the table. It showed him in the centre of the Beershorn Wanderers Football Club. His young man's limbs, sleek in their dark male pride, seemed to disdain the covering offered them by the brief shorts and striped jersey. His body might have been naked, like his full, muscled throat, which rose, round and proud as the male organ of a flower, from the neck of his sweater.

'He is a thought too fat, but really very handsome,' mused Flora, following Judith's glance. 'I don't suppose he plays football any more – probably mollocks instead.'

'Aye,' suddenly whispered Judith, 'look at him – the shame of our house. Cursed be the day I brought him forth and the nourishment he drew from my bosom, and the wooing tongue God gave him to bring disgrace upon weak women.'

She stood up and looked out into the drizzling rain.

**The cries from the little hut had stopped. An exhausted silence, brimmed with the enervating weakness which follows a stupendous effort, mounted from the stagnant air in the yard, like a miasma. All the surrounding surface of the countryside – the huddled Downs lost in rain, the wet fields fanged abruptly with flints, the leafless thorns thrust sideways by the eternal pawing of the wind, the lush breeding miles of meadow through which the lifeless river wandered – seemed to be folding inwards upon themselves. Their dumbness said: 'Give up'. There is no answer to the riddle; only that bodies return exhausted, hour by hour, minute by minute, to the all-forgiving and all-comprehending primeval slime.

'Well, Cousin Judith, if you really think she will be about again in a few days, perhaps I might look in at her hut this morning and arrange about the curtains,' said Flora, preparing to go. Judith did not answer at first.

'The fourth time,' she whispered at last. 'Four of them. Love-children. Pah! That animal, and love! And he – '

Here Flora realized that the conversation was not likely to take a turn in which she could join with any benefit, so she went quickly away.

'So they all belong to Seth,' she thought, while putting on her mackintosh in her bedroom. 'Really, it is too bad. I suppose on any other farm one would say that it set a bad

65

example, but of course that does not apply here. I must see, I think, what can be done about Seth . . .'

She picked her way through the mud and rancid straw which carpeted the yard without encountering anyone except a person whom she took from his employment to be Reuben himself. He was feverishly collecting the feathers dropped by the chickens straying about the yard, and comparing them in number with the empty feather-sockets on the bodies of the chickens; this, she supposed, must be a precautionary measure, to prevent any feathers being taken away by Mark Dolour to his daughter Nancy.

Reuben (if it were he) was so engrossed that he did not observe Flora.

CHAPTER 6

FLORA approached the hut in some trepidation. Her practical experience of confinements was non-existent, for such of her friends as were married had not yet any children, and most of them were still too young to think of marriage as anything but a state infinitely remote.

But she had a lively acquaintance with confinements through the works of women novelists, especially those of the unmarried ones. Their descriptions of what was coming to their less fortunate married sisters usually ran to four or five pages of close print, or eight or nine pages of staccato lines containing seven words, and a great many dots arranged in threes.

Another school dismissed confinements with a careful brightness, a 'So-sorry-I'm-late-darling-I've-just-been-having-a-baby-where-shall-we-go-for-supper-afterwards?' sangfroid which Flora, curiously enough, found equally alarming.

She sometimes wondered whether the old-fashioned, though doubtless lazy, method of describing the event in the phrase, 'She was brought to bed of a fine boy,' was not the best way of putting it.

A third type of woman novelist combined literature and motherhood by writing a good, serious first novel when they were twenty-six; then marrying and having a baby, and, the confinement over, writing articles for the Press on 'How I Shall Bring Up My Daughter', by Miss Gwenyth Bludgeon, the brilliant young novelist, who gave birth to a daughter this morning. Miss Bludgeon is in private life Mrs Neil McIntish.

Some of Flora's friends had been exceedingly frightened, not to say revolted, by these painstaking descriptions of confinements; and had been compelled to rush off to the Zoo and bribe the keepers to assure them that the lionesses, at least, got through the Greatest Event of Their Lives in decent solitude. It was comforting, too, to watch the lionesses cuffing their fubsy cubs about in the sunlight. The lionesses, at least, did not write articles for the papers on how they would Bring Up their Cubs.

Flora had also learned the degraded art of 'tasting' unread books, and now, whenever her skimming eye lit on a phrase about heavy shapes, or sweat, or howls, or bedposts, she just put the book back on the shelf, unread.

Musing thus, she was relieved when a voice replied: 'Oo's there?' to her tap upon the door of the hut.

'Miss Poste from the farm,' she answered composedly. 'May I come in?'

There was a silence; a startled one, Flora felt. At length the voice called suspiciously:

'What do 'ee want wi' me and mine?'

Flora sighed. It was curious that persons who lived what the novelists called a rich emotional life always seemed to be a bit slow on the uptake. The most ordinary actions became, to such persons, entangled in complicated webs of apprehension and suspicion. She prepared to make a long explanatory statement – but suddenly changed her mind. Why should she explain? Indeed, what was there to explain?

She pushed the door open and walked in.

To her relief, there were no sweat nor howls nor bedposts.

There was only a young woman whom she presumed to be Meriam, the hired girl, sitting over an oil stove and reading what Flora, who had a nice sense of atmosphere, at once identified as *Madame Olga's Dream Book*. Baby there was none, and she was puzzled. But she was too relieved to wonder much what the explanation could be.

The hired girl (who was, of course, rather sullen looking and like a ripe fruit) was staring at her.

'Good morning,' Flora began pleasantly, 'are you feeling better? Mrs Starkadder seems to think you will be about again in a day or two, and if you feel well enough, I want you to wash the curtains in my bedroom. When can you come up to the farm and fetch them?'

The hired girl huddled closer over the oil stove, looking at Flora in what the latter interestedly recognized as the Tortured Dumb Beast manner. When she spoke, her voice was low and drawling:

'Why do ye come here, mockin' me in me shame – and me only out of me trouble yesterday?'

Flora started, and stared a little.

'Yesterday? I thought it was to-day? Surely you – er – didn't I hear? – that is, weren't you crying out, only about ten minutes ago? Mrs Starkadder and I both heard you.'

The beginnings of a sullen smile, rather like a plum in quality, touched the hired girl's sensual lips.

'Aye, I moithered out a bit. I was rememberin' me trouble yesterday. Mrs Starkadder she weren't in the kitchen when me time came on me. How should she know what I bin through, and when I bin through it? Not that I ever say much while it's goin' on. 'Taint so bad as some people make out. Mother says it's because I keeps me spirits up and eats hearty aforehand.'

Flora was pleasantly surprised to hear this, and for a second wondered if the women novelists had been mis-informed about confinements. But no; she recollected that they usually left themselves a loophole by occasionally creat-ing a primitive woman, a creature who was as close to the earth as a bloomy greengage and rather like one to look at and talk to, and this greengage creature never had any bother with her confinements, but just took them in her stride, as it were. Evidently, Meriam belonged to the greengage category.

'Indeed,' said Flora, 'I am glad to hear it. When can you take the curtains down? The day after to-morrow?'

'I never said as I'd wash your curtains. Haven't I enough to bear, wi' three children to find food for, and me mother lookin' after a fourth? And who's to know what will happen to me when the sukebind is out in the hedges again and I feels so strange on the long summer evenings – ?'

'Nothing will happen to you, if only you use your intelligence and see that it doesn't,' retorted Flora firmly. 'And if I may sit down on this stool – thank you, no, I will use my handkerchief as a cushion – I will tell you how to see that nothing happens. And never mind about the sukebind for a minute (what *is* this sukebind, anyway?). Listen to me.'

And carefully, in detail, in cool phrases, Flora explained exactly to Meriam how to forestall the disastrous effect of too much sukebind and too many long summer evenings upon the female system.

Meriam listened, with eyes widening and widening.

' 'Tes wickedness! 'Tes flying in the face of Nature!' she burst out fearfully at last.

'Nonsense!' said Flora. 'Nature is all very well in her place, but she must not be allowed to make things untidy. Now remember, Meriam – no more sukebind and summer evenings without some preparations beforehand. As for your children, if you will wash the curtains for me, I will pay you, and that can go towards buying some of whatever it is children have to eat.'

Meriam seemed unconvinced by the argument for coping with sukebind, but she finally agreed to wash the curtains on the next day, much to Flora's satisfaction.

While Flora was making the final arrangements, her glance was wandering thoughtfully round the hut. It was of the variety known as 'miserable', but it was plain to Flora's experienced eyes that, unlikely as this seemed, somebody had been tidying it up. She was sure that the greengage had never even heard of such a process and wondered very much who had been at work.

While she was drawing on her gloves, there came a sharp tap at the door.

' 'Tes mother,' said Meriam, and she called: 'Come in, mother.'

The door then opened and on the threshold, taking in Flora from heels to beret with snapping little black eyes, stood a rusty black shawl with a hat alighting perilously upon the knob of hair which crowned the top of its head.

'Good morning, miss. A nasty day,' snapped the shawl, furling a large umbrella.

Flora was so startled at being addressed in a respectful and normal manner by anyone in Sussex that she almost forgot to answer, but habit is strong, and she recovered her wits sufficiently to agree graciously that the day was, indeed, nasty.

'She comes from up at the farm. She wants me to wash her bedroom curtains – and me with me trouble only a day behind me,' said Meriam.

'Who's "she"? The cat's mother?' snapped the shawl. 'Speak properly to the young lady. You must excuse her, miss; she's more like father's side o' the family. Ah! it was a black day for me when I took up with Agony Beetle and left Sydenham for Sussex (all my people live in Sydenham, miss, and have these forty years). Wash them? Well, I never thought I'd live to hear of anyone up at Cold Comfort wanting a bit of washing done. They might begin on that old Adam of theirs, or whatever he calls himself, and no harm would be done, I'll lay. She'll wash them for you, miss. I'll bring them along myself to-morrow afternoon and put them up for you.'

Flora replied that this would do very well, and it says much for the cumulative effect of the atmosphere of Cold Comfort that she felt almost moved as she spoke the words to one who seemed to possess some of the attributes of an ordinary human being, and who seemed to perceive (however dimly) that curtains must be washed and life generally tidied up before anyone could even begin to think of enjoying it.

She wondered if she should inquire after the welfare of the baby, and had just decided that this might be a little tactless when Mrs Beetle demanded of her daughter:

'Well, ain't you going to ask me 'ow 'e is?'

'I knows. There ain't no need to ask. He'll be doing fine. They allus does,' was the sullen reply.

'Well, you needn't sound as though you wished they wouldn't,' said the shawl, tartly. 'Lord knows, they wasn't very welcome, pore little innercents; but now they *are* 'ere, we may as well bring them up right. And I will, too. It's to me advantage. Come another four years and I can begin makin' use of them.'

'How?' asked Flora, pausing at the door. Was a flaw about to disclose itself in the hitherto admirable character of the shawl?

'Train the four of them up into one of them jazz-bands,' replied Mrs Beetle, promptly. 'I seen in the *News of People* that they earns as much as six pounds a night playin' up West in night-clubs. Well, I thought, here's a jazz-band ready-made to me 'and, as you may say; and it's better still now there's four of them. I've got 'em all under me 'and in one family, so's I can keep an eye on the lot of them while they're learning to play. So that's why I'm bringing them up right, on plenty of milk, and seein' they get to bed early. They'll need all their strength if they 'ave to sit up till the cows come 'ome playin' in them night-clubs.'

Flora was rather shocked, but she felt that, though Mrs Beetle's scheme might be a little *callous*, it was at least *organized*, which was more than could be said of any other life which the four embryo musicians might lead if their upbringing were left to their mother or (a yet darker thought) to Grandfather Agony Beetle himself.

So she went off, after a pleasant farewell to Meriam and mother, and a statement that she would come in some time to see the new baby.

**After she had gone the hut sank into a dim trough of languor, pierced only by the shrill beam shed by the personality of Mrs Beetle, which seemed to gather into one all the tenuous threads of the half-formulated desires of the two women which throbbed about them.

Meriam huddled on her stool, the coarsened lines of her body spreading like some natural growth born of the travail of the endlessly teeming fields. In thick, lewd whispers, she began to tell her mother what Flora had advised her to do. Her voice rose ... fell ... rose ... fell ..., its guttural syllables punctuated by the swish of Mrs Beetle's broom. Once Mrs Beetle flung open a window, muttering that the place was enough to choke a black, but save for this interruption Meriam's voice droned on like the voice of the earth itself.

'Well, you needn't sw-sw-sw-sw about it as though you was talkin' to someone from the Vicarage,' observed Mrs Beetle at the conclusion of her confidences. 'It's no news to me, though I wasn't quite sure 'ow it was done nor 'ow much they cost ... Anyway, we know now; thanks to Miss Interference from the 'ill. And I'll lay she's no better than she ought to be, a bit of a kid like 'er sailing in 'ere as bold as brass and talkin' to you about such things. Still, she does look as if she washed 'erself sometimes, and she ain't painted up like a dog's dinner, like most of them nowadays. Not that I 'old with wot she told you, mind you. It ain't right.'

'Aye,' agreed her daughter, heavily, ' 'tes wickedness. 'Tes flyin' in the face of Nature.'

'That's right.'

A pause, during which Mrs Beetle stood with her broom suspended, looking firmly at the oil stove. Then she added:

'All the same, it might be worth tryin'.'

FLORA's spirits were usually equable, but by lunch-time the next day the combined forces of the unceasing rain, the distressing manner in which the farm-house and its attendant buildings seemed sinking into decay before her eyes, and the appearance and characters of her relatives, had produced in her a feeling of gloom which was as unusual as it was disagreeable.

'This will not do,' she thought, as she looked out on the soaking countryside from her bedroom window, whence she had retreated to arrange some buds and branches which she had picked on her morning walk. 'I am probably hungry; lunch will restore my spirits.'

And yet, on second thoughts, it seemed probable that lunch cooked by a Starkadder and partaken of in solitude would only make her worse.

She had managed yesterday's meals successfully. Judith had provided a cutlet and some junket for her at one o'clock, served beside a smoky fire, in a little parlour with faded green wallpaper, next door to the dairy. Here, too, Flora had partaken of tea and supper. These two meals were served by Mrs Beetle – an agreeable surprise. It appeared that Mrs Beetle came in to the farm and did her daughter's work on those occasions when Meriam was being confined. Flora's arrival had coincided with one of these times, which, as we know, were frequent. Mrs Beetle also came in each day to prepare Aunt Ada Doom's meals.

So Flora had thus far escaped meeting Seth and Reuben or any of the other male Starkadders. Judith, Adam, Mrs Beetle, and an occasional glimpse of Elfine represented her whole knowledge of the inhabitants and servants of the farm.

But she was not satisfied. She wished to meet her young cousins, her Aunt Ada Doom, and Amos. How could she tidy up affairs at Cold Comfort if she did not meet any of the Starkadders? And yet she shrank from boldly entering

the kitchen where the family sat at the manger, and introducing herself. Such a move would lower her dignity, and,
hence, her future power. It was all very difficult. Perhaps
Judith did not actively intend to keep Flora from meeting
the rest of the family, but she had so far achieved just this
result.

But to-day, Flora had decided, she would meet her
cousins, Seth and Reuben. She thought that tea-time would
present a good opportunity on which to carry out her inten-
tion. If the Starkadders did not partake of tea (and it was
probable that they did not) she would prepare it herself, and
tell the Starkadders that she intended with their nominal
permission to do so every afternoon during her visit.

But this point could be considered later. At the moment,
she was going down into Howling to see if there was a pub
in which she could lunch. In any other household such a
proceeding would be enough to terminate her stay. Here,
they probably would not even notice her absence.

At one o'clock, therefore, Flora was in the saloon bar of
the Condemn'd Man, the only public-house in Howling,
asking Mrs Murther the landlady if she 'did' lunches?

A smile indicating a shuddering thankfulness, as of one
who peers into a pit into which others have fallen while she
has escaped, passed over the face of Mrs Murther, as she
replied that she did not.

'At least, only for two days in August, and not always
then,' she added, gladly.

'Couldn't you pretend it is August now?' demanded
Flora, who was ravenous.

'No,' replied Mrs Murther, simply.

'Well, if I buy a steak at the butcher's, will you cook it
for me?'

Mrs Murther unexpectedly said that she would; and
added even more surprisingly that Flora could have some
of what they was having themselves, an offer which Flora a
little rashly accepted.

What they was having themselves proved to be apple tart
and vegetables, so Flora did quite well. She obtained her

steak after some little delay with the butcher, who thought she was mad; and it seemed to her that a surprisingly short time elapsed between the purchasing of the steak and her sitting down before it, browned and savoury, in the parlour of the Condemn'd Man.

Nor did the hovering presence of Mrs Murther cast an atmosphere sufficiently dismal to spoil her appetite. Mrs Murther seemed resigned, rather than despairing. Her face and manner suggested the Cockney phrase dear and familiar to Flora in London: 'Oh, well, mustn't grumble', though Flora knew better than to expect to hear it in Howling, where everybody felt that they must grumble, and all the time at that.

'Now I must be off and see to my other gentleman's dinner,' said Mrs Murther, having hovered long enough to see that Flora had all the salt and pepper, bread, forks, and the rest of it that she wanted.

'Have you another gentleman?' asked Flora.

'Yes. Stayin' here. A book-writer,' rejoined Mary Murther.

'He would be,' muttered Flora. 'What's his name?' (for she wondered if she knew him).

'Mybug,' was the improbable answer.

Flora simply did not believe this, but she was too busy eating to start a long and exhausting argument. She decided that Mr Mybug must be a genius. A person who was merely talented would have weakly changed his name by deed-poll.

What a bore it was, she thought. Had she not enough to do at Cold Comfort without there being a genius named Mybug staying a mile away from the farm who would probably fall in love with her? For she knew from experience that intellectuals and geniuses seldom fell for females of their own kidney, who had gone all queer about the shoes and coiffure, but concentrated upon reserved but normal and properly dressed persons like herself, who were both repelled and alarmed (not to say bored) by the purposeful advances of the said geniuses and intellectuals.

'Well – what kind of books does he write?' she asked.

'He's doin' one now about another young fellow who

wrote books, and then his sisters pretended *they* wrote them, and then they all died of consumption, poor young mommets.'

'Ha! A life of Branwell Brontë,' thought Flora. 'I might have known it. There has been increasing discontent among the male intellectuals for some time at the thought that a woman wrote *Wuthering Heights*. I thought one of them would produce something of this kind, sooner or later. Well, I must just avoid him, that's all.'

And she fell to finishing her apple tart a little more quickly than was comfortable, for she was nervous lest Mr Mybug should come in, and fall in love with her.

'Don't you 'urry yourself; 'e's never in afore half past two,' soothed Mrs Murther, reading her thoughts with disconcerting readiness. 'He's up on the Downs in all weathers, and a nice old lot of mud 'e brings into the 'ouse too. Was everything all right? That'll be one and sixpence, please.'

Flora felt better on her return walk to the farm. She decided that she would spend the afternoon arranging her books.

There were sounds of life in the yard as she crossed it. Buckets clattered in the cowshed, and the hoarse bellow of the bull came from his dark shed. ('I don't believe he's ever let out into the fields when the sun's shining,' thought Flora, and made a note to see about him, as well as about the Starkadders.) Belligerent noises came from the henhouse, but nobody was to be seen.

At four o'clock she came downstairs to look for some tea. She did not bother to glance into her little parlour to see if her own tea were on the table. She went straight into the kitchen.

Of course, there were no preparations for tea in the kitchen; she realized, as soon as she saw the ashy fire and the crumbs and fragments of carrot left on the table from dinner, that it was rather optimistic of her to have expected any.

But she was not daunted. She filled the kettle, put some wood on the fire and set the kettle on it, flicked the reminders of dinner off the table with Adam's drying-up towel (which she held in the tongs), and set out a ring of cups and saucers about the dinted pewter teapot. She found a loaf and some butter, but no jam, of course, or anything effeminate of that sort.

Just as the kettle boiled and she darted forward to rescue it, a shadow darkened the door and there stood Reuben, looking at Flora's gallant preparations with an expression of stricken amazement mingled with fury.

'Hullo,' said Flora, getting her blow in first. 'I feel sure you must be Reuben. I'm Flora Poste, your cousin, you know. How do you do? I'm so glad to see somebody has come in for some tea. Do sit down. Do you take milk? (No sugar . . . of course . . . or do you? I do, but most of my friends don't.)'

***The man's big body, etched menacingly against the bleak light that stabbed in from the low windows, did not move. His thoughts swirled like a beck in spate behind the sodden grey furrows of his face. A woman . . . Blast! Blast! Come to wrest away from him the land whose love fermented in his veins, like slow yeast. She-woman. Young, soft-coloured, insolent. His gaze was suddenly edged by a fleshy taint. Break her. Break. Keep and hold and hold fast the land. The land, the iron furrows of frosted earth under the rain-lust, the fecund spears of rain, the swelling, slow burst of seed-sheaths, the slow smell of cows and cry of cows, the trampling bride-path of the bull in his hour. All his, his . . .

'Will you have some bread and butter?' asked Flora, handing him a cup of tea. 'Oh, never mind your boots. Adam can sweep the mud up afterwards. Do come in.'

Defeated, Reuben came in.

He stood at the table facing Flora and blowing heavily on his tea and staring at her. Flora did not mind. It was quite interesting: like having tea with a rhinoceros. Besides, she was rather sorry for him. Amongst all the Starkadders, he looked as though he got the least kick out of life. After

77

all, most of the family got a kick out of something. Amos got one from religion, Judith got one out of Seth, Adam got his from cowdling the dumb beasts, and Elfine got hers from dancing about on the Downs in the fog in a peculiar green dress, while Seth got his from mollocking. But Reuben just didn't seem to get a kick out of anything.

'Is it too hot?' she asked, and handed him the milk, with a smile.

The opaque curve purred softly down into the teak depths of the cup. He went on blowing it, and staring at her. Flora wanted to set him at ease (if he had an ease?), so she composedly went on with her tea, wishing there were some cucumber sandwiches.

After a silence which lasted seven minutes by a covert glance at Flora's watch, a series of visible tremors which passed across the expanse of Reuben's face, and a series of low, preparatory noises which proceeded from his throat, persuaded her that he was about to speak to her. Cautious as a camera-man engaged in shooting a family of fourteen lions, Flora made no sign.

Her control was rewarded. After another minute Reuben brought forth the following sentence:

'I ha' scranleted two hundred furrows come five o'clock down i' the bute.'

It was a difficult remark, Flora felt, to which to reply. Was it a complaint? If so, one might say, 'My dear, how too sickening for you!' But then, it might be a boast, in which case the correct reply would be, 'Attaboy!' or more simply, 'Come, that's capital.' Weakly she fell back on the comparatively safe remark:

'Did you?' in a bright, interested voice.

She saw at once that she had said the wrong thing. Reuben's eyebrows came down and his jaw came out. Horrors! He thought she was doubting his word!

'Aye, I did, tu. Two hundred. Two hundred from Ticklepenny's Corner down to Nettle Flitch. Aye, wi'out hand to aid me. Could you ha' done that?'

'No, indeed,' replied Flora, heartily, and her guardian

angel (who must, she afterwards decided, have been doing a spot of overtime) impelled her to add: 'But then, you see, I shouldn't want to.'

This seemingly innocent confession had a surprising effect on Reuben. He banged down his cup and thrust his face forward, peering intently into hers.

'Wouldn't you, then? Ah, but you'd pay a hired man good money to do it for you, I'll lay – wastin' the farm's takin's.'

Flora was now beginning to see what was the matter. He thought she had designs on the farm!

'Indeed I wouldn't,' she retorted promptly. 'I wouldn't care if Ticklepenny's Corner wasn't scranleted at all. I don't want to have anything to do with Nettle Flitch. I'd let' – she smiled pleasantly up to Reuben – 'I'd let you do it all instead.'

But this effort went sour on her, to her dismay.

'Let!' shouted Reuben, thumping the table. 'Let! A mirksy, capsy word to use to a man as has nursed a farm like a sick mommet – and a man as knows every inch of soil and patch o' sukebind i' the place. Let . . . aye, a fine word – '

'I really think we had better get this straight,' interrupted Flora. 'It will make things so much easier. I don't want the farm. Really, I don't. In fact' – she hesitated whether she should tell him that it seemed incredible to her that anyone could possibly want it, but decided that this would be rude as well as unkind – 'well, such an idea never came into my head. I know nothing about farming, and I don't want to. I would much rather leave it to people who do know everything about it, like you. Why, just think what a mess I should make of the sukebind harvest and everything. You must see that I am the last person in the world who would be any use at scranleting. I am sure you will believe me.'

A second series of tremors, of a slightly more complicated type than the first, passed across Reuben's face. He seemed about to speak, but in the end he did not. He slapped down his cup, gave a last stare at Flora, and stumped out of the kitchen.

This was an unsatisfactory end to the interview, which had begun well; but she was not disturbed. It was obvious that, even if he did not believe her, he wanted to; and that was half the battle. He had even been on the verge of believing her when she made that lucky remark about not wanting to scranlet; and only his natural boorishness and his suspicious nature had prevented him. The next time she assured him that she was not after Cold Comfort Farm, Reuben would be convinced that she spoke the truth.

The fire was now burning brightly. Flora lit a candle, which she had brought down from her bedroom, and took up some sewing with which to beguile the time until supper in her own room. She was making a petticoat and decorating it with drawn threadwork.

A little later, as she sat peacefully sewing, Adam came in from the yard. He wore, as a protection from the rain, a hat which had lost – in who knows what dim hintermath of time – the usual attributes of shape, colour, and size, and those more subtle race-memory associations which identify hats as hats, and now resembled some obscure natural growth, some moss or sponge or fungus, which had attached itself to a host.

He was carrying between finger and thumb a bunch of thorn twigs, which Flora presumed that he had just picked from one of the trees in the yard; and he held them ostentatiously in front of him, like a torch.

He glanced spitefully at Flora from under the brim of the hat as he crossed the kitchen, but said nothing to her. As he placed the twigs carefully on a shelf above the sink, he glanced round at her, but she went on sewing, and said never a word. So after rearranging the twigs once or twice, and coughing, he muttered:

'Aye, them'll last me till Michaelmas to cletter the dishes wi' – there's nothing like a thorn twig for cletterin' dishes. Aye, a rope's as good as a halter to a willin' horse. Curses, like rookses, flies home to rest in bosomses and barnses.'

It was clear that he had not forgotten Flora's advice about using a little mop to clean the dishes. As he shuffled away, she thought that she must remember to buy one for him the next time she went into Howling.

Flora had scarcely time to get over this before there sounded a step in the yard outside, and there entered a young man who could only be Seth.

Flora looked up with a cool smile.

'How do you do? Are you Seth? I'm your cousin, Flora Poste. I'm afraid you're too late for any tea . . . unless you would like to make some fresh for yourself.'

He came over to her with the lounging grace of a panther, and leaned against the mantelpiece. Flora saw at once that he was not the kind that could be fobbed off with offers of tea. She was for it.

'What's that you're making?' he asked. Flora knew that he hoped it was a pair of knickers. She composedly shook out the folds of the petticoat and replied that it was an afternoon tea-cloth.

'Aye . . . woman's nonsense,' said Seth, softly. (Flora wondered why he had seen fit to drop his voice by half an octave.) 'Women are all alike — ay fussin' over their fal-lals and bedazin' a man's eyes, when all they really want is man's blood and his heart out of his body and his soul and his pride . . .'

'Really?' said Flora, looking in her work-box for her scissors.

'Aye.' His deep voice had jarring notes which were curiously blended into an animal harmony like the natural cries of stoat or weasel. 'That's all women want – a man's life. Then when they've got him bound up in their fal-lals and bedazin' ways and their softness, and he can't move because of the longin' for them as cries in his man's blood – do you know what they do then?'

'I'm afraid not,' said Flora. 'Would you mind passing me that reel of cotton on the mantelpiece, just by your ear? Thank you so much.' Seth passed it mechanically, and continued.

'They eat him, same as a hen-spider eats a cock-spider. That's what women do – if a man lets 'em.'

'Indeed,' commented Flora.

'Aye – but I said "if" a man lets 'em. Now I – I don't let no women eat me. I eats them instead.'

Flora thought an appreciative silence was the best policy to pursue at this point. She found it difficult, indeed, to reply to him in words, since his conversation, in which she had participated before (at parties in Bloomsbury as well as in drawing-rooms in Cheltenham), was, after all, mainly a kind of jockeying for place, a shifting about of the pieces on the board before the real game began. And if, in her case, one of the players was merely a little bored by it all and was wondering whether she would be able to brew some hot milk before she went to bed that night, there was not much point in playing.

True, in Cheltenham and in Bloomsbury gentlemen did not say in so many words that they ate women in self-defence, but there was no doubt that that was what they meant.

'That shocks you, eh?' said Seth, misinterpreting her silence.

'Yes, I think it's dreadful,' replied Flora, good-naturedly meeting him half-way.

He laughed. It was a cruel sound like the sputter of the stoat as it sinks its feet into the neck of a rabbit.

'Dreadful . . . aye! You're all alike. You're just the same as the rest, for all your London ways. Mealy-mouthed as a school-kid. I'll lay you don't understand half of what I've been saying, do you? . . . Liddle innercent.'

'I am afraid I wasn't listening to all of it,' she replied, 'but I am sure it was very interesting. You must tell me all about your work some time . . . What do you do, now, on the evenings when you aren't – er – eating people?'

'I goes over to Beershorn,' replied Seth, rather sulkily. The dark flame of his male pride was a little suspicious of having its leg pulled.

'To play darts?' Flora knew her A. P. H.

'Noa . . . me play that kid's game with a lot of old men? That's a good 'un, that is. No. I goes to the talkies.'

And something in the inflection which Seth gave to the last word of his speech, the lingering, wistful, almost cooing note which invaded his curiously animal voice, caused Flora to put down her sewing in her lap and to glance up at him. Her gaze rested thoughtfully upon his irregular but handsome features.

'The talkies, do you? Do you like them?'

'Better nor anything in the whoal world,' he said, fiercely. 'Better nor my mother nor this farm nor Violet down at the Vicarage, nor anything.'

'Indeed,' mused his cousin, still eyeing his face thoughtfully. 'That's interesting. Very interesting indeed.'

'I've got seventy-four photographs o' Lotta Funchal,' confided Seth, becoming in his discussions of his passion like those monkeys which are described as 'almost human'. 'Aye, an' forty o' Jenny Carrol, and fifty-five o' Laura Vallee, and twenty o' Carline Heavytree, and fifteen of Sigrid Maelstrom. Aye, an' ten o' Panella Baxter. Signed ones.'

Flora nodded, displaying courteous interest, but showing nothing of the plan which had suddenly occurred to her; and Seth, after a suspicious glance at her, suddenly decided that he had been betrayed into talking to a woman about something else than love, and was angry.

So, muttering that he was going off to Beershorn to see 'Sweet Sinners' (he was evidently inflamed by this discussion of his passion), he took himself off.

The rest of the evening passed quietly. Flora supped off an omelette and some coffee, which she prepared in her own sitting-room. After supper she finished the design upon the breast of her petticoat, read a chapter of *Macaria, or Altars of Sacrifice*, and went to bed at ten o'clock.

All this was pleasant enough. And while she was undressing, she reflected that her campaign for the tidying up of Cold Comfort was progressing quite well, when she thought that she had only been there two days. She had made overtures to Reuben. She had instructed Meriam, the hired girl, in the precautionary arts, and she had gotten her bedroom curtains washed (they hung full and crimson in the candle-light). She had discovered the nature of Seth's *grande passion*, and it was not Women, but the Talkies. She had had a plan for making the most of Seth, but she could think that out in detail later. She blew out the candle.

But (she thought, settling her cool forehead against the cold pillow) this habit of passing her evenings in peaceful solitude in her own sitting-room must not make her forget her plan of campaign. It was clear that she must take some of her meals with the Starkadders, and learn to know them.

She sighed: and fell asleep.

CHAPTER 8

SHE found some difficulty during the ensuing week in meeting her Cousin Amos, while no one so much as breathed a word about introducing her to Aunt Ada Doom. Each morning, at nine o'clock, Flora watched Mrs Beetle stagger upstairs with a tray laden with sausages, marmalade, porridge, a kipper, a fat black pot of strong tea, and what Flora caustically thought of as half a loaf; but when once Mrs Beetle had entered Aunt Ada's bedroom, the door was shut for good. And when Mrs Beetle came out she was not communicative. Once she observed to Flora, seeing the latter regarding the empty tray which had come out of Mrs Stark-adder's bedroom:

'Yes . . . we're a bit off our feed this morning, as you might say. We've only 'ad two goes of porridge, two soft-boiled eggs, a kipper just on the turn, and 'alf that pot o' jam Adam stole from the Vicarage bazaar larst summer. Still, there's room for it where it goes, 'eaven knows, and we keep 'ealthy enough on it.'

'I have not met my aunt yet,' said Flora.

Mrs Beetle replied sombrely that Flora 'adn't missed

much, and they said no more on the matter. For Flora was not the type of person who questions servants.

And even if she had been, it was plain to her that Mrs Beetle was not the type of person who gives away secrets. Flora gathered that she did not altogether disapprove of old Mrs Starkadder. She had been heard to say that at least there was one of 'em at Cold Comfort as knew her own mind, even if she 'ad seen something narsty in the woodshed when she was two. Flora had no idea what this last sentence could possibly mean. Possibly it was a local idiom for going cuckoo.

In any case, she could not demand to see her aunt if her aunt did not want to see her; and surely if she had wanted to see her she would have commanded that Flora be brought into the Presence. Perhaps old Mrs Starkadder knew that Flora was out to tidy up the farm, and intended to adopt a policy of passive resistance. In which case an attempt must sooner or later be made to invade the enemy's fort. But that could wait.

Meanwhile, there was Amos.

She learnt from Adam that he preached twice a week to the Church of the Quivering Brethren, a religious sect which had its headquarters in Beershorn. It occurred to her that she might ask to accompany him there one evening, and begin working on him during the long drive down to the town.

Accordingly, when Thursday evening came during her second week at the farm, she approached her cousin as he entered the kitchen after tea (for he would never partake of that meal, which he thought finicking) and said resolutely:

'Are you going down into Beershorn to preach to the Brethren to-night?'

Amos looked at her, as though seeing her for the first, or perhaps the second time. ***His huge body, rude as a wind-tortured thorn, was printed darkly against the thin mild flame of the declining winter sun that throbbed like a sallow lemon on the westering lip of Mockuncle Hill, and sent its pale, sharp rays into the kitchen through the open door.

The brittle air, on which the fans of the trees were etched like ageing skeletons, seemed thronged by the bright, invisible ghosts of a million dead summers. The cold beat in glassy waves against the eyelids of anybody who happened to be out in it. High up, a few chalky clouds doubtfully wavered in the pale sky that curved over against the rim of the Downs like a vast inverted *pot-de-chambre*. Huddled in the hollow, like an exhausted brute, the frosted roofs of Howling, crisp and purple as broccoli leaves, were like beasts about to spring.

'Aye,' said Amos at last. He was encased in black fustian, which made his legs and arms look like drain-pipes, and he wore a hard little felt hat. Flora supposed that some people would say that he walked in a lurid, smoky hell of his own religious torment. In any case, he was a rude old man.

'They'll all burn in hell,' added Amos in a satisfied voice, 'and' I mun surelie tell them so.'

'Well, may I come too?'

He did not seem surprised. Indeed, she caught in his eye a triumphant light, as though he had been long expecting her to see the error of her ways and come to him and the Brethren for spiritual comfort.

'Aye . . . ye can come . . . ye poor miserable creepin' sinner. Maybe ye think ye'll escape hell fire if ye come along o' me, and bow down and quiver. But I'm tellin' ye no. 'Tes too late. Ye'll burn wi' the rest. There'll be time to say what yer sins have been, but there'll be no time for more.'

'Do I have to say them out aloud?' asked Flora, in some trepidation. It occurred to her that she had heard of a similar custom from friends of hers who were being educated at that great centre of religious life, Oxford.

'Aye, but not to-night. Nay, there'll be too many sayin' their sins aloud to-night; there'll be no time for the Lord to listen to a new sheep like you. And maybe the spirit won't move ye.'

Flora was pretty sure it would not; so she went upstairs to put on her hat and coat.

She did wonder what the Brethren would look like. In novels, persons who turned to religion to obtain the colour and excitement which everyday life did not give them were all grey and thwarted. Probably the Brethren would be all grey and thwarted ... though it was too true that life as she is lived had a way of being curiously different from life as described by novelists.

The yard was painted in sharp layers of gold light and towering shadows, by the rays of the new-lit-mog's-lantern (this was used especially for carrying round the chicken-house at night to see if there were any stray cats after the hens: hence the name).

Viper, the great gelding, was harnessed to the trap; and Adam, who had been called from the cowshed to get the brute between the shafts, was being swung up and down in the air as he hung on to the reins.

The great beast, nineteen hands high, jerked his head wickedly, and Adam's frail body flew up into the darkness beyond the circle of grave, gold light painted by the mog's-lantern, and was lost to sight.

Then down he came again, a twisted grey moth falling into the light as Viper thrust his head down to snuff the reeking straw about his feet.

'Git up,' said Amos to Flora.

'Is there a rug?' she asked, hanging fire.

'Nay. The sins burnin' in yer marrow will keep yer warm.'

But Flora thought otherwise, and darting into the kitchen, she returned with her leather coat, in the lining of which she had been mending a tiny tear.

Adam whisked past her head as she put her foot on the step, piping in his distress like a very old peewit. His eyes were shut. His grey face was strained into an exalted mask of martyrdom.

'*Do* let go of the reins, Adam,' urged Flora, in some distress. 'He'll hurt you in a minute.'

'Nay ... 'tes exercisin' our Viper,' said Adam feebly; and then, as Amos struck Viper on the shanks and the brute jerked his head as though he had been shot, Adam was flung out of the circle of light into the thick darkness, and was seen no more.

'There . . . you see!' said Flora reproachfully.

But muttering, 'Aye, let un be for a moithering old fool,' Amos struck the horse again and the gig plunged forward.

Flora quite enjoyed the drive into Beershorn. The coat kept her pleasantly warm, and the cold wind dashing past her cheeks was exhilarating. She could see nothing except the muddy road directly under the swinging mog's-lantern, and the large outlines of the Downs against the starless sky, but the budding hedges smelt fresh, and there was a feeling that spring was coming.

Amos was silent. Indeed, none of the Starkadders had any general conversation; and Flora found this particularly try-ing at meal-times. Meals at the farm were eaten in silence. If anyone spoke at all during the indigestible twenty minutes which served them for dinner or supper, it was to pose some awkward questions which, when answered, led to a blazing row; as, for example: 'Why has not – (whichever member of the family was absent from table) – come in to her food?' or 'Why has not the barranfield been gone over a second time with the pruning snoot?' On the whole, Flora liked it better when they were silent, though it did rather give her the feeling that she was acting in one of the less cheerful German highbrow films.

But now she had Amos to herself; and the opportunity was golden. She began:

'It must be so interesting to preach to the Brethren, Cousin Amos. I quite envy you. Do you prepare your ser-mon beforehand, or do you just make it up as you go along?'

An apparent increase in Amos's looming bulk, after this question had had time to sink in, convinced her in the midst of a disconcerting and ever-lengthening pause that he was swelling with fury. Cautiously she glanced over the side of the trap to see if she could jump out should he attempt to smite her. The ground looked disagreeably muddy and far off; and she was relieved when Amos at last replied in a tolerably well-controlled voice:

'Doan't 'ee speak o' the word o' the Lord in that godless way, as though 'twere one o' they pagan tales in the *Family Herald*. The word is not prepared beforehand; it falls on me mind like the manna fell from heaven into the bellies of the starving Israelites.'

'Really! How interesting. Then you have no idea what you are going to say before you get there?'

'Aye ... I allus knows 'twill be summat about burnin' ... or the eternal torment ... or sinners comin' to judgement. But I doan't know exactly what the words will be until I gets up in me seat and looks round at all their sinful faces, awaitin' all eager for to hear me. Then I knows what I mun say, and I says it.'

'Does anyone else preach, or are you the only one?'

'Oanly me. Deborah Checkbottom, she tried onceways to get up and preach. But 'tweren't no good. Her couldn't.'

'Wouldn't the spirit work or something?'

'Nay, it worked. But I wouldn't have it. I reckoned the Lord's ways is dark and there'd be a mistake, and the spirit that was meant for me had fallen on Deborah. So I just struck her down wi' the gurt old Bible, to let the devil out of her soul.'

'And did it come out?' asked Flora, endeavouring with some effort to maintain the proper spirit of scientific inquiry.

'Aye, he came out. We heard no more o' Deborah's tryin' to preach. Now I preaches alone. No one else gets the word like I do.'

Flora detected a note of complacency and took her opportunity.

'I am looking forward so much to hearing you, Cousin Amos. I suppose you like preaching very much?'

'Nay. 'Tes a fearful torment and a groanin' to me soul's marrow,' corrected Amos. (Like all true artists, thought Flora, he was unwilling to admit that he got no end of a kick out of his job.) 'But 'tes my mission. Aye, I mun tell the Brethren to prepare in time for torment, when the roarin' red flames will lick round their feet like the dogs lickin' Jezebel's blood in the Good Book. I mun tell everybody' – here he moved slightly round in his seat, and Flora presumed that he was fixing her with a meaning stare – 'o' hell fire. Aye, the word burns in me mouth and I mun blow it out on the whoal world like flames.'

'You ought to preach to a larger congregation than the Brethren,' suggested Flora, suddenly struck by a very good idea. 'You mustn't waste yourself on a few miserable sinners in Beershorn, you know. Why don't you go round the country with a Ford van, preaching on market days?'

For she was sure that Amos's religious scruples were likely to be in the way when she began to introduce the changes she desired to bring about at the farm, and if she could get him out of the way on a long preaching tour her task would be simpler.

'I mun till the field nearest my hand before I go into the hedges and by-ways,' retorted Amos austerely. 'Besides, 'twould be exaltin' meself and puffin' meself up if I was to go preachin' all over the country in one o' they Ford vans. 'Twould be thinkin' o' my own glory instead o' the glory o' the Lord.'

Flora was surprised to find him so astute, but reflected that religious maniacs derived considerable comfort from digging into their motives for their actions and discovering discreditable reasons which covered them with good, satisfying sinfulness in which they could wallow to their hearts' content. She thought she heard a note of wistfulness, however, in the words, 'one o' they Ford vans', and gathered that the idea of such a tour tempted him considerably. She returned to the attack:

'But, Cousin Amos, isn't that rather putting your own miserable soul before the glory of the Lord? I mean, what does it matter if you *do* puff yourself up a bit and lose your holy humility if a lot of sinners are converted by your preaching? You must be *prepared*, I think, to sin in order to save others – at least, that is what *I* should be prepared to do if *I* were going round the country preaching from a Ford van. You see what I mean, don't you? By *seeming* to be humble, and dismissing the idea of making this tour, you are *in reality* setting more value on your soul than on the spreading of the word of the Lord.'

She was proud of herself at the conclusion of this speech. It had, she thought, the proper over-subtle flavour, that air of triumphantly pointing out an undetected and perfectly enormous sin lying slap under the sinner's nose which distinguishes all speeches intended to lay bare the workings of the religious mind.

Anyway, it produced the right effect on Amos. After a pause, during which the buggy rapidly passed the houses on the outskirts of the town, he observed in a hoarse, stifled voice:

'Aye, there's truth in what ye say. Maybe it is me duty to seek a wider field. I mun think of it. Aye, 'tes terrible. A sinner never knows how the devil may dress himself up to deceive. 'Twill be a new sin to wrestle with, the sin of carin' whether me soul is puffed up or not. And how can I tell, when I am feelin' puffed up when I preach, whether I'm sinnin' in me pride or whether I'm doin' right by savin' souls and therefore it woan't matter if I *am* puffed up? Aye, and what right have I to puff meself up if I *do* save them? Aye, 'tes a dark and bewilderin' way.'

All this was muttered in so low a voice that Flora could only just hear what he was saying, but she distinguished enough to make her reply firmly:

'Yes, Cousin Amos, it is all very difficult. But I do think, in spite of the difficulties, that you ought to consider seriously the possibility of letting hundreds more people hear your sermons. You have a Call, you know. No one should neglect a Call. Wouldn't you *like* to preach to thousands?'

'Aye, dearly. But 'tes vainglorious to think on't,' he replied wistfully.

'There you go again,' reproved his youthful companion. 'What does it matter if it *is* vainglorious – what does your soul matter compared with the souls of thousands of sinners, who might be saved by your preaching?'

At this moment the trap came to a halt outside a public-house, in a small yard opening off the High Street, and Flora was relieved, for the conversation seemed to have entered one of those vicious circles to which only the death or collapse from exhaustion of one of the participants can put an end.

Amos left Flora to get down from the trap as best she could.

'Hurry up,' he called. 'We mun hasten and leave the devil's house,' glancing back disapprovingly at the warmly-lit windows of the pub, which Flora thought looked rather nice.

'Is the chapel far from here?' she asked, following him down the High Street, where coarse yellow rays from the little shops shone out into the wintry dark.

'Nay – 'tes here.'

They stopped in front of a building which Flora at first took to be an unusually large dog-kennel. The doors were open, and inside could be seen the seats and walls of plain pitch-pine. Some of the Brethren were already seated, and others were hurrying in to take their places.

'We mun wait till the chapel is full,' whispered Amos.

'Why?'

''Tes frittenin' for them to see their preacher among them like any simple soul,' he whispered, standing some-what in the shadows. 'They fear to have me among them, breathin' warnin's o' hell fire and torment. 'Tes frittenin' in a way, when I stands up on the platform, bellowin', but 'tes not so cruel frittenin' as if I was to stand among them before I begin to preach, like any one of them, sharin' a hymn-book, maybe, or fixin' one of them wi' my eye to read her thoughts.'

'But I thought you wanted to frighten them?'

'Aye, so I do, but in a grand, glorifyin' kind of way. And I doan't want to fritten 'em so much that they won't never come back to hear me preach again.'

Flora, observing the faces of the Brethren as they crowded into the dog-kennel, thought that Amos had probably underestimated the strength of their nerves. Seldom had she seen so healthy and solid-looking an audience.

As an audience, it compared most favourably with audiences she had studied in London; and particularly with an audience seen once – but only once – at a Sunday afternoon meeting of the Cinema Society to which she had, somewhat unwillingly, accompanied a friend who was interested in the progress of the cinema as an art.

That audience had run to beards and magenta shirts and original ways of arranging its neckwear; and not content with the ravages produced in its over-excitable nervous system by the remorseless workings of its critical intelligence, it had sat through a film of Japanese life called 'Yĕs', made by a Norwegian film company in 1915 with Japanese actors, which lasted an hour and three-quarters and contained twelve close-ups of water-lilies lying perfectly still on a scummy pond and four suicides, all done extremely slowly.

All round her (Flora pensively recalled) people were muttering how lovely were its rhythmic patterns and what an exciting quality it had and how abstract was its formal decorative shaping.

But there was one little man sitting next to her, who had not said a word; he had just nursed his hat and eaten sweets out of a paper bag. Something (she supposed) must have linked their auras together, for at the seventh close-up of a large Japanese face dripping with tears, the little man held out to her the bag of sweets, muttering:

'Peppermint creams. Must have something.'

And Flora had taken one thankfully, for she was extremely hungry.

When the lights went up, as at last they did, Flora had observed with pleasure that the little man was properly and conventionally dressed; and, for his part, his gaze had dwelt upon her neat hair and well-cut coat with incredulous joy, as of one who should say: 'Dr Livingstone, I presume?'

He then, under the curious eyes of Flora's highbrow friend, said that his name was Earl P. Neck, of Beverly

Hills, Hollywood; and he gave them his 'cyard' very ceremoniously and asked if they would go and have tea with him? He seemed the nicest little creature, so Flora disregarded the raised eyebrows of her friend (who, like all loose-living persons, was extremely conventional) and said that they would like to very much, so off they went.

At tea, Mr Neck and Flora had exchanged views on various films of a frivolous nature which they had seen and enjoyed (for of 'Yes' they could not yet trust themselves to speak), and Mr Neck had told them that he was a guest-producer at the new British studios at Wendover, and would Flora and her friend come and visit the studios some time? It must be soon, said Mr Neck, because he was returning to Hollywood with the annual batch of England's best actors and actresses in the autumn.

Somehow she had never found time to visit Wendover, though she had dined twice with Mr Neck since their first meeting, and they liked each other very much. He had told Flora all about his slim, expensive mistress, Lily, who made boring scenes and took up the time and energy which he would much sooner have spent with his wife, but he had to have Lily, because in Beverly Hills, if you did not have a mistress, people thought you were rather queer, and if, on the other hand, you spent all your time with your wife, and were quite firm about it, and said that you liked your wife, and, anyway, why the hell shouldn't you, the papers came out with repulsive articles headed 'Hollywood Czar's Domestic Bliss', and you had to supply them with pictures of your wife pouring your morning chocolate and watering the ferns.

So there was no way out of it, Mr Neck said.

Anyway, his wife quite understood, and they played a game called 'Dodging Lily', which gave them yet another interest in common.

Now Mr Neck was in America, but he would be flying over to England, so his last letter told Flora, in the late spring.

Flora thought that when he came she would invite him

to spend a day with her in Sussex. There was somebody about whom she wished to talk to him.

She was reminded of Mr Neck, as she stood pensively watching the Brethren going into the chapel, by the spectacle of the Majestic Cinema immediately opposite. It was showing a stupendous drama of sophisticated passion called 'Other Wives' Sins'. Probably Seth was inside, enjoying himself.

The dog-kennel was nearly full.

Somebody was playing a shocking tune on the poor little wheezy organ near the door. Except for this organ, Flora observed, peering over Amos's shoulder, the chapel looked like an ordinary lecture hall, with a little round platform at the end farthest from the door, on which stood a chair.

'Is that where you preach, Cousin Amos?'

'Aye.'

'Does Judith or either of the boys ever come down to hear you preach?' She was making conversation because she was conscious of a growing feeling of dismay at what lay before her, and did not wish to give way to it.

Amos frowned.

'Nay. They struts like Ahab in their pride and their eyes drip fatness, nor do they see the pit digged beneath their feet by the Lord. Aye, 'tes a terrible wicked family I'm cursed wi', and the hand o' the Lord it lies heavy on Cold Comfort, pressin' the bitter wine out o' our souls.'

'Then why don't you sell it and buy another farm on a really *nice* piece of land, if you feel like that about it?'

'Nay ... there have always been Starkadders at Cold Comfort,' he answered, heavily. ''Tes old Mrs Starkadder – Ada Doom as she was, before she married Fig Starkadder. She's sot against us leavin' the farm. She'd never see us go. 'Tes a curse on us. And Reuben sits awaitin' for me to go, so as he can have the farm. But un shall niver have un. Nay, I'll leave it to Adam first.'

Before Flora could convey to him her lively sense of dismay at the prospect indicated in this threat, he moved

95

forward saying, "Tes nearly full. We mun go in,' and in they went.

Flora took a seat at the end of a row near the exit; she thought it would be as well to sit near the door in case the double effect of Amos's preaching and no ventilation became more than she could bear.

Amos went to a seat almost directly in front of the little platform, and sat down after directing two slow and brooding glances, laden with promise of terrifying eloquence to come, upon the Brethren sitting in the same row.

The dog-kennel was now packed to bursting, and the organ had begun to play something like a tune. Flora found a hymn-book being pressed into her hand by a female on her left.

'It's number two hundred, "Whatever shall we do, O Lord",' said the female, in a loud conversational voice.

Flora had supposed from impressions gathered during her wide reading, that it was customary to speak only in whispers in a building devoted to the act of worship. But she was ready to learn otherwise, so she took the book with a pleasant smile and said, 'Thank you so much'.

The hymn went like this:

> Whatever shall we do, O Lord,
>   When Gabriel blows o'er sea and river,
> Fen and desert, mount and ford?
>   The earth may burn, but we will quiver.

Flora approved of this hymn, because its words indicated a firmness of purpose, a clear path in the face of a disagreeable possibility, which struck an answering note in her own character. She sang industriously in her pleasing soprano. The singing was conducted by a surly, excessively dirty old man with long, grey hair who stood on the platform and waved what Flora, after the first incredulous shock, decided was a kitchen poker.

'Who is that?' she asked her friend.

"Tes Brother Ambleforth. He leads the quiverin' when we begins to quiver.'

'And why does he conduct the music with a poker?'

'To put us in mind of hell fire,' was the simple answer, and Flora had not the heart to say that as far as she was concerned, at any rate, this purpose was not achieved.

After the hymn, which was sung sitting down, everybody crossed their legs and arranged themselves more comfortably, while Amos rose from his seat with terrifying deliberation, mounted the little platform, and sat down.

For some three minutes he slowly surveyed the Brethren, his face wearing an expression of the most profound loathing and contempt, mingled with a divine sorrow and pity. He did it quite well. Flora had never seen anything to touch it except the face of Sir Henry Wood when pausing to contemplate some late-comers into the stalls at the Queen's Hall just as his baton was raised to conduct the first bar of the 'Eroica'. Her heart warmed to Amos. The man was an artist.

At last he spoke. His voice jarred the silence like a broken bell.

'Ye miserable, crawling worms, are ye here again, then? Have ye come like Nimshi, son of Rehoboam, secretly out of yer doomed houses to hear what's comin' to ye? Have ye come, old and young, sick and well, matrons and virgins (if there is any virgins among ye, which is not likely, the world bein' in the wicked state it is), old men and young lads, to hear me tellin' o' the great crimson lickin' flames o' hell fire?'

A long and effective pause, and a further imitation of Sir Henry. The only sound (and it, with the accompanying smell, was quite enough) was the wickering hissing of the gas flares which lit the hall and cast sharp shadows from their noses across the faces of the Brethren.

Amos went on:

'Aye, ye've come.' He laughed shortly and contemptuously. 'Dozens of ye. Hundreds of ye. Like rats to a granary. Like field-mice when there's harvest home. And what good will it do ye?'

Second pause, and more Sir Henry stuff.

97

'Nowt. Not the flicker of a whisper of a bit o' good.'

He paused and drew a long breath, then suddenly leaped from his seat and thundered at the top of his voice:

'*Ye're all damned!*'

An expression of lively interest and satisfaction passed over the faces of the Brethren, and there was a general re-arranging of arms and legs, as though they wanted to sit as comfortably as possible while listening to the bad news.

'Damned,' he repeated, his voice sinking to a thrilling and effective whisper. 'Oh, do ye ever stop to think what that word *means* when ye use it every day, so lightly, o' yer wicked lives? No. Ye doan't. Ye never stop to think what anything means, do ye? Well, I'll tell ye. It means endless horrifyin' torment, with yer poor sinful bodies stretched out on hot gridirons in the nethermost fiery pit of hell, and demons mockin' ye while they waves cooling jellies in front of ye, and binds ye down tighter on yer dreadful bed. Aye, an' the air'll be full of the stench of burnt flesh and the screams of your nearest and dearest . . .'

He took a gulp of water, which Flora thought he more than deserved. She was beginning to feel that she could do with a glass of water herself.

Amos's voice now took on a deceptively mild and con-versational note. His protruding eyes ranged slowly over his audience.

'Ye know, doan't ye, what it feels like when ye burn yer hand in takin' a cake out of the oven or wi' a match when ye're lightin' one of they godless cigarettes? Aye. It stings wi' a fearful pain, doan't it? And ye run away to clap a bit o' butter on it to take the pain away. Ah, but' (an impressive pause) '*there'll be no butter in hell!* Yer whoal body will be burnin' and stingin' wi' that unbearable pain, and yer blackened tongues will be stickin' out of yer mouth, and yer cracked lips will try to scream out for a drop of water, but no sound woan't come because yer throat is drier nor the sandy desert and yer eyes will be beatin' like great red-hot balls against yer shrivelled eyelids . . .'

It was at this point that Flora rose quietly and with an

apology to the woman sitting next to her, passed rapidly across the narrow aisle to the door. She opened it, and went out. The details of Amos's description, the close atmosphere and the smell of the gas made the inside of the chapel quite near enough to hell, without listening to Amos's conducted tour of the place thrown in. She felt that she could pass the evening more profitably elsewhere.

But where? The fresh air smelled deliciously sweet. She regained her composure while she stood in the porch putting on her gloves. She wondered if she should drop in to see 'Other Wives' Sins', but thought not; she had heard enough about sin for one evening.

What, then, should she do? She could not return to the farm except with Amos in the buggy, for it was seven miles from Beershorn, and the last bus to Howling left at half past six during the winter months. It was now nearly eight o'clock and she was hungry. She looked crossly up and down the street; most of the shops were shut, but one a few doors from the cinema was open.

It was called Pam's Parlour. It was a tea-shop, and Flora thought it looked pretty grim; there were cakes in its windows all mixed up with depressing little boxes made of white wood and raffia bags and linen bags embroidered with hollyhocks. But where there were cakes there might also be coffee. She crossed the road and went in.

No sooner did she stand inside than she realized that she had gone out of hell fire into an evening of boredom. For someone was seated at one of the tables whom she recognized. She seemed to remember meeting him at a party given by a Mrs Polswett in London. And he could only be Mr Mybug. That was who he looked like, and that, of course, was who he was. There was no one else in the shop. He had a clear field, and she could not escape.

CHAPTER 9

HE glanced up at her as she came in and looked pleased. He had some books and papers in front of him and had been busily writing.

By now Flora was really cross. Surely she had endured enough for one evening without having to listen to intelligent conversation! Here was an occasion, she thought, for indulging in that deliberate rudeness which only persons with habitually good manners have the right to commit; she sat down at the table with her back to the supposed Mr Mybug, picked up a menu which had gnomes painted on it, and hoped for the best . . .

A waitress in a long frilly chintz dress which needed ironing had brought her coffee, some plain biscuits, and an orange, which she had dressed with sugar and was now enjoying. The waitress had warned her that we were closed, but as this did not seem to prevent Flora sitting in the shop and enjoying her sugared orange, she did not mind if we were.

She was just beginning on her fourth biscuit when she became conscious of a presence approaching her from behind, and before she could collect her faculties the voice of Mr Mybug said:

'Hullo, Flora Poste. Do you believe that women have souls?' And there he was, standing above her and looking down at her with a bold yet whimsical smile.

Flora was not surprised at being asked this question. She knew that intellectuals, like Mr Kipling's Bi-coloured Python-Rock-Snake, always talked like this. So she replied pleasantly, but from her heart: 'I am afraid I'm not very interested.'

Mr Mybug gave a short laugh. Evidently he was pleased. She spooned out some more orange juice and wondered why.

'Aren't you? Good girl . . . we shall be all right if only you'll be frank with me. As a matter of fact, I'm not very interested in whether they have souls either. Bodies matter more than souls. I say, may I sit down? You do remember me, don't you? We met at the Polswetts in October. Look here, you don't think this is butting in or anything, do you? The Polswetts told me you were staying down here, and I wondered if I should run into you. Do you know Billie Polswett well? She's a charming person, I think . . . so simple and gay, and such a genius for friendship. He's charming, too . . . a bit homo, of course, but quite charming. I say, that orange does look good . . . I think I'll have one, too. I adore eating things with a spoon. May I sit here?'

'Do,' said Flora, seeing that her hour was upon her and that there was no escape.

Mr Mybug sat down and, turning round, beckoned to the waitress, who came and told him that we were closed.

'I say, that sounds vaguely indelicate,' laughed Mr Mybug, glancing round at Flora. 'Well, look here, miss, never mind that. Just bring me an orange and some sugar, will you?'

The waitress went away, and Mr Mybug could once more concentrate upon Flora. He leaned his elbows on the table, sank his chin in his hands, and looked steadily at her. As Flora merely went on eating her orange, he was forced to open the game with, 'Well?' (A gambit which Flora, with a sinking heart, recognized as one used by intellectuals who had decided to fall in love with you.)

'You are writing a book, aren't you?' she said, rather hastily. 'I remember that Mrs Polswett told me you were. Isn't it a life of Branwell Brontë?' (She thought it would be best to utilize the information artlessly conveyed to her by Mrs Murther at the Condemn'd Man, and conceal the fact that she had met Mrs Polswett, a protégée of Mrs Smiling's, only once, and thought her a most trying female.)

'Yes, it's goin' to be dam' good,' said Mr Mybug. 'It's a psychological study, of course, and I've got a lot of new matter, including three letters he wrote to an old aunt in Ireland, Mrs Prunty, during the period when he was working on *Wuthering Heights.*'

He glanced sharply at Flora to see if she would react by a

laugh or a stare of blank amazement, but the gentle, interested expression upon her face did not change, so he had to explain.

'You see, it's obvious that it's his book and not Emily's. No woman could have written that. It's male stuff . . . I've worked out a theory about his drunkenness, too – you see, he wasn't really a drunkard. He was a tremendous genius, a sort of second Chatterton – and his sisters hated him because of his genius.'

'I thought most of the contemporary records agree that his sisters were quite devoted to him,' said Flora, who was only too pleased to keep the conversation impersonal.

'I know . . . I know. But that was only their cunning. You see, they were devoured by jealousy of their brilliant brother, but they were afraid that if they showed it he would go away to London for good, taking his manuscripts with him. And they didn't want him to do that because it would have spoiled their little game.'

'Which little game was that?' asked Flora, trying with some difficulty to imagine Charlotte, Emily, and Anne engaged in a little game.

'Passing his manuscripts off as their own, of course. They wanted to have him under their noses so that they could steal his work and sell it to buy more drink.'

'Who for – Branwell?'

'No – for themselves. They were all drunkards, but Anne was the worst of the lot. Branwell, who adored her, used to pretend to get drunk at the Black Bull in order to get gin for Anne. The landlord wouldn't let him have it if Branwell hadn't built up – with what devotion, only God knows – that false reputation as a brilliant, reckless, idle drunkard. The landlord was proud to have young Mr Brontë in his tavern; it attracted custom to the place, and Branwell could get gin for Anne on tick – as much as Anne wanted. Secretly, he worked twelve hours a day writing *Shirley* and *Villette* – and, of course, *Wuthering Heights*. I've proved all this by evidence from the three letters to old Mrs Prunty.'

'But do the letters,' inquired Flora, who was fascinated

by this recital, 'actually say that he is writing *Wuthering Heights*?'

'Of course not,' retorted Mr Mybug. 'Look at the question as a psychologist would. Here is a man working fifteen hours a day on a stupendous masterpiece which absorbs almost all his energy. He will scarcely spare the time to eat or sleep. He's like a dynamo driving itself on its own demoniac vitality. Every scrap of his being is concentrated on finishing *Wuthering Heights*. With what little energy he has left he writes to an old aunt in Ireland. Now, I ask you, would you expect him to mention that he was working on *Wuthering Heights*?'

'Yes,' said Flora.

Mr Mybug shook his head violently.

'No – no – no! Of course he wouldn't. He'd want to get away from it for a little while, away from this all-obsessing work that was devouring his vitality. Of course he wouldn't mention it – not even to his aunt.'

'Why not even to her? Was he so fond of her?'

'She was the passion of his life,' said Mr Mybug, simply, with a luminous gravity in his voice. 'Think – he'd never seen her. She was not like the rest of the drab angular women by whom he was surrounded. She symbolized mystery ... woman ... the eternal unsolvable and unfindable X. It was a perversion, of course, his passion for her, and that made it all the stronger. All we have left of this fragile, wonderfully delicate relationship between the old woman and the young man are these three short letters. Nothing more.'

'Didn't she ever answer them?'

'If she did, her letters are lost. But his letters to her are enough to go on. They are little masterpieces of repressed passion. They're full of tender little questions ... he asks her how is her rheumatism ... has her cat, Toby, "recovered from the fever" ... what is the weather like at Derrydownderry ... at Haworth it is not so good ... how is Cousin Martha (and what a picture we get of Cousin Martha in those simple words, a raw Irish chit, high-cheekboned, with limp black hair and clear blood in her lips!) . . . It didn't matter to Branwell that in London the Duke was jockeying Palmerston in the stormy Corn Reforms of the "forties". Aunt Prunty's health and welfare came first in interest.'

Mr Mybug paused and refreshed himself with a spoonful of orange juice. Flora sat pondering on what she had just heard. Judging by her personal experience among her friends, it was not the habit of men of genius to refresh themselves from their labours by writing to old aunts; this task, indeed, usually fell to the sisters and wives of men of genius, and it struck Flora as far more likely that Charlotte, Anne, or Emily would have had to cope with any old aunts who were clamouring to be written to. However, perhaps Charlotte, Anne, or Emily had all decided one morning that it really *was* Branwell's turn to write to Aunt Prunty, and had sat on his head in turn while he wrote the three letters, which were afterwards posted at prudently spaced intervals.

She glanced at her watch.

It was half past eight. She wondered what time the Brethren came out of the dog-kennel. There was no sign of their release so far; the kennel was thundering to their singing, and at intervals there were pauses, during which Flora presumed that they were quivering. She swallowed a tiny yawn. She was sleepy.

'What are you going to call it?'

She knew that intellectuals always made a great fuss about the titles of their books. The titles of biographies were especially important. Had not *Victorian Vista*, the scathing life of Thomas Carlyle, dropped stone cold last year from the presses because everybody thought it was a boring book of reminiscences, while *Odour of Sanctity*, a rather dull history of Drainage Reform from 1840 to 1873, had sold like hot cakes because everybody thought it was an attack on Victorian morality.

'I'm hesitating between *Scapegoat; A Study of Branwell Brontë*, and *Pard-spirit; A Study of Branwell Brontë* – you know . . . A pard-like spirit, beautiful and swift.'

Flora did indeed know. The quotation was from Shelley's

'Adonais'. One of the disadvantages of almost universal education was the fact that all kinds of persons acquired a familiarity with one's favourite writers. It gave one a curious feeling; it was like seeing a drunken stranger wrapped in one's dressing-gown.

'Which do you like best?' asked Mr Mybug.

'*Pard-spirit*,' said Flora, unhesitatingly, not because she did, but because it would only lead to a long and boring argument if she hesitated.

'Really . . . that's interesting. So do I. It's wilder somehow, isn't it? I mean, I think it does give one something of the feeling of a wild thing bound down and chained, eh? And Branwell's colouring carries out the analogy – that wild reddish-leopard colouring. I refer to him as the Pard throughout the book. And then, of course, there's an undercurrent of symbolism . . .'

He thinks of everything, reflected Flora.

'A leopard can't change his spots, and neither could Branwell, in the end. He might take the blame for his sisters' drunkenness and let them, out of some perverted sense of sacrifice, claim his books. But in the end his genius has flamed out, blackest spots on richest gold. There isn't an intelligent person in Europe to-day who really believes Emily wrote the *Heights*.'

Flora finished her last biscuit, which she had been saving, and looked hopefully across at the dog-kennel. It seemed to her that the hymn now being sung had a sound like the tune of those hymns which are played just before people come out of church.

In the interval of outlining his work, Mr Mybug had been looking at her very steadily, with his chin lowered, and she was not surprised when he said, abruptly:

'Do you cah about walking?'

Flora was now in a dreadful fix, and earnestly wished that the dog-kennel would open and Amos, like a fiery angel, come to rescue her. For if she said that she adored walking, Mr Mybug would drag her for miles in the rain while he talked about sex, and if she said that she liked it only in moderation, he would make her sit on wet stiles, while he tried to kiss her. If, again, she parried his question and said that she loathed walking, he would either suspect that she suspected that he wanted to kiss her, or else he would make her sit in some dire tea-room while he talked more about sex and asked her what she felt about it.

There really seemed no way out of it, except by getting up and rushing out of the shop.

But Mr Mybug spared her this decision by continuing in the same low voice:

'I thought we might do some walks together, if you'd cah to? I'd better warn you – I'm – pretty susceptible.'

And he gave a curt laugh, still looking at her.

'Then perhaps we had better postpone our walks until the weather is finer,' said she, pleasantly. 'It would be too bad if your book were held up by your catching a cold, and if you really have a weak chest you cannot be too careful.'

Mr Mybug looked as though he would have given much to have brushed this aside with a brutal laugh. He had planned that his next sentence should be, in an even lower voice:

'You see, I believe in utter frankness about these things – Flora.'

But somehow he did not say it. He was not used to talking to young women who looked as clean as Flora looked. It rather put him off his stroke. He said instead, in a toneless voice: 'Yes ... oh, yes, of course,' and gave her a quick glance.

Flora was pensively drawing on her gauntlets and keeping her glance upon the stream of Brethren now issuing from the dog-kennel. She feared to miss Amos.

Mr Mybug rose abruptly, and stood looking at her with his hands thrust into his pockets.

'Are you with anybody?' he asked.

'My cousin is preaching at the Church of the Quivering Brethren opposite. He is driving me home.'

Mr Mybug murmured his, 'dear, how amusing.' He then said:

'Oh . . . I thought we might have walked it.'

'It is seven miles, and I am afraid my shoes are not stout enough,' countered Flora firmly.

Mr Mybug gave an ironical smile and muttered something about 'Check to the King', but Flora had seen Amos coming out of the kennel and knew that rescue had come, so she did not mind who was checked.

She said, pleasantly, 'I must go, I am afraid; there is my cousin looking for me. Good-bye, and thank you so much for telling me about your book. It's been so interesting. Perhaps we shall meet again sometime . . .'

Mr Mybug leapt on this remark, which slipped out unintentionally from Flora's social armoury, before she could prevent it, and said eagerly that it would be great fun if they could meet again. 'I'll give you my card.' And he brought out a large, dirty, nasty one, which Flora with some reluctance put into her bag.

'I warn you,' added Mr Mybug, 'I'm a queer moody brute. Nobody likes me. I'm like a child that's been rapped over the knuckles till it's afraid to shake hands – but there's something there if you cah to dig for it.'

Flora did not cah to dig, but she thanked him for his card with a smile, and hurried across the road to join Amos, who stood towering in the middle of it.

As she came up to him he drew back, pointed at her, and uttered the single word:

'Fornicator!'

'No – dash it, Cousin Amos, that wasn't a stranger; it was a person I'd met before at a party in London,' protested Flora, her indignation a little roused by the unjustness of the accusation, especially when she thought of her real feelings for Mr Mybug.

''Tes all one – aye, and worse too, comin' from London, the devil's city,' said Amos, grimly.

However, his protest had apparently been a matter more of form than of feeling. He said nothing more about it, and they drove home in silence, save for a single remark from him to the effect that the Brethren had been mightily stirred by his preaching and that Flora had missed a good deal by not staying for the quivering.

To which Flora replied that she was sure she had, but that his eloquence had been altogether too much for her weak and sinful spirit. She added firmly that he really ought to see about going round on that Ford van; and he sighed heavily, and said that no doubt she was a devil sent to tempt him.

Still, the seeds were sown. Her plans were maturing.

It was not until she glanced at Mr Mybug's card in the candle-light of her own room that she discovered that his name was not Mybug, but Meyerburg, and that he lived in Charlotte Street – two facts which were not calculated to raise her spirits. But such had been the varied excitements of the day that her subsequent sleep was deep and unbroken.

CHAPTER 10

IT was now the third week in March. Fecund dreams stirred the yearlings. The sukebind was in bud. The swede harvest was over; the beet harvest not yet begun. This meant that Micah, Urk, Amos, Caraway, Harkaway, Mizpah, Luke, Mark and four farm-hands who were not related to the family had a good deal of time on their hands in one way and another. Seth, of course, was always busiest in the spring. Adam was employed about the beastenhousen with the yearling lambs. Reuben was preparing the fields for the harvest after next; he never rested, however slack the season of the year. But the other Starkadders were simply ripe for rows and mischief.

As for Flora, she was quite enjoying herself. She was mixed up in a good many plots. Only a person with a candid mind, who is usually bored by intrigues, can appreciate the full fun of an intrigue when they begin to manage one for the first time. If there are several intrigues and there is a certain danger of their getting mixed up and spoiling each other, the enjoyment is even keener.

Of course, some of the plots were going better than others. Her plot to make Adam use a little mop to clean the dishes with, instead of a thorn twig, had gone sour on her.

One day, when Adam came into the kitchen just after breakfast, Flora had said to him:

'Oh, Adam, here's your little mop. I got it in Howling this afternoon. Look, isn't it a nice little one? You try it and see.'

For a second she had thought he would dash it from her hand, but gradually, as he stared at the little mop, his expression of fury changed to one more difficult to read.

It was, indeed, rather a nice little mop. It had a plain handle of white wood with a little waist right at the tip, so that it could be more comfortably held in the hand. Its head was of soft white threads, each fibre being distinct and comely instead of being matted together in an unsightly lump like the heads of most little mops. Most taking of all, it had a loop of fine red string, with which to hang it up, knotted round its little waist.

Adam cautiously put out his finger and poked at it. ''Tes mine?'

'Aye – I mean, yes, it's yours. Your very own. Do take it.'

He took it between his finger and thumb and stood gazing at it. His eyes had filmed over like sightless Atlantic pools before the flurry of the storm breath. His gnarled fingers folded round the handle.

'Aye ... 'tes mine,' he muttered. 'Nor house nor kine, and yet 'tes mine ... My little mop!'

He undid the thorn twig which fastened the bosom of his shirt and thrust the mop within. But then he withdrew it again, and replaced the thorn. 'My little mop!' He stood staring at it in a dream.

'Yes. It's to cletter the dishes with,' said Flora, firmly, suddenly foreseeing a new danger on the horizon.

'Nay ... nay,' protested Adam. ''Tes too pretty to cletter

those great old dishes wi'. I mun do that with the thorn twigs; they'll serve. I'll keep my liddle mop in the shed, along wi' our Pointless and our Feckless.'

'They might eat it,' suggested Flora.

'Aye, aye, so they might, Robert Poste's child. Ah, well, I mun hang it up by its liddle red string above the dish-washin' bowl. Niver put my liddle pretty in that gurt old greasy washin'-up water. Aye, 'tes prettier nor apple-blooth, my liddle mop.'

And shuffling across the kitchen, he hung it carefully on the wall above the sink, and stood for some time admiring it. Flora was justifiably irritated, and went crossly out for a walk.

She was frequently cheered by letters from her friends in London. Mrs Smiling was now in Egypt, but she wrote often. When abroad in hot climates she wore a great many white dresses, said very little, and all the men in the hotel fell in love with her. Charles also wrote in reply to Flora's little notes. Her short, informative sentences on two sides of deep blue note-paper brought details in return from Charles about the weather in Hertfordshire and messages from his mother. What little else he wrote about, Flora seemed to find mightily satisfying. She looked forward to his letters. She also heard from Julia, who collected books about gangsters, from Claud Hart-Harris, and from all her set in general. So, though exiled, she was not lonely.

Occasionally, while taking her daily walk on the Downs, she saw Elfine: a light, rangy shape which had the plastic contours of a choir-boy etched by Botticelli, drawn against the thin cold sky of spring. Elfine never came near her and this annoyed Flora. She wanted to get hold of Elfine and to give her some tactful advice about Dick Hawk-Monitor.

Adam had confided to Flora his fears about Elfine. She did not think he had done it consciously. He was milking at the time, and she was watching him, and he was talking half to himself.

'She's ay a-peerin' at the windows of Hautcouture Hall' (he pronounced it 'Howchiker', in the local man-

ner) 'to get a sight of that young chuck-stubbard, Mus'
Richard,' he had said.

Something earthly, something dark and rooty as the bar-
ran that thrust its tenacious way through the yeasty soil
had crept into the old man's voice with the words. He was
moved. Old tides lapped his loins.

'Is that the young squire?' asked Flora, casually. She
wanted to get to the bottom of this business without seeming inquisitive.

'Aye – blast un fer a capsy, set-up yearling of a woman-
izer.' The reply came clotted with rage, but behind the rage
were traces of some other and more obscure emotion; a
bright-eyed grubbing in the lore of farmyard and bin, a
hint of the casual lusts of chicken-house and duck-pond, a
racy, yeasty, posty-toasty interest in the sordid drama of
man's eternal blind attack and woman's inevitable yielding
and loss.

Flora had experienced some distaste, but her wish to tidy
up Cold Comfort had compelled her to pursue her inquiries.

She asked when the young people were to be married,
knowing full well what the answer would be. Adam gave a
loud and unaccustomed sound which she had with some
difficulty interpreted as a mirthless laugh.

'When apples grow on the sukebind ye may see lust buy
hissen a wedding garment,' he had replied meaningfully.

Flora nodded, more gloomily than she felt. She thought
that Adam took too black a view of the case. Probably,
Richard Hawk-Monitor was only mildly attracted by Elfine, and the thought of behaving as Adam feared had
never occurred to him. Even if it had, it would have been
instantly dismissed.

Flora knew her hunting gentry. They were what the
Americans, bless them! call dumb. They hated fuss.
Poetry (Flora was pretty sure Elfine wrote poetry) bored
them. They preferred the society of persons who spoke
once in twenty minutes. They liked dogs to be well trained
and girls to be well turned out and frosts to be of short

duration. It was most unlikely that Richard was planning a Lyceum betrayal of Elfine. But it was even less likely that he wanted to marry her. The eccentricity of her dress, behaviour, and hairdressing would put him off automatically. Like most other ideas, the idea would simply not have entered his head.

'So, unless I do something about it,' thought Flora, 'she will simply be left on my hands. And heaven knows nobody will want to marry her while she looks like that and wears those frocks. Unless, of course, I fix her up with Mr Mybug.'

But Mr Mybug was, temporarily at least, in love with Flora herself, so that was another obstacle. And was it quite fair to fling Elfine, all unprepared, to those Bloomsbury-cum-Charlotte-Street lions which exchanged their husbands and wives every other week-end in the most broad-minded fashion? They always made Flora think of the description of the wild boars painted on the vases in Dickens's story – 'each wild boar having his leg elevated in the air at a painful angle to show his perfect freedom and gaiety'. And it must be so discouraging for them to find each new love exactly resembling the old one: just like trying balloon after balloon at a bad party and finding they all had holes in and would not blow up properly.

No. Elfine must not be thrown into Charlotte Street. She must be civilized, and then she must marry Richard.

So Flora continued to look out for Elfine when she went out for walks on the Downs.

Aunt Ada Doom sat in her room upstairs ... alone.

There was something almost symbolic in her solitude. She was the core, the matrix; the focusing-point of the house ... and she was, like all cores, utterly alone. You never heard of two cores to a thing, did you? Well, then. Yet all the wandering waves of desire, passion, jealousy, lust, that throbbed through the house converged, web-like, upon her core-solitude. She felt herself to be a core ... and utterly, irrevocably alone.

The weakening winds of spring fawned against the old house. The old woman's thoughts cowered in the hot room where she sat in solitude ... She would not see her niece ... Keep her away ...

Make some excuse. Shut her out. She had been here a month and you had not seen her. She thought it strange, did she? She dropped hints that she would like to see you. You did not want to see her. You felt ... you felt some strange emotion at the thought of her. You would not see her. Your thoughts wound slowly round the room like beasts rubbing against the drowsy walls. And outside the walls the winds rubbed like drowsy beasts. Half-way between the inside and the outside walls, winds and thoughts were both drowsy. How enervating was the warm wind of the coming spring ...

When you were very small – so small that the lightest puff of breeze blew your little crinoline skirt over your head – you had seen something nasty in the woodshed.

You'd never forgotten it.

You'd never spoken of it to Mamma – you could smell, even to this day, the fresh betel-nut with which her shoes were always cleaned – but you'd remembered all your life.

That was what had made you ... different. That – what you had seen in the tool-shed – had made your marriage a prolonged nightmare to you.

Somehow you had never bothered about what it had been like for your husband ...

That was why you had brought your children into the world with loathing. Even now, when you were seventy-nine, you could never see a bicycle go past your bedroom window without a sick plunge at the apex of your stomach ... in the bicycle shed you'd seen it, something nasty, when you were very small.

That was why you stayed in this room. You had been here for twenty years, ever since Judith had married and her husband had come to live at the farm. You had run away from the huge, terrifying world outside these four walls against which your thoughts rubbed themselves like drowsy yaks. Yes, that was what they were like. Yaks. Exactly like yaks.

Outside in the world there were potting-sheds where nasty things could happen. But nothing could happen here. You saw to that. None of your grandchildren might leave the farm. Judith might not leave. Amos might not leave. Caraway might not leave. Urk might not leave. Seth might not leave. Micah might not leave. Ezra might not leave. Mark and Luke might not leave. Harkaway might leave sometimes because he paid the proceeds of the farm into the bank at Beershorn every Saturday morning, but none of the others might leave.

None of them must go out into the great dirty world where there were cow-sheds in which nasty things could happen and be seen by little girls.

You had them all. You curved your old wrinkled hand into a brown shell, and laughed to yourself. You held them like that ... in the hollow of your hand, as the Lord held Israel. None of them had any money except what you gave them. You allowed Micah, Urk, Caraway, Mark, Luke, and Ezra tenpence a week each in pocket-money. Harkaway had a shilling, to cover his fare by bus down into Beershorn and back. You had your heel on them all. They were your washpot, and you had cast your shoe out over them.

Even Seth, your darling, your last and loveliest grandchild, you held in the hollow of your old palm. He had one and sixpence a week pocket-money. Amos had none. Judith had none.

How like yaks were your drowsy thoughts, slowly winding round in the dim air of your quiet room. The winter landscape, breaking upon spring's pressure, beat urgently against the panes.

So you sat here, living from meal to meal (Monday, pork; Tuesday, beef; Wednesday, toad-in-the-hole; Thursday, mutton; Friday, veal; Saturday, curry; Sunday, cutlets). Sometimes ... you were so old ... how could you know?

... you dropped soup on yourself ... you whimpered ... Once Judith brought up the kidneys for your breakfast and they were too hot and burned your tongue ... Day slipped into day, season into season, year into year. And you sat here, alone. You ... Cold Comfort Farm.

Sometimes Urk came to see you, the second child of your sister's man by marriage, and told you that the farm was rotting away.

No matter. There have always been Starkadders at Cold Comfort.

Well, let it rot ... You couldn't have a farm without sheds (cow, wood, tool, bicycle, and potting), and where there were sheds things were bound to rot ... Besides, so far as you could see from your bi-weekly inspection of the farm account books, things weren't doing too badly ... Anyway, here you were, and here they all stayed with you.

You told them you were mad. You had been mad since you saw something nasty in the woodshed, years and years and years ago. If any of them went away, to any other part of the country, you would go much madder. Any attempt by any of them to get away from the farm made one of your attacks of madness come on. It was unfortunate in some ways but useful in others ... The woodshed incident had twisted something in your child-brain seventy years ago.

And seeing that it was because of that incident that you sat here ruling the roost and having five meals a day brought up to you as regularly as clockwork, it hadn't been such a bad break for you, that day you saw something nasty in the woodshed.

CHAPTER II

THE bull was bellowing. The steady sound went up into the air in a dark red column. Seth leaned moodily on the hoot-piece, watching Reuben, who was slowly but deftly repairing a leak in the midden-rail. Not a bud broke the dark feathery faces of the thorns, but the air whined with spring's passage. It was eleven in the morning. A bird sang his idiotic recitative from the dairy roof.

Both brothers looked up as Flora came across the yard dressed for her walk upon the Downs. She looked inquiringly at the shed, whence issued the shocking row made by Big Business, the bull.

'I think it would be a good idea if you let him out,' she said. Seth grinned and nudged Reuben, who coloured dully.

'I don't mean for stud purposes. I meant simply for air and exercise,' said Flora. 'You cannot expect a bull to produce healthy stock if he is shut up in the smelly dark all day.'

Seth disapproved of the impersonal note which the conversation had taken, so he lounged away. But Reuben was always ready to listen to advice which had the good of the farm at heart, and Flora had discovered this. He said, quite civilly:

'Aye, 'tes true. We mun let un out in the great field tomorrow.' He returned to his repairing of the midden-rail, but just as Flora was walking away he looked up again and remarked:

'So ye went wi' the old devil, eh?'

Flora was learning how to translate the Starkadder argot, and took this to mean that she had, last week, accompanied her Cousin Amos to the Church of the Quivering Brethren. She replied in tones just tinged with polite surprise:

'I am not quite sure what you mean, but if you mean did I go with Cousin Amos to Beershorn, yes, I did.'

'Aye, ye went. And did the old devil say anything about me?'

Flora could only recall a remark about dead men's shoes, which it would scarcely be prudent to repeat, so she replied that she did not remember much of what had been said because the sermon had been so powerful that it had driven everything else out of her head.

'I was advising Cousin Amos,' she added, 'to address his

116

sermons to a wider audience. I think he ought to go round the country on a lorry, preaching –'

'Frittenin' the harmless birds off the bushes, more like,' interposed Reuben, gloomily.

'– at fairs and on market days. You see, if Cousin Amos were away a good deal it would mean that someone else would have to take charge of the farm, wouldn't it?'

'Someone else will have to take charge of it, in any case, when the old devil dies,' said Reuben. Stark passion curdled the whites of his eyes and his breath came thraw.

'Yes, of course,' said Flora. 'He talks of leaving it to Adam. Now, I don't think that would be at all wise, do you? To begin with, Adam is ninety. He has no children (at least, he has none as far as I know, and, of course, I do not listen to what Mrs Beetle says), and I should not think he is likely to marry, should you? Nor has he the legal type of mind. I shouldn't imagine he would trouble to make a will, for example. And if he did make one, who knows who he would leave the farm to? He might leave it to Feckless, or even to Aimless, and that would mean a lot of legal trouble, for I doubt if two cows can inherit a farm. Then, again, Pointless and Graceless might put in a claim for it, and that could easily mean an endless lawsuit in which all the resources of the farm would be swallowed up. Oh, no, I hardly think it would do for Cousin Amos to leave the farm to Adam. I think it would be much better if he were persuaded to go on a preaching tour round England, or perhaps to retire to some village a long way off and write a nice long book of sermons. Then whoever was left in charge of the farm could get a good grip of affairs here, and when Cousin Amos did come back at last, he would see that the management of the farm must be left in the hands of that person in order to save all the bother of getting things reorganized. You see, Reuben, Cousin Amos could not think of leaving the farm to Adam then, because the person who had been managing it would obviously be the person to leave it to.'

She faltered a little towards the end of her speech as she recalled that the Starkadders rarely did what was obvious, though they were only too embarrassingly ready to do what was natural. Nor did her remarks have the wished-for effect upon Reuben. He said, in a voice thick with fury:

'Meanin' you?'

'No, indeed. I've already told you, Reuben, that I should be no use at all at running the farm. I do think you might believe me.'

'If ye doan't mean you, who do you mean?'

Flora abandoned diplomacy, and said, 'You.'

'Me?'

'Aye, you.' She patiently dropped into Starkadder.

He stared thickly at her. She observed with distaste that his chest was extremely hairy.

''Tes impossible,' he said at last. 'The old lady would never let him go.'

'Why not?' asked Flora. 'Why should he not go? Why does Aunt Ada Doom like to keep you all here, as though you were all children?'

'She – she – she's ill,' stammered Reuben, casting a fleeting glance at the closed, dusty windows of the farm high above his head, where the lin-tits were already building under the eaves. 'If any on us says we'll leave the farm, she gets an attack. There have always been Starkadders at Cold Comfort. None of us mun go, except Harkaway, when he takes the money down to the bank at Beershorn every Saturday morning.'

'But you all go into Beershorn sometimes.'

'Aye, but 'tes a great risk. If she knew, 'twould bring on an attack.'

'An attack? What of?' Flora was getting a little impatient. Unlike Charles she deplored a gloomy mystery.

'Her – her illness. She – she ain't like other people's grandmothers. When she was no bigger than a linnet, she saw –'

'Oh, Reuben, do hurry up and tell me, there's a good

soul. All the sun will be gone by the time I get up on to the Downs.'

'She – she's mad.'

Fat and dark, the word lay between them in the indifferent air. Time, which had been behaving normally lately, suddenly began to spin upon a bright point in endless space. It never rains but it pours.

'Oh,' said Flora, thoughtfully.

So that was it. Aunt Ada Doom was mad. You would expect, by all the laws of probability, to find a mad grandmother at Cold Comfort Farm, and for once the laws of probability had not done you down and a mad grandmother there was.

Flora observed, tapping her shoe with her walking-stick, that it was very awkward.

'Aye,' said Reuben, ''tes terrible. And her madness takes the form of wantin' to know everything as goes on. She has to see all the books twice a week: the milk book an' the chicken book an' the pig book and corn book. If we keeps the books back, she has an attack. 'Tes terrible. She's the head of the family, ye see. We mun keep her alive at all costs. She never comes downstairs but twice a year – on the first of May and on the last day of the harvest festival. If anybody eats too much, she has an attack. 'Tes terrible.'

'It is indeed,' agreed Flora. It struck her that Aunt Ada Doom's madness had taken the most convenient form possible. If everybody who went mad could arrange in what way it was to take them, she felt pretty sure they would all choose to be mad like Ada Doom.

'Is that why she doesn't want to see me?' she asked. 'I've been here nearly a month, you know, and I have never seen her yet.'

'Aye ... maybe.' said Reuben, indifferently. His long speech seemed to have exhausted him. His face was sodden, sunk in on itself in defensive folds.

'Well, anyway,' said Flora, briskly, 'because Aunt Ada is mad there is no reason why you should not try to persuade Cousin Amos to go on a preaching tour, and then manage the farm while he is away. You have a stab at it.'

'Do you think,' said Reuben, slowly, 'that if I was to look after th' farm while the old devil was away, moitherin' about hell fire to a lot of frittened birds and cows a long way off, he'd come back and see as I could do it, and maybe leave it to me for my own when he's gone?'

'Yes, I do,' said Flora, firmly.

Reuben's face became contorted with a number of emotions, and suddenly, even as she watched him, victory was hers!

'Aye,' he said hoarsely, 'dang me if I doan't din into the old devil how he must be off speechifyin' this very week.'

And much to her surprise he held out his hand to her. She took it and shook it warmly. This was the first sign of humanity she had encountered among the Starkadders, and she was moved by it. She felt like stout Cortez or Sir James Jeans on spotting yet another white dwarf.

She was cheerful as she walked away towards the downland path. If Reuben did not overdo the persuading stunt (and this was a real danger, for Amos was astute and would soon see through any obvious attempt to get rid of him) her plan should succeed.

It was a fresh, pleasant morning and she felt the more disposed to enjoy her walk because Mr Mybug (she could not learn to think of him as Meyerburg) was not with her. For the last three mornings he had been with her, but this morning she had said that he really ought to do some work. Flora did not see why, but one excuse was as good as another to get rid of him.

It cannot be said that Flora really enjoyed taking walks with Mr Mybug. To begin with, he was not really interested in anything but sex. This was understandable, if deplorable. After all, many of our best minds have had the same weakness. The trouble about Mr Mybug was that ordinary subjects, which are not usually associated with sex even by our best minds, did suggest sex to Mr Mybug, and he pointed them out and made comparisons and asked Flora what she thought about it all. Flora found it difficult to reply because she was not interested. She was therefore obliged merely to be polite, and Mr Mybug mistook her lack of enthusiasm and thought it was due to inhibitions. He remarked how curious it was that most Englishwomen (most young Englishwomen, that was, Englishwomen of about nineteen to twenty-four) were inhibited. Cold, that was what young Englishwomen from nineteen to twenty-four were.

They used sometimes to walk through a pleasant wood of young birch trees which were just beginning to come into bud. The stems reminded Mr Mybug of phallic symbols and the buds made Mr Mybug think of nipples and virgins. Mr Mybug pointed out to Flora that he and she were walking on seeds which were germinating in the womb of the earth. He said it made him feel as if he were trampling on the body of a great brown woman. He felt as if he were a partner in some mighty rite of gestation.

Flora used sometimes to ask him the name of a tree, but he never knew.

Yet there were few occasions when he was not reminded of a pair of large breasts by the distant hills. Then, he would stand looking at the woods upon the horizon. He would wrinkle up his eyes and breathe deeply through his nostrils and say that the view reminded him of one of Poussin's lovely things. Or he would pause and peer in a pool and say it was like a painting by Manet.

And, to be fair to Mr Mybug, it must be admitted he was sometimes interested by the social problems of the day. Only yesterday, while he and Flora were walking through an alley of rhododendrons on an estate which was open to the public, he had discussed a case of arrest in Hyde Park. The rhododendrons made him think of Hyde Park. He said that it was impossible to sit down for five minutes in Hyde Park after seven in the evening without being either accosted or arrested.

There were many homosexuals to be seen in Hyde Park. Prostitutes, too. God! those rhododendron buds had a phallic, urgent look!

Sooner or later we should have to tackle the problem of homosexuality. We should have to tackle the problem of Lesbians and old maids.

God! that little pool down there in the hollow was shaped just like somebody's navel! He would like to drag off his clothes and leap into it. There was another problem . . . We should have to tackle that, too. In no other country but England was there so much pruriency about nakedness. If we all went about naked, sexual desire would automatically disappear. Had Flora ever been to a party where everybody took off all their clothes? Mr Mybug had. Once a whole lot of us bathed in the river with nothing on and afterwards little Harriet Belmont sat naked in the grass and played to us on her flute. It was delicious; so gay and simple and natural. And Billie Polswett danced a Hawaiian love-dance, making all the gestures that are usually omitted in the stage version. Her husband had danced too. It had been lovely; so warm and natural and *real*, somehow.

So, taking it all round, Flora was pleased to have her walk in solitude.

She passed a girl riding on a pony and two young men walking with knapsacks and sticks, but no one else. She went down into a valley, filled with bushes of hazel and gorse, and made her way towards a little house built of grey stones, its roof painted turquoise-green, which stood on the other side of the Down. It was a shepherd's hut; she could see the stone hut close to it in which ewes were kept at lambing-time and a shallow trough from which they drank.

If Mr Mybug had been there, he would have said that the ewes were paying the female thing's tribute to the Life Force. He said a woman's success could only be estimated by the success of her sexual life, and Flora supposed he would say the same thing about a ewe.

Oh, she *was* so glad he wasn't there!

She went skipping round the corner of the little sheep-house and saw Elfine, sitting on a turf and sunning herself.

Both cousins were startled. But Flora was quite pleased. She wanted a chance to talk to Elfine.

Elfine jumped to her feet and stood poised; she had something of the brittle grace of a yearling foal. A dryad's smile played on the curious sullen purity of her mouth, and her eyes were unawake and unfriendly. Flora thought, 'What a dreadful way of doing one's hair; surely it must be a mistake.'

'You're Flora – I'm Elfine,' said the other girl simply. Her voice had a breathless, broken quality that suggested the fluty sexless timbre of a choir-boy's notes (only choir-boys are seldom sexless, as many a harassed vicaress knows to her cost).

'No prizes offered,' thought Flora, rather rudely. But she said politely: 'Yes. Isn't it a delicious morning. Have you been far?'

'Yes . . . No . . . Away over there . . .' The vague gesture of her outflung arm sketched, in some curious fashion, illimitable horizons. Judith's gestures had the same barrier-less quality; there was not a vase left anywhere in the farm.

'I feel stifled in the house,' Elfine went on, shyly and abruptly. 'I hate houses.'

'Indeed?' said Flora.

She observed Elfine draw a deep breath, and knew that she was about to get well away on a good long description of herself and her habits, as these shy dryads always did if you gave them half a chance. So she sat down on another turf in the sun and composed herself to listen, looking up at the tall Elfine.

'Do you like poetry?' asked Elfine, suddenly. A pure flood of colour ran up under her skin. Her hands, burnt and bone-modelled as a boy's, were clenched.

'Some of it,' responded Flora, cautiously.

'I adore it,' said Elfine, simply. 'It says all the things I can't say for myself . . . somehow . . . It means . . . oh, I don't know. Just everything, somehow. It's *enough*. Do you ever feel that?'

Flora replied that she had, occasionally, felt something of the sort, but her reply was limited by the fact that she was not quite sure exactly what Elfine meant.

'I write poetry,' said Elfine. (So I was right! thought Flora.) 'I'll show you some . . . if you promise not to laugh. I can't bear my children being laughed at . . . I call my poems my children.'

Flora felt that she could promise this with safety.

'And love, too,' muttered Elfine, her voice breaking and changing shyly like the Finnish ice under the first lusty rays and wooing winds of the Finnish spring. 'Love and poetry go together, somehow . . . out here on the hills, when I'm alone with my dreams . . . oh, I can't tell you how I feel. I've been chasing a squirrel all the morning.'

Flora said severely:

'Elfine, are you engaged?'

Her cousin stood perfectly still. Slowly the colour receded from her face. Her head dropped. She muttered: 'There's someone . . . We don't want to spoil things by having any- thing definite and binding . . . it's horrible . . . to bind any- one down.'

'Nonsense. It is a very good idea,' said Flora, austerely, 'and it is a good thing for you to be bound down, too. Now, what do you suppose will happen to you if you don't marry this Someone?'

Elfine's face brightened. 'Oh . . . but I've got it all planned out,' she said, eagerly. 'I shall get a job in an arts and crafts shop in Horsham and do barbola work in my spare time. I shall be all right . . . and later on I can go to Italy and per- haps learn to be a little like St Francis of Assisi . . .'

'It is quite unnecessary for a young woman to resemble St Francis of Assisi,' said Flora coldly; 'and in your case it would be downright suicidal. A large girl like you *must* wear clothes that *fit*; and Elfine, *whatever* you do, always wear court shoes. Remember – c-o-u-r-t. You are so handsome that you can wear the most conventional clothes and look very well in them; but do, for heaven's sake, avoid orange linen jumpers and hand-wrought jewellery. Oh, and shawls in the evening.'

She paused. She saw by Elfine's expression that she had been progressing too quickly. Elfine looked puzzled and extremely wretched. Flora was penitent. She had taken a fancy to the ridiculous chit. She said in a very friendly tone, drawing her cousin down to sit beside her:

'Now, what is it? Tell me. Do you hate being at home?'

'Yes . . . but I'm not often there,' whispered Elfine. 'No . . . it's Urk.'

Urk . . . That was the foxy-looking little man who was always staring at Flora's ankles or else spitting into the well.

'What about Urk?' she demanded.

'He . . . they . . . I think he wants to marry me,' stammered Elfine. 'I think Grandmother means me to marry him when I am eighteen. He . . . he . . . climbs the apple-tree outside my window and tries to watch me going to . . . to bed. I had to hang up three face-towels over the window, and then he poked them down with a fishing-rod and laughed and shook his fist at me . . . I don't know what to do.'

Flora was justly indignant, but concealed her nasty temper. It was at this moment that she resolved to adopt Elfine and rescue her in the teeth of all the Starkadders of Cold Comfort.

'And does Someone know this?' she asked.

'Well . . . I told him.'

'What did he say?'

'Oh . . . he said, "Rotten luck, old girl".'

'It's Dick Hawk-Monitor, isn't it?'

'Oh . . . how did you know? Oh . . . I suppose everybody knows by now. It's beastly.'

'Things are certainly in rather a mess, but I do not think we need go so far as to say they are beastly,' said Flora, more calmly. 'Now, you must forgive my asking you these questions, Elfine, but has the young Hawk-Monitor actually *asked* you to marry him?'

'Well . . . he said he thought it would be a good idea if we did.'

'Bad . . . bad . . .' muttered Flora, shaking her head. 'Forgive me, but does he seem to love you?'

'He . . . he does when I'm there, Flora, but I don't some-how think he thinks much about me when I'm not there.'

'And I suppose you care enough for him, my dear, to wish to become his wife?'

Elfine after some hesitation admitted that she had some-times been selfish enough to wish that she had Dick all to herself. It appeared that there was a dangerous cousin named Pamela, who often came down from London for week-ends. Dick thought she was great fun.

Flora's expression did not change when she heard this piece of news, but her spirits sank. It would be difficult enough to win Dick for Elfine as it was; it would be a thousandfold more difficult with a rival in the field.

But her spirit was of that rare brand which becomes cold and pleased at the prospect of a battle, and her dismay did not last.

Elfine was saying:

'. . . And then there's this dance. Of course, I hate dancing unless it's in the woods with the wind-flowers and the birds, but I did rather want to go to this one, because, you see, it's Dick's twenty-first birthday party and . . . somehow . . . I think it would be rather fun.'

'Amusing or diverting . . . not "rather fun",' corrected Flora, kindly. 'Have you been invited?'

'Oh, no . . . You see, Grandmother does not allow the Starkadders to accept invitations, unless it is to funerals or the churching of women. So now no one sends us invitations. Dick did say he wished that I was coming, but I think he was only being kind. I don't think he really thought for a minute that I should be able to.'

'I suppose it would be of no use asking your grandmother for permission to go? In dealing with old and tyrannical persons it is wise to do the correct thing whenever one can; they are then less likely to suspect when one does something incorrect.'

'Oh, I am sure she would never let me go. She quarrelled with Mr Hawk-Monitor nearly thirty years ago and she hates Dick's mother. She would be mad with rage if she thought that I even knew Dick. Besides, she thinks dancing is wicked.'

'An interesting survival of medieval superstition,' commented Flora. 'Now listen, Elfine, I think it would be an excellent move if you went to this dance. I will try and see if I can manage it. I shall go, too, and keep an eye on you. It may be a little difficult to secure invitations for us, but I will do my best. And when we have got our invitations, I will take you up to Town with me and we will buy you a frock.'

'Oh, Flora!'

Flora was pleased to see that the wild-bird-cum-dryad atmosphere which hung over Elfine like a pestilential vapour was wearing thin. She was talking quite naturally. If this was the good effect of a little ordinary feminine gossip and a little interest in her poor childish affairs, the effect of a well-cut dress and a brushed and burnished head of hair might be miraculous. Flora could have rubbed her hands with glee.

'When is this dance?' she asked. 'Will many people be asked?'

'It's on the twenty-first of April, just a month from to-morrow. Oh, yes, it will be very big; they are holding it in the Assembly Rooms at Godmere, and all the county will be asked, because, you see, it is Dick's twenty-first birthday.'

'All the better,' thought Flora. 'It will be easier to work an invitation.' She had so many friends in London; surely there must be among them someone who knew these Hawk-Monitors? And Claud Hart-Harris could come down to partner her, because he waltzed so well, and who could be an escort for Elfine?

'Does Seth dance?' she asked.

'I don't know. I hate him,' replied Elfine, simply.

'I cannot say that I like him much myself,' confessed Flora, 'but if he dances, I think it would be as well if he came with us. You must have a partner, you know. Or perhaps you could ask some other man?'

But Elfine, being a dryad, naturally knew no other men;

127

and the only man Flora could think of who would be sure to be available for April 21st was Mr Mybug. She had only to ask *him*, she knew, and he would come bounding along to partner Elfine. It was dreadful to have no choice but Seth or Mr Mybug, but Sussex was like that.

'Well, we can arrange these details later,' she said. 'What I must do now is to find out if anyone in London among my friends know these Hawk-Monitors. I will ask Claud; he knows positive herds of people who live in country houses. I will write to him this afternoon.'

She was well disposed enough towards Elfine, but she really did not wish to spend with her the rest of an exquisite morning. So she rose to her feet and with a pleasant smile (having promised her cousin to let her know how matters were progressing) she went on her way.

CHAPTER 12

CLAUD HART-HARRIS wrote from his house at Chiswick Mall a few days later in reply to Flora's letter. He knew the Hawk-Monitors. Papa was dead, Mamma was a darling old bird whose hobby was the Higher Thought. There was a son who was easy on the eye but slow on the uptake, and a healthy sort of daughter named Joan. He thought he could arrange four invitations for Flora, if she was sure she wanted them. Would it not be rather a tiresome affair? But if she really wanted to go, he would write to Mrs Hawk-Monitor and tell her that a friend of his was in exile in a farm-house at Howling, and that she would love to come to the ball and bring her girl cousin and two young men. He, Claud, would of course be charmed to partner Flora, but, candidly, Seth sounded pretty squalid. Need he come?

'Squalid or not,' said the small, clear voice of Flora, fifty miles away (for she thought she would answer his letter by telephone, as she was in a hurry to get the affair arranged), 'he is all we can find, unless we have that Mr Mybug I told you about. I would really rather we did not have him, Claud. You know how dreadful intelligent people are when you take them to dances.'

Claud twisted the television dial and amused himself by studying Flora's fair, pensive face. Her eyes were lowered and her mouth compressed over the serious business of arranging Elfine's future. He fancied she was tracing a pattern with the tip of her shoe. She could not look at him, because public telephones were not fitted with television dials.

'Oh, yes, we certainly don't want a lot of intelligent conversation,' he said, decidedly. 'I think we will rule out the Mybug. Well, then, I will write to Mrs Hawk-Monitor today, and let you know as soon as I hear. Or perhaps I had better ask her to send the invitations direct to you, shall I?'

And so it was arranged.

Flora came out of the post office at Beershorn into the pleasant sunshine feeling a little ashamed of her schemes. Claud had said Mrs Hawk-Monitor was a darling. Flora was planning to palm off Elfine on the darling's only son. She strained her imagination, but found that it refused to present her with a picture of Mrs Hawk-Monitor welcoming Elfine with joy as a daughter-in-law. Mrs Hawk-Monitor's hobby might be the Higher Thought, but Flora felt sure she would be practical enough when it was a question of considering a wife for Richard. She would not be sympathetic, in spite of her own leanings, with Elfine's artiness. Elfine would have to be transformed, inside and out, before Mrs Hawk-Monitor could consider her suitable; and even if the transformation were made, Mrs Hawk-Monitor could not possibly approve Elfine's family. Who, indeed, could approve of such figures of rugged but slightly embarrassing grandeur as Micah and Judith?

And the Starkadders themselves would be sure, when the engagement was announced, to kick up one hell of a shine.

Difficult times lay ahead.

But this was what Flora liked. She detested rows and scenes, but enjoyed quietly pitting her cool will against opposition. It amused her; and when she was defeated, she withdrew in good order and lost interest in the campaign. She had little or no sporting spirit. Bloody battles to the death bored her, nor did she like other people to win.

But it was no fun to fight a darling. Flora herself, had she been sixty-five and Mrs Hawk-Monitor, would have felt most bitter towards a girl who planted an Elfine into the midst of a quiet country family.

There was only one way of soothing her tiresome conscience. Elfine must be transformed indeed; her artiness must be rooted out. Her mind must match the properly groomed head in which it was housed. Her movements must be made less frequent, and her conversation less artless. She must write no more poetry nor go for any long walks unless accompanied by the proper sort of dog to take on long walks. She must learn to be serious about horses. She must learn to laugh when a book or a string quartet was mentioned, and to confess that she was not brainy. She must learn to be long-limbed and clear-eyed and inhibited. The first two qualities she possessed already, and the last she must set to work to acquire at once.

And there were only twenty-seven days in which to teach her all these things!

Flora walked down the High Street towards the place where the buses started, planning how she would begin Elfine's education. She looked at the clock on the Town Hall, which said twelve, and realized that she had half an hour to wait for a bus. It was a Saturday morning and the town was full of people who had come in from outlying farms and villages to do their shopping for the week-end; some of them were already waiting for the bus, and Flora walked across the Market Place, prepared to wait with them.

But then she became aware that someone, a man, was trying to attract her attention. She was very properly not looking at him when something in his appearance seemed familiar to her; he looked like a Starkadder (there were so many of them that one of her minor worries was a fear of not recognizing one when she met him in the street). Sure enough, it was Harkaway. He had just come out of the bank, into which he had been paying the weekly takings of the farm. In a second Flora recognized him, and said 'Good morning' with a bow and a smile.

He returned her greeting in the Starkadder manner, that is, with a suspicious stare. He looked as though he would have liked to ask her what she was doing in Beershorn. She decided that if he did she would undo the parcel of pale green silk she carried and shake it in his face all down the High Street.

Harkaway stopped in front of her and out-manoeuvred her in her advance on the bus.

'You'm a long way from whoam,' he muttered.

'So are you,' retorted Flora. She was rather cross.

'Aye, but I ha' business to do in Beershorn every Saturday. I comes down every Saturday morning in the year, wi' Viper,' and he jerked his head towards that large and disagreeable beast, which Flora now observed anchored to the buggy a little way farther on.

'Indeed. I came by bus.'

A slow, secret smile crept into Harkaway's face. It was wolfish, ursine, vulpine. He softly jangled some coins in his pocket. He seemed as though he bathed in some secret satisfaction of his own. This was because he had driven down to Beershorn in the buggy, and saved the shilling his grandmother gave him every week for the fare.

'Aye, th' bus . . . ' he repeated, drawlingly.

'Yes, the bus. There isn't another one until half past twelve.'

'Happen I might drive you home with me,' he suggested, as Flora had meant him to do. Her disinclination to sit in the damp, smelly bus had fought with her disinclination to drive home with a Starkadder, and the bus had lost. Besides, she was always glad to see more of the private lives of the Starkadders. Harkaway might be able to tell her something about Urk, who was supposed to be going to marry Elfine.

'That would be very kind of you,' she said, and they moved off together to the buggy.

She looked at him meditatively as the buggy passed rapidly between the hedges. She wondered what was his particular nastiness? She could hardly distinguish him from Urk and Caraway, Ezra, Luke, and Mark. Never mind, probably she would get them sorted out in time.

She began to make conversation.

'How is the well getting on?' (Not that she cared.)

"Tes all collapsed. 'Tes terrible.'

'Oh, I am so sorry! What a pity. The last time I saw it, it was nearly finished. How did it happen?'

"Twas Mark. He and our Micah was argyfyin' who should lay the last brick, and we was all standin' round waitin' to see which would hit t'other first. And Mark, he pushed Micah down th' well, and pushed th' bricks down on top of 'un. Laugh! We fair lay on th' ground.'

'Was – is Micah – er – is he badly hurt?'

'Nay. Mark dived in after un and rescued un. But th' bricks was lost.'

'A pity, indeed,' commented Flora.

She was much surprised when Harkaway burst out:

'Aye, 'tis a pity. There's some at Cold Comfort would do better for a few bricks thrown at their heads. I names no names but I know what I think.'

The coins jingled softly again in his pocket. The ursine smile touched his lips.

'Who?' asked Flora.

'Her . . . th' old lady. My grand-aunt. Her as has us all under her thumb.' He jingled the coins again.

'Ah, yes, my aunt,' said Flora, thoughtfully. She found Harkaway comparatively easy to talk to. Nor did he seem unfriendly.

'I cannot understand,' she resumed, 'why you do not break away from her. I suppose she has all the money.'

'Aye . . . and she's mad. If any on us was to leave th' farm, she'd go madder yet. 'Twould be a terrible disgrace on us. We mun keep the head of the family alive and in her right mind. There have always been – '

'I know, I know,' said Flora, hastily. 'Such a comfort, I always feel, don't you? But really, Harkaway, I do think it is carrying authority a little too far when grown men are prevented from marrying – '

Harkaway laughed shortly, rather to Flora's dismay; she feared he was going to make a farmyard joke. But he said, much more surprisingly:

'Nay, nay. Some of us is married right enough. But th' old lady, she mun never see our women-folk, or she'd go right away mad. The women-folk of the Starkadders keep themselves to themselves. They lives down in the village and only comes up when there's a gatherin' or th' old lady comes downstairs. There's Micah's Susan, Mark's Phoebe, Luke's Prue, Caraway's Letty, Ezra's Jane. Urk, he'm a bachelor. Me . . . I've got me own troubles.'

Flora longed to ask what his own troubles were, but feared that the question might bring forth a flood of embarrassing confidences. Perhaps he was in love with Mrs Beetle? Meanwhile, his news was so surprising that she could only stare and stare again.

'And do you mean to say that they all live down in the village. Five women?'

'Six women,' corrected Harkaway, in a low voice. 'Aye, there's – another. There's poor daft Rennet.'

'Really? What relation is she to the others?'

'She'm own daughter to Micah's Susan by her first marriage. Her marriage to Mark, I mean; and Mark, he's own half-brother to Amos, who is Micah's cousin. So 'tes rather confusin', like. Aye, poor Rennet . . .'

'What is the matter with *her*?' inquired Flora, rather tartly. She was exceedingly dismayed at the news that there was a whole horde of female Starkadders whom she had not seen. It really seemed as though her task would be too much for her.

'She were disappointed o' Mark Dolour, ten years ago. She's never married. She's queer, like, in her head. Sometimes, when the sukebind hangs heavy from the passin' wains, she jumps down th' well. Aye, an' twice she's tried to choke Meriam, the hired girl. 'Tes Nature, you may say, turned sour in her veins.'

Flora was really quite glad when the buggy stopped outside the farm. She wanted to hear no more. She felt that she could not undertake to rescue Susan, Letty, Phoebe, Prue, Jane, and Rennet as well as Elfine. Dash it, the women must take their chance. She would rescue Elfine, and as soon as that was accomplished, she would try to have a show-down with Aunt Ada, but beyond this she would make no promises.

For the next three weeks she was so busy with Elfine that she had no time to worry about the unknown female Starkadders.

She spent most of her time with Elfine. She expected at first that someone would interfere, and try to stop Elfine and her from going for their morning walk along the top of the Downs and from spending the afternoons in Flora's little green parlour. These habits were innocent, but that was not enough to keep the Starkadders from trying to stop them. Nay, their very innocency was more likely to set the grand, rugged Starkadder machinery in motion. For it is a peculiarity of persons who lead rich emotional lives and who (as the saying is) live intensely and with a wild poetry, that they read all kinds of meanings into comparatively simple actions, especially the actions of other people, who do not live intensely and with a wild poetry. Thus you may find them weeping passionately on their bed, and be told that you – you alone – are the cause because you said that awful thing to them at lunch. Or they wonder why you like going to concerts; there must be more in it than meets the eye.

So the cousins usually slipped out for their walks when no one was about.

Flora had learned, by experience, that she must ask permission of the Starkadders if she wanted to go down into Beershorn, or if (as she did a week or so after her arrival) she wanted to buy a pot of apricot jam for tea. On this occasion she had found Judith lying face downwards in the furrows of Ticklepenny's Corner, weeping. In reply to her question, Judith had said that anybody might do anything they pleased, so long as she was left alone with her sorrow. Flora took this generous statement to mean that she might pay for the jam.

And so she did; but on the whole she spent little money at Cold Comfort, and so she had nearly eighty pounds to spend on Elfine. She decided that they would go up to London together the day before the ball and buy her gown and get her hair cut correctly.

She was pleased to be spending eighty pounds on Elfine. If she succeeded in making Dick Hawk-Monitor propose to Elfine it would be a successful *geste* in the face of the Starkadders. It would be a triumph of the Higher Common Sense over Aunt Ada Doom. It would be a victory for Flora's philosophy of life over the subconscious life-philosophy of the Starkadders. It would be like a splendid deer stepping haughtily across a ploughed field.

For three weeks she forced Elfine as a gardener skilfully forces a flower in a hothouse. Her task was difficult, but might have been much more so. For Elfine's peculiarities of dress, outlook, and behaviour were due only to her own youthful tastes. They had not been ground into her, for years, by older people. She was ready to shed them if something better was shown to her. Also, she was only seventeen years old, and docile; when Flora planed away all the St Francis-cum-barbola-work crust, she found beneath it an honest child, capable of loving calmly and deeply, friendly and sweet-tempered and fond of pretty things.

'Have you always admired St Francis?' asked Flora, as they sat one rainy afternoon in the little green parlour, towards the end of the first week. 'I mean, who told you about him, and who taught you to wear those shocking clothes?'

'I wanted to be like Miss Ashford. She kept the Blue Bird's Cage down in Howling for a month or two last summer. I went in there to tea once or twice. She was very kind to me. She used to have lovely clothes – that is, I mean, they weren't what you would call lovely, but I used to like them. She had a smock – '

'Embroidered with hollyhocks,' said Flora, resignedly. 'And I'll bet she wore her hair in shells round her ears and a pendant made of hammered silver with a bit of blue enamel in the middle. And did she try to grow herbs?'

'How did you know?'

'Never mind, I do know. And she talked to you about Brother Wind and Sister Sun and the wind on the heath, didn't she?'

'Yes . . . She had a picture of St Francis feeding the birds. It was lovely.'

'And did you want to be like her, Elfine?'

'Oh, yes . . . She never tried to make me like her, of course, but I did want to be. I used to copy her clothes . . .'

'Yes, well, never mind that now. Go on with your reading.'

And Elfine obediently resumed her reading aloud of 'Our Lives from Day to Day' from an April number of *Vogue*. When she had finished, Flora took her, page by page, through a copy of *Chiffons*, which was devoted to descriptions and sketches of lingerie. Flora pointed out how these graceful petticoats and night-gowns depended upon their pure line and delicate embroidery for their beauty; how all gross romanticism was purged away, or expressed only in a fold or a flute of material. She then showed how the same delicacy might be found in the style of Jane Austen, or a painting by Marie Laurencin.

'It is that kind of beauty,' said Flora, 'that you must learn to look for and admire in everyday life.'

'I like the night-gowns and "Persuasion",' said Elfine, 'but I don't like "Our Lives" very much, Flora. It's all rather in a hurry, isn't it, and wanting to tell you how nice it was?'

'I do not propose that you shall found a life-philosophy upon "Our Lives from Day to Day", Elfine. I merely make you read it because you will have to meet people who do that kind of thing, and you must on no account be all dewy and awed when you do meet them. You can, if you like, secretly despise them. Nor must you talk about Marie Laurencin to people who hunt. They will merely think she is your new mare. No. I tell you of these things in order that you may have some standards, within yourself, with which secretly to compare the many new facts and people you will meet if you enter a new life.'

She did not tell Elfine of *The Higher Common Sense*, but quoted one or two of the *Pensées* to her, from time to time, and resolved to give her H. B. Mainwaring's excellent translation of *The Higher Common Sense* as a wedding present.

Elfine progressed. Her charming nature and Flora's wise advice met and mingled naturally. Only over poetry was there a little struggle. Flora warned Elfine that she must write no more poetry if she wanted to marry into the county.

'I thought poetry was enough,' said Elfine, wistfully. 'I mean, I thought poetry was so beautiful that if you met someone you loved, and you told them you wrote poetry, that would be enough to make them love you, too.'

'On the contrary,' said Flora, firmly, 'most young men are alarmed on hearing that a young woman writes poetry. Combined with an ill-groomed head of hair and an eccentric style of dress, such an admission is almost fatal.'

'I shall write it secretly, and publish it when I am fifty,' said Elfine, rebelliously.

Flora coldly raised her eyebrows, and decided that she would return to the attack when Elfine had had her hair cut and seen her beautiful new dress.

They entered upon the third week in hopeful spirits. At first, Elfine had been bewildered and unhappy in the new worlds into which Flora led her. But as she grew at home in them, and became fond of Flora, she was happy, and bloomed like a rose-peony. She fed upon hope; and even Flora's confident spirit faltered before the thought of what a weltering ruin, what a desert, must ensue if those hopes were never achieved.

But they must be achieved! Flora wrote as much to her ally, Claud Hart-Harris. She had chosen him, rather than

Charles, as her escort to the Hawk-Monitors' ball, because she felt that she would need all her powers of concentration to see herself and Elfine safely through the evening; and if Charles came to partner her she would be conscious of a certain interest in their own personal relationship, a current of unsaid speeches, which would distract her feelings and perhaps confuse a little her thoughts.

Claud had written to say that she might expect the invitation on April 19th or so. So she came down to breakfast in the kitchen on the morning of the nineteenth with a pleasant sensation of excitement and anticipation.

It was half past eight. Mrs Beetle had finished sweeping the floor and was shaking the mat out in the yard, in the sunshine. (It always surprised Flora to see the sun shining into the yard at Cold Comfort; she had a feeling that the rays ought to be short-circuited just outside the wall by the atmosphere of the farm-house.)

'Ni smorning,' screamed Mrs Beetle, adding that we could do with a bit of it.

Flora smilingly agreed and went across to the cupboard to take down her own little green teapot (a present from Mrs Smiling) and tin of China tea. She glanced out into the yard and was pleased to see that none of the male Starkadders were about. Elfine was out on a walk. Judith was probably lying despairingly across her bed, looking with leaden eyes at the ceiling across which the first flies of the year were beginning monotonously to circle and crawl.

The bull suddenly bellowed his thick, dark-red note. Flora paused, with the teapot in her hand, and looked thoughtfully out across the yard towards his shed.

'Mrs Beetle,' she said firmly, 'the bull ought to be let out. Could you help me do it? Are you afraid of bulls?'

'Yes,' said Mrs Beetle, 'I am afraid o' bulls. And you don't let 'im out, miss, not if I stand 'ere till midnight. In all respect, Miss Poste, though you was to kill me for it.'

'We could guide him towards the gate with the bull-fork, or whatever it is called,' suggested Flora, glancing at the implement which lay across two hooks at the side of the shed.

'No, miss,' said Mrs Beetle.

'Well, I shall open the gate and try to drive him through it,' said Flora, who was utterly terrified of bulls, and cows too, for that matter. 'You must wave your apron at him, Mrs Beetle, and shout.'

'Yes, miss. I'll go up to your bedroom window,' said Mrs Beetle, 'and shout at 'im from there. The sound'll carry better.'

And she nipped away like lightning before Flora could stop her. A few seconds later Flora heard her shouting shrilly from the window overhead.

'Go on, Miss Poste. I'm 'ere!'

Flora was now rather dismayed. The situation seemed to have developed much more quickly than she had thought it would. She was extremely afraid. She stood there, idly waving the teapot, and trying to remember all she had ever read about the habits of bulls. They ran at red. Well, they would not run at her; she was all green. They were savage, especially in spring (it was the middle of April, and the trees were in bud). They gored you . . .

Big Business bellowed again. It was a harsh, mournful sound; there were old swamps and rotting horns buried in it. Flora ran across the yard and pushed open the gate leading into the big field facing the farm, fastening it back. Then she took down the bull-prong, or whatever it called itself, and, standing at a comfortable distance from the shed, manoeuvred the catch back, and saw the door swing open.

Out came Big Business. It was a much less dramatic affair than she had supposed it would be. He stood for a second or two bewildered by the light, with his big head swaying stupidly. Flora stood quite still.

'Eeee-yer! Go on, yer old brute!' shrieked Mrs Beetle.

The bull lumbered off across the yard, still with his head down, towards the gate. Flora followed cautiously, holding the bull-prong. Mrs Beetle screeched to her for the dear's sake to be careful. Once Big Business half turned towards her, and she made a determined movement with the prong. Then, to her relief, he went through the gate into the grassy field, and she swung it to and shut it before he had time to turn round.

'There!' said Mrs Beetle, reappearing at the kitchen door with the speed of a newspaper proprietor explaining his candidate's failure at a by-election. 'I told you so!'

Flora replaced the bull-prong and went back into the kitchen to make her breakfast. It was nine o'clock. The postman should arrive at any minute now.

So she sat down to her breakfast in a position that gave her, through the kitchen window, a view of the path leading up to the farm, for she did not want any one of the Starkadders to get the letters from the postman before she had seen whether the invitation to the Hawk-Monitor ball was among them.

But, to her dismay, just as the figure of the postman appeared at that point of the path where it curved over the hill towards the farm-house, it was joined by another figure. Flora craned her eyes above her cup to see who it might be. It was somebody who was hung about with a good many dead rabbits and pheasants in one way and another, so that his features were obscured from view. He stopped, said something to the postman, and Flora saw something white pass from hand to hand. The rabbit-festooned Starkadder, whoever he might be, had forestalled her. She bit crossly into a piece of toast and continued to observe the approaching figure. He soon came close enough for her to see that it was Urk.

She was much disconcerted. It could not have been worse.

'Turns you up, don't it, seein' ter-day's dinner come in 'anging round someone's neck like that?' observed Mrs Beetle, who was loading a tray with food to take up to Mrs Doom. 'Ter-morrer's, too, for all I know, and the day after's. Give me cold storage, any day.'

Urk opened the door of the kitchen and came slowly into the room.

140

He had been shooting rabbits. His narrow nostrils were slightly distended to inhale the blood-odour from the seventeen which hung round his neck. Their cold fur brushed his hands lightly and imploringly like little pleas for mercy, and his buttocks were softly brushed by the draggled tail-feathers of five pheasants which hung from the pheasant-belt encircling his waist. He felt the weight of the twenty-five dead animals he bore (for there was a shrew or two in his breast pocket) pulling him down, like heavy, dark-blooded roots into the dumb soil. He was drowsy with killing, in the mood of a lion lying on a hippopotamus with its mouth full.

He held the letters in front of him, looking down at them with a sleepy stare. Flora saw, with a start of indignation, that his thumb had left a red mark upon an envelope addressed in Charles's neat hand.

This was quite intolerable. She rose quickly to her feet, holding out her hand.

'My letters, please,' she said, crisply.

Urk pushed them across the table to her, but he kept one in his hand, turning it over curiously to look at a crest upon the back of the envelope. ('Oh, Lord!' thought Flora.)

'I think that one is for me, too,' she said.

Urk did not answer. He looked at her, then down at the letter, then across at Flora again. When his voice came, it was a throaty snarl:

'Who's writing to you from Howchiker?'

'Mary, Queen of Scots. Thanks,' said Flora, with deplorable pertness, and twitched it out of his hand. She slipped it into the pocket of her coat, and sat down to finish her breakfast. But the low, throaty snarl cut once more across the silence:

'Ye're smart, aren't yer? Think I don't know what's going on . . . wi' books from London and all that rot. Now you listen to me. She's mine, I tell you . . . mine. She's my woman, same as a hen belongs to a cock, and no one don't have her except me, ye see? She were promised to me the day she were born, by her Grandmother. I put a cross in water-vole's blood on her feedin'-bottle when she was an hour old, to mark her for mine, and held her up so's she might see it and know she was mine . . . And every year since then, on her birthday, I've taken her up to Ticklepenny's Corner and we've hung over th' old well until we see a water-vole, and I've said to her, I've said, "Remember". And all she would say was: "What, Cousin Urk?" But she knows all right. She knows. When the water-voles mate under the may trees this summer I'll make her mine. Dick Hawk-Monitor . . . what's he? A bit of a boy? Playin' at horses in a red coat, like his daddy afore him. Many a time I've lay and laughed at 'em . . . fools. Me and the water-voles, we can afford to wait for what we want. So you heed what I say, miss. Elfine's mine. I doan't mind her bein' a bit above me' (here his voice thickened in a manner which caused Mrs Beetle to make a sound resembling 't-t-t-t-'), "cause a man likes his piece to be a bit dainty. But she's mine –'

'We heard,' said Flora; 'you said it before.'

'– and God help the man or woman who tries to take her from me. Me and the water-voles, we'll get her back.'

'Are those water-voles round your neck?' asked Flora, interestedly. 'I've never seen any before. What a lot of them all at once!'

He turned from her, with a peculiar stooping, stealthy, swooping movement, and padded out of the kitchen.

'Well, I never,' said Mrs Beetle, loudly; 'there's a narsty temper for you.'

Flora placidly agreed that it was, but she made up her mind that Elfine must be taken up to Town that very day, instead of to-morrow, as she had planned.

She had meant to take Elfine up on the day before the ball, but there was no time to be lost. If Urk suspected that they were going to the ball he would probably try to stop them. They must be sure of the dress, and of Elfine's shorn head, whatever happened. They must go at once. She rose, leaving her breakfast unfinished, and hurried upstairs to

Elfine's room. She found Elfine just returned from her walk.

Flora quickly told her of the change in their plans and left her to get ready while she hurried downstairs to try to find Seth, and to ask him to drive them down to the station. They could just catch the ten fifty-nine to Town.

Seth was hanging over the fence round the great field, looking sullenly at Big Business, who was cantering round and round bellowing.

'Someone's let the bull out,' said Seth, pointing.

'I know. I did. And quite time, too,' said Flora. 'But never mind that now. Seth, will you drive Elfine and me down to Beershorn, to catch the ten fifty-nine?'

Her request was made in a cool, pleasant voice. Yet the softly burning, perpetual ruby flame of romance in Seth responded to some tremor of urgency in her tones. Besides, he wanted to go to the Hawk-Monitors' dance, and see if it was at all like the hunt ball scene in 'Silver Hoofs', the stupendous drama of English country life which Intro-Pan-National had made a year or two ago, and he guessed that Flora was taking Elfine up to London to buy her dress. He did not want anything to interfere with the preparations for the ball.

He said 'Aye', he would, and lounged away with his curious animal grace to get out the buggy.

Adam appeared at the door of the cow shed, where he had been milking Graceless, Pointless, Feckless, Aimless, and Fury. His old body was bent like a thorn against a sharp dazzle of sticky buds bursting from the boughs of a chestnut-tree which hung over the yard.

'Eh, eh – someone's let the bull out,' he said. "Tes terrible . . . I – I mun soothe our Feckless. She'm not herself. Who let un out?'

'I did,' said Flora, buckling the belt of her coat.

And distant shouts came from the back of the farm, where Micah and Ezra were busy setting up the hittenpiece which supported the bucket above the well.

'Th' bull's out!'

'Who let out Big Business?'

'Who let un loose?'

'Ay, 'tes terrible!'

Flora had been writing on a leaf from her pocket-diary, which she now gave to Adam, and instructed him to pin it on the door of the kitchen where it could be seen by everyone as they came hurrying into the yard. It said:

'I did. F. Poste.'

The buggy came out into the yard with Viper in the shafts and Seth holding the reins, just as Elfine, wearing a deplorable blue cape, appeared at the kitchen door.

'Jump up, my dear. We have no time to waste,' cried Flora, mounting the step of the buggy.

'Who let th' bull out?' thundered Reuben, starting from the pig-pen, where he had been delivering a sow who was experienced enough, heaven knows, to deliver herself, but who enjoyed being fussed over.

Flora pointed silently to the note pinned upon the kitchen door. Seth signed to Adam to open the gate of the yard, which Adam did.

'Who let th' bull out?' screamed Judith, putting her head out from an upper window. The question was repeated by Amos, who burst from the chicken-run where he had been collecting eggs.

Flora hoped that they would all see the note and have their curiosity satisfied, or else they would all go blaming each other, and when she came home there would be a shocking atmosphere of rows and uncomfortableness.

But now they were off. Seth struck Viper on the flanks, and they shot forward. Flora repressed an inclination to raise her hat and bow from side to side as they passed through the gate. She felt that someone should have shouted loyally: 'God bless the young squire!'

CHAPTER 13

THEY passed a pleasant day in London.

Flora first took Elfine to Maison Viol, of Brass Street, in Lambeth, to have her hair cut. Short hair was just coming back into fashion, yet it was still new enough to be distinguished. M. Viol himself cut Elfine's hair, and dressed it in a careless, simple, fiendishly expensive way that showed the tips of her ears.

Flora then took Elfine to Maison Solide. M. Solide had dressed Flora for the last two years and did not despise her as much as he despised most of the women whom he dressed. His eyes widened when he saw Elfine. He looked at her broad shoulders and slim waist and long legs. His fingers made the gestures of a pair of scissors, and he groped blindly towards a roll of snow-coloured satin which a well-trained assistant put into his arms.

'White?' ventured Flora.

'But what else?' screamed M. Solide, ripping the scissors across the satin. 'It is to wear white that God, once in a hundred years, makes such a young girl.'

Flora sat and watched for an hour while M. Solide worried the satin like a terrier, tore it into breadths, swathed and caped and draped it. Flora was pleased to see that Elfine did not seem nervous or bored. She seemed to take naturally to the atmosphere of a world-famous dressmaker's establishment. She bathed delightedly in white satin, like a swan in foam. She twisted her neck this way and that, and peered down the length of her body, as though down a snow slope, to watch the assistants like busy black ants pinning and rearranging the hem a thousand feet below.

Flora opened a new romance, and became absorbed in it, until Julia arrived at one o'clock to take them to lunch.

M. Solide, pale and cross after his orgy, assured Flora that the dress would be ready by to-morrow morning. Flora said that they would call for it. No, he must not send it. It was too rare. Would he post a picture by Gauguin to Australia? A thousand evils might befall it on the way.

But, secretly, she wished to protect the dress from Urk. She was sure that he would destroy it if he got a glimmer of a chance.

'Well, do you like your dress?' she asked Elfine, as they sat at lunch in the New River Club.

'It's heavenly,' said Elfine, solemnly. She, like M. Solide, was pale with exhaustion. 'It's better than poetry, Flora.'

'It is not at all like the sort of thing St Francis of Assisi wore,' pointed out Julia, who considered Flora was doing a lot for Elfine and should be appreciated.

Elfine blushed, and bent her head over her cutlet. Flora looked at her benignly. The dress had cost fifty guineas, but Flora did not grudge the sum. She felt at this moment that any sum would have been sacrificed by her to score off the Starkadders.

This feeling was increased by the pleasure she felt in the casual yet delicate appointments of the New River Club. It was the most haughty club in London. No one with an income of more than seven hundred and forty pounds a year might join. Its members were limited to a hundred and twenty. Each member must be nominated by a family with sixteen quarterings. No member might be divorced; if he or she were, membership was forfeited. The Selection Committee was composed of seven of the wildest, proudest, most talented men and women in Europe. The club combined the austerities of a monastic order with the tender peace of a home.

Flora had engaged rooms for Elfine and herself at the club; it was necessary for them to spend the night in Town as they had to call for Elfine's dress the next morning. Flora welcomed the opportunity to indulge herself in some civilized pleasures, from which she had long been absent, and, accordingly, went in the afternoon to hear a concert of Mozart's music at the State Concert Hall in Bloomsbury, leaving Julia to take Elfine to buy a petticoat, some shoes and stockings and a plain evening coat of white velvet. In the evening she proposed that the three of them should visit the Pit Theatre, in Stench Street, Seven Dials, to see a new play by Brandt Slurb called 'Manallalive-O!', a Neo-Expressionist attempt to give dramatic form to the mental reactions of a man employed as a waiter in a restaurant who dreams that he is the double of another man who is employed as a steward on a liner, and who, on awakening and realizing that he is still a waiter employed in a restaurant and not a steward employed on a liner, goes mad and shoots his reflection in a mirror and dies. It had seventeen scenes and only one character. A pest-house, a laundry, a lavatory, a court of law, a room in a lepers' settlement, and the middle of Piccadilly Circus were included in the scenes.

'Why,' asked Julia, 'do you want to see a play like that?'

'I don't, but I think it would be so good for Elfine, so that she will know what to avoid when she is married.'

But Julia thought it would be a much better idea if they went to see Mr Dan Langham in 'On Your Toes!' at the New Hippodrome, so they went there instead and had a nice time instead of a nasty one.

In that entranced pause when the lights of the theatre fade, and upon the crimson of the yet unraised curtain the footlights throw up their soft glow, Flora glanced at Elfine, unobserved, and was pleased with what she saw.

A noble yet soft profile was lifted seriously towards the stage. The light wings of gold hair blew back from either cheek towards the ears; this gave the head a classic look like that of a Greek charioteer pressing his team forward to victory in the face of a strong wind. The beautiful bones, the youth of the face were now revealed.

Flora was satisfied.

She had done what she had hoped to do. She had made Elfine look groomed and normal, yet had preserved in her personality a suggestion of cool, smoothly blowing winds and of pine trees and the smell of wild flowers. She had conceived just such a change, and M. Viol and M. Solide, her instruments, had carried it out.

An artist in living flesh could ask for no more, and the auguries for the evening of the dance were good.

She leaned back in her seat with a contented sigh as the curtains parted.

The cousins reached the farm about five o'clock on the evening of the next day. Much to Flora's surprise, Seth had been at the station to meet their train with the buggy, and he drove them back. They stopped at a large garage in the town on the way home to arrange for a car to call at the farm on the following evening to take them to Godmere. It was to be at Cold Comfort at half past seven, but first it was to meet the six-thirty train and pick up a Mr Hart-Harris, who was arriving at that time.

Having made these arrangements, Flora hopped cheerfully back into the buggy and settled herself into her own black and green plaid rug at Seth's side. Elfine tucked her in. (By this time Elfine was quite devoted to her, and divided the time between devising schemes for Flora's comfort and looking with delight at the picture of her own altered head in the shop windows which they passed.)

'Are you looking forward to it, Seth?' asked Flora.

'Aye,' he drawled softly, in his warm voice, "twill be th' first time I've ever been to a dance wheer all the women wasn't after me. Happen I can enjoy meself a bit, fer a change.'

Flora doubted whether he really would, for the county would probably fall for Seth as inevitably as did the villages. But there was no point in alarming him beforehand.

'But I thought you liked having girls after you?'

'Nay. I only likes the talkies. I don't mind takin' a girl out if she will let me, but many's the girl I've niver seen again because she worried me in the middle of a talkie. Aye, they're all the same. They must have yer blood and yer breath and ivery bit of yer time and yer thoughts. But I'm not like that. I just likes the talkies.'

Flora reflected, as they drove home through the lanes, that Seth's problem was the next one to tackle. She thought of a letter in her handbag. It was from Mr Earl P. Neck, and it said that he would be motoring down within the next few days to see some friends who lived at Brighton, and he proposed to motor over and see her, too. She was going to introduce Seth to him.

It was five o'clock on the afternoon of the next day. The weather favoured the cousins. Flora had pessimistically presumed that it would be pelting with rain, but it was not. It was a mild, rosy spring evening in which blackbirds sang on the budding boughs of the elms and the air smelled of leaves and freshness.

The cousins were having a fiendish business getting themselves dressed.

The intelligent and sensitive reader will doubtless have wondered at intervals throughout this narrative how Flora managed about a bathroom. The answer is simple. At Cold Comfort there was no bathroom. And when Flora had asked Adam how the family themselves managed for baths, he had replied coldly: 'We manages w'hout,' and the vision of dabblings and chillinesses and inadequacies thus conjured had so repelled Flora that she had pursued her inquiries no further.

She had discovered, however, that that refreshing woman, Mrs Beetle, owned a hip-bath, in which she would permit Flora to bathe every other evening at eight o'clock for a small weekly sum, and this Flora did, and the curtailment of her seven weekly baths to four was by far the most unpleasant experience she had so far had to endure at the farm.

But this evening, just when baths were needed, baths were impossible. So Flora put two enormous noggins of water on the stove in the kitchen to get hot, and hoped for the best.

Her absence from the farm with Elfine had not been commented upon. She doubted if they had noticed it. What with the bull getting out, and Meriam, the hired girl, having so far got through the spring without entering upon

149

her annual interesting condition, and the beginning of the carrot harvest which was even longer and more difficult to do than the swede harvest, the Starkadders had enough to absorb them without noticing where a couple of girls had got to. Besides, it was their habit to avoid seeing each other for days at a time, and the absence of Flora and Elfine seemed fortunately to have coincided with one of these hibernations on the part of the family.

But Aunt Ada – did she know? Elfine said she knew everything. She shuddered as she spoke. If Aunt Ada found out that they were going to the ball . . .

'She had best not pull any Cinderella stuff on me,' said Flora coldly, peering into the nearest noggin to see if the water were done.

'It is just possible that she may come downstairs one of these evenings,' said Elfine timidly. 'She sometimes does, in the spring.'

Flora said that she hoped it kept fine for her.

But she did rather wonder why the kitchen was decorated with a wreath of deadly nightshade round the mantelpiece and large bunches of the evil-smelling pussy's dinner arranged in jam-jars on the mantelpiece. And round the dim, ancient portrait of Fig Starkadder, which hung above the fireplace, was a wreath of a flower which was unfamiliar to Flora. It had dark green leaves and long, pink, tightly closed buds. She asked Elfine what it was.

'That's the sukebind,' said Elfine fearfully. 'Oh, Flora, is the water done?'

'Just on, my dove. Here, you take one,' and she handed it to Elfine. 'So that's sukebind, is it? I suppose when it opens all the trouble begins?'

But Elfine was already away with the hot water to Flora's room, where her dress lay upon the bed, and Flora must follow her up.

CHAPTER 14

PERHAPS something, some pregnant quality, in the mildly restless air of the spring evening had infused itself into the room where old Mrs Starkadder sat before the huge bed of glowing cinders in the grate. For she struck suddenly, fiercely, upon the little bell that stood ever at her elbow (at least, it was at her elbow whenever she sat in that particular chair).

A plan which she had been pondering for days, and had even hinted at to Seth, had suddenly matured. The shrill sound leapt through the tepid air of the room. It roused Judith, who was standing at the window looking with sodden eyes at the inexorable fecundity of the advancing spring.

'I mun go downstairs,' said the old woman.

'Mother . . . you're mistaken. 'Tes not the first o' May nor the seventeenth o' October. You'd better bide here,' protested her daughter.

'I tell you I mun go downstairs. I mun feel you all about me – all of you: Micah, Urk, Ezra, Harkaway, Caraway, Amos, Reuben, and Seth. Aye and Mark and Luke. None of you mun ever leave me. Give me my liberty bodice, girl.'

Silently Judith gave it her.

The old house was silent. The dying light lay quietly upon its walls, and the sound of the blackbird's song came into the still, empty rooms. Aunt Ada's thoughts spun like Catherine wheels as she laboriously dressed herself.

Once . . . when you were a little girl . . . you had seen something nasty in the woodshed. Now you were old, and could not move easily. You leaned heavily on Judith's shoulder as she pressed her foot into the small of your back to lace your corsets.

Flora drew the curtains and lit the lamp. Elfine's dress lay on the bed, a lovely miracle, and Elfine must be dressed before Flora could begin to think of her own toilet.

It took an hour to dress Elfine. Flora washed her young

cheeks with scalding water until they burned with angry roses, and brushed back the wings of hair, slipped the foam of the petticoat over her head and brushed again, stood on a chair to drop the dress over her head, and then brushed again. Then she put on the stockings and shoes, and wrapped Elfine in the white coat, put the fan and bag into her waiting hands, and made her sit on the bed, out of dust and danger.

'Oh, Flora . . . do I look nice?'

'You look extremely beautiful,' returned Flora, solemnly looking up at her. 'Mind you behave properly.'

But to herself she was thinking, in the words of the Abbé Fausse-Maigre, 'Condole with the Ugly Duckling's mother. She has fathomed the pit of amazement.'

Flora's own dress was in harmonious tones of pale and dark green. She wore no jewels, and her long coat was of viridian velvet. She would not permit Elfine to wear jewels, either, though Elfine begged for at least her little string of pearls.

Now they were ready. It was only half past six. There was a whole hour to wait before they could creep down to the waiting car. In order to calm their nerves, Flora seated herself upon the bed and read aloud from the *Pensées*:

'Never arrive at a house at a quarter past three. It is a dreadful hour; too early for tea and too late for luncheon . . .'

'Can we be sure that an elephant's real name is elephant? Only mankind presumes to name God's creatures; God himself is silent upon the matter.'

Yet the *Pensées* failed to have their usual calming effect. Flora was a little agitated. Would the car arrive safely? Would Claud Hart-Harris miss the train? (He usually did!) How would Seth look in a dinner-jacket? Above all, would Richard Hawk-Monitor propose to Elfine? Even Flora did not dare to imagine what would happen if they returned from the ball and he had not spoken. He *must* speak! She conjured the god of love by the spring evening, by the blackbird's song, by the triumphant beauty of Elfine.

(Now you were putting on your elastic-sided boots. You had not worn them since Fig died. Fig . . . a prickly beard, a smell of flannel, a stumbling, urgent voice in the larder. Your boots smelled nasty. Where was the lavender water? You made Judith sprinkle some, inside and out. So. Now your first petticoat.)

'Flora,' said Elfine, 'I am afraid I feel sick.'

Flora looked sternly at her and read aloud: 'Vanity can rule the queasiest stomach.'

Suddenly there was a tap at the door. Elfine looked at Flora in terror, and Flora noted how her eyes became dark blue when she was moved. It was a good line.

'Shall I open it?' whispered Elfine.

'I expect it's only Seth.'

Flora got off the bed and tiptoed to the door, which she opened an eighth of an inch. Indeed, it was Seth in a ready-made dinner-jacket which in no way destroyed his animal grace; he merely looked like a panther in evening dress. He whispered to Flora that a car was coming up the hill and that perhaps they had best come downstairs.

'Is Urk anywhere about?' asked Flora, for she knew that if he could mess things up he would.

'I saw un hanging over th' well up at Ticklepenny's talkin' to the water-voles an hour ago,' replied Seth.

'Oh, then, he is safe for another half-hour at least,' said Flora. 'I think we might go down, then. Elfine, are you ready? Now, not a sound! Come along.'

By the light of a candle which Seth carried they made their way safely down into the kitchen, which was deserted. The door leading into the yard was open, and they saw a big car, just visible in the twilight, drawn up outside the gate at the other end of the yard. The chauffeur was just getting down to open the gate, and Flora saw, much to her relief, that another person, who must be Claud, was peering out of the car window. She waved reassuringly to him, and caught the words 'too barbarous' floating across the still evening air. She motioned frantically to him not to make a noise.

'I'll carry Elfine. She mustn't spoil them shoes,' whispered Seth, with unexpected thoughtfulness, and picked his sister up and strode off with her across the yard. He made a second journey for Flora, and she hardly had time to decide whether or not he was holding her unnecessarily tightly when she found herself safely popped into the car, and squeezing the outstretched hands of Claud, with Elfine smiling prettily in the corner.

'My dear, why all this Fall-of-the-House-of-Usher stuff?' inquired Claud. 'I mean, this is too good to be true. Where do we go from here?'

Seth was giving the chauffeur his instructions, and in this pause just before their adventure really began, Flora gazed up searchingly at the windows of the farm-house. ***They were dead as the eyes of fishes, reflecting the dim, pallid blue of the fading west. The crenellated line of the roof thrust blind ledges against a sky into which the infusion of the darkness was already beginning to seep. The livid silver tongues of the early stars leaped between the shapes of the chimney-pots, backwards and forwards, like idiot children dancing to a forgotten tune. As Flora watched, a dim light flowered slowly behind a drawn blind in the window of a room immediately above the kitchen, and she saw a shadow move hesitatingly, as though it had lost a bootlace and was searching dumbly for it, across the blind. The light was like the waxing and waning of the eye in the head of a dying beast. The house seemed to settle deeper into the yard as darkness came. Not a sound broke its quiescence. But the light, strangely naked and innocent, burned waveringly on in the deepening gloom.

The car moved forward, and Flora, for one, was immensely bucked to be off.

'Well, Flora, you look extremely nice,' said Claud, studying her. 'That dress is quite charming. As for your protégée,' he added in a lower tone, 'she is beautiful. Now tell me all about it.'

So, also lowering her voice, Flora told him. He was amused and interested, but a little discontented with his own role. 'I feel,' he complained, 'like a minor character out of "Cinderella".'

Flora soothed him by telling him that this excursion into the hinterland of Sussex should afford him a pleasant change from the excessive urbanity of those circles in which he habitually moved, and the rest of their journey passed pleasantly enough. Seth was inclined to swagger, as he was nervous of Claud's tail coat and white waistcoat and irritated by his casual voice, but he was too excited and looking forward too much to the dance to make himself really disagreeable.

The Assembly Rooms at Godmere were reached by the party without mishap. The High Street was crowded with traffic, for most of the guests had come in from outlying villages and houses in their cars, and a big crowd had come in by bus, from miles round, to gather outside the doors in the Market Place to see the guests going in.

The party from Cold Comfort was fortunate in being in the hands of a competent chauffeur. He actually found a site in a narrow cul-de-sac just round a turning close to the Rooms where he parked their car. Flora instructed him to return at twelve o'clock, when the ball was over, and inquired how he proposed to spend the rest of his evening.

'I shall go to the talkies, madam,' he replied respectfully.

'Aye, there's Marie Rambeau in "Red Heels" at th' Orpheum,' broke in Seth eagerly.

'Yes, well, that will do very well,' said Flora graciously, frowning slightly at Seth; and she slipped her fingers within the arm of Claud, and they moved slowly off through the crowd to the Rooms.

A red carpet had been placed down the flight of steps leading up to the entrance and along the pavement as far as the kerb. On either side of this carpet was assembled a large crowd of sightseers, whose interested and admiring faces were illuminated by two flambeaux which burned at either side of the entrance.

Just as Flora's party was mounting the first steps amid a murmur of admiration from the crowd, she thought she

155

heard someone say her name, and, looking in the direction from which the sound came, she perceived none other than Mr Mybug, perilously poised upon the plinth of a lamp-post, and accompanied by another gentleman of disordered dress and wild appearance, whom she judged to be one of his intellectual peers.

Mr Mybug waved gaily to Flora, and he looked cheerful enough, but she (foolish creature) felt a little sorry for him because he was rather fat and his clothes were not very good, and when she compared his personal appearance with that of Charles, who was always so neat except when a lock of his black hair descended over his forehead while he was playing tennis or otherwise agitated, she felt that Mr Mybug was one of our more desolate figures, and almost wished that he were coming to the ball.

'Who is that?' inquired Claud, glancing in the direction of her gaze.

'A Mr Mybug. I met him in London.'

'Good God!' observed Claud, in a tone of deep distaste.

Had Flora been alone, she would have called pleasantly to Mr Mybug across the heads of the crowd:

'How do you do? . . . How amusing to see you here! Are you copy-hunting?'

But she felt that upon this occasion she stood in the rela-tion of a chaperone and sponsor to Elfine, and that her own conduct must be carefully regulated so as not to give rise to a breath of adverse comment.

She contented herself, therefore, with bowing very pleas-antly to Mr Mybug, who looked rather miserable and tried to pull down his cardigan, which had worked up all wrinkly round his waist.

Mr Aubrey Featherweight, who had designed the Assem-bly Rooms of Godmere in the year 1830, had not been content to provide them with one broad and not unshapely flight of steps as an approach. He had constructed another flight leading down into the large ballroom, which was built slightly below the level of the street.

Now when Flora, emerging from the draughty ladies'

cloak-room immediately within the entrance hall of the Rooms accompanied by the stately and beautiful Elfine, saw this second staircase and realized that it led down into the ballroom, so intense a glow of gratitude filled her heart that she could have fallen upon her knees and thanked Fate.

Did not the Abbé F.-M. say: 'Lost is that man who sees a beautiful woman descending a noble staircase,' and were not both these ingredients here, and ready to her hand? What else but a staircase could so perfectly set off the jewel she had made of Elfine?

A handsome lady of some sixty years stood at the head of the staircase to welcome those guests who passed from the hall on their way to the ballroom, and at her side, aiding her in the task of welcoming each guest, stood a large young woman in a cruel shade of electric blue, whom Flora rightly judged to be Mrs Hawk-Monitor's daughter Joan.

The four young people slowly approached their hostess.

Flora's fine eyes, that were so observant, noticed how propitious was this moment for their entry.

The hour was nearly nine. All the guests of importance had already arrived, and the fine flower of the county of Sussex was circling to the strains of the 'Twelve Sweet Hours' waltz in the ballroom below, the gowns of the young women and the elegant dark purple and white of the young men's clothes being admirably set off by the florid crimson walls, the slender white pillars capped by gold acanthus leaves, and the banks of dark green foliage which decorated the alcoves of the room.

Claud moved forward to present Flora and Elfine to Mrs Hawk-Monitor, who received Flora with a gracious smile, and whose sudden, startled glance at Elfine was all that Flora could wish; and then Elfine, in response to a gentle motion from Flora (who had been detained for a moment in conversation by Joan Hawk-Monitor), began to descend the crimson-covered stairs.

It was at this moment that the sweet, leisurely last notes of the 'Twelve Hours' waltz ceased, and the dancers below slowly came to a standstill and stood clapping and smiling.

Then a startled hush fell upon the clapping. All eyes were turned upon the staircase. A low hum of admiration, the most delightful sound in the world that a woman's ears can receive, rose into the stillness.

Here was beauty. It silenced all comment except that of eager praise. A generation that had admired piquante women, boyish women, ugly, smart, and fascinating women was now confronted by simple beauty, pure and undeniable as that of the young Venus whom the Greeks loved to carve; and responded immediately, in delighted and surprised homage, to its challenge.

Just as no human creature who has eyes to see can deny the beauty of an almond-tree in full flower, no human eyes could deny beauty to Elfine. The slow descent of this young girl down the staircase was like the descent of a sunlit cloud down the breast of a mountain. Her candid beauty, set off by the snowy-silver of her simple dress, refreshed the dancers who stood silently looking up at her as the sight of a cluster of flowers or a moonlight expanse of sea refreshes the eyes.

And Flora, silently watching from the head of the staircase, saw that a tall young man who stood just at its foot was looking up at Elfine as the young shepherd must once have looked at the moon goddess; and she was satisfied.

The entranced pause was broken by music. The orchestra began to play a gay polka, and the young man (who was Richard Hawk-Monitor himself) came forward to give his hand to Elfine and lead her into the mazes of the dance.

Flora and Claud (who was much amused by all this) came down the stairs into the ballroom a little later and also joined the dancers.

Flora had every reason to feel smug and satisfied with her evening's work as she floated round the room in the arms of Claud, who danced admirably. Without seeming to take so obvious an interest in the movements of Elfine and her partner that her gaze became ill-bred, she observed their every action.

What she saw pleased her much. Richard appeared to be deeply in love. It is usual to see a young man looking down

into the face of a girl with whom he is dancing with an expression of soft admiration, and Flora was used to such
spectacles. But she had not often seen a young man's face
so rapt, so almost awed, with adoration and another emotion
which can only be defined as gratitude, as was the face of
Richard Hawk-Monitor. Wonder, too, was in his expression.
He held Elfine preciously, as a man might hold a flowering
branch of some rare tree which he has seen for the first
time and is bringing back to his cave.

The miracle for which she had conjured the love god had
befallen. Richard had realized, not that Elfine was beautiful,
but that he loved Elfine. (Young men frequently need this
fact pointed out to them, as Flora knew by observing the
antics of her friends.)

Now she must wait patiently until the end of the ball,
when Elfine would tell her whether Richard had proposed
marriage. She felt that the anxiety of waiting to know
whether her diplomacy had succeeded might impair the
pleasure of the evening for her, but resolved to bear the
trial with calmness.

However, as it turned out, she began to enjoy the ball so
much that she almost forgot her anxiety.

The ball was, indeed, a very agreeable one. Perhaps it
was more by luck than by judgement that Mrs Hawk-
Monitor had combined two of the essentials for a successful
ball (too many guests in a smallish room), but both were
there, and then these were combined with the elegance and
lavishness of the supper-tables and the sober richness of the
appointments, and the fact that most of the people who
were present knew each other slightly, all the ingredients
for success were present, and success was achieved.

Flora overheard many comments upon Elfine's beauty,
and was asked several times who her lovely companion was.
She smilingly replied that she was a cousin, a Miss Starkadder, and would say no more save that Elfine lived in the
neighbourhood. She did not make the mistake of snobbishly
embroidering upon Elfine's ancestry and charm. She let
Elfine's serious beauty do its own work, and very well it did

it. Elfine danced most of the dances with Richard Hawk-Monitor, but she gave many others to the group of eager young men who gathered round her as soon as the music paused.

Flora observed that Mrs Hawk-Monitor, from her position in an alcove on the balcony above the ballroom, was beginning to look vaguely anxious, especially during those dances that Elfine gave to Richard.

Flora divided her dances chiefly between Claud and Seth. Seth appeared to be enjoying the evening immensely. In one way and another he had nearly as spectacular a success as Elfine. A group of some nine young persons whose dress proclaimed that they had come down from London for the ball took possession of Seth early in the evening, and would not let him go. Flora overheard two or three of the young women telling each other that their dears, he was *too* credit-able, and *merely* body-thrilling, and Seth just smiled his slow, warm smile and drawled; 'Aye' and 'Nay' when asked if he did not adore farming, and what he wanted from life, and didn't he think the important thing was to experience *everything*?

Several young men approached Flora, and seemed anxious to appropriate her company after they had danced with her, and all this was very satisfactory, but she had resolved that for this evening at any rate she must keep herself in the background and make no attempt to rival Elfine. So she danced mostly with Claud, after Seth had been carried off to supper by his adoring tribe of young girls. Flora knew that she did not look so beautiful as Elfine, but, then, she did not want to. She knew that she looked distinguished, elegant, and interesting. She asked for nothing more.

Only one disagreeable incident marred the pleasure of the evening. Just as she and Claud were making their way to the supper-tables in an adjoining room a disturbance broke out in the balcony above their heads, and Flora looked up in time to see the back of a gentleman, which was only too familiar to her, being hustled out through the entrance with some haste by two of the flunkeys.

'Somebody tried to gate-crash,' called a laughing young man to Claud, in passing, as he came running down the stairs. He had been giving the flunkeys a hand.

Flora felt rather distressed. She sat down at the little table which Claud had reserved for them, which was charmingly wreathed with spring leaves and flowers, with a sober expression on her face.

'My dear Flora, was that a friend of yours?' asked Claud, motioning the waiter to open some champagne.

'It was Mr Mybug,' said Flora, simply; 'and I cannot help feeling, Claud, that if I had thought of trying to get him an invitation he would not have had to try and gate-crash.'

'It is a good thing that everybody who hasn't got invitations for things doesn't have to try and gate-crash,' observed Claud.

'I cannot help feeling,' pursued Flora, picking up her fork to begin on the crab *mousse*, 'rather sorry for Mr Mybug.'

'We are purified by suffering,' said Claud, helping himself to crab.

But Flora went on: 'You see, he is rather fat. I always feel sorry for people who are fat. And I haven't got the heart to tell him that's why I won't let him kiss me. He thinks it's because I'm inhibited.'

'But, my dear, he would. Don't distress yourself. Have some more crab.'

And Flora did, and telling herself that it was her duty to look pleasant, for Elfine's sake, she thought no more of Mr Mybug that evening.

Flora and Claud lingered long over the supper-table, enjoying the spectacle of the brilliantly lit, elegantly decorated apartment filled with young persons of both sexes, most of them handsome and all of them happy. Claud, who had served in the Anglo-Nicaraguan wars of '46, was at his ease in the comfortable silence in which they sat, and allowed the irony and grief of his natural expression to emerge from beneath the mask of cheerful idiocy with which he usually covered his sallow, charming face. He had seen his friends die in anguish in the wars. For him, the whole of the rest of his life was an amusing game which no man of taste and intelligence could permit himself to take seriously.

Much as Flora was enjoying the ball, she was doing so more as a spectator than as a participant. She wished regretfully that some others of her friends might have been present: Mrs Smiling, looking vague in a white gown; the handsome Julia; Charles, in the severe tail coat of darkest blue which so well became his height and gravity.

As at all good parties, an atmosphere, impalpable as a perfume yet as real, rose above the heads of the laughing guests. It was the aroma of enjoyment and gaiety. No one could inhale it without instinctively smiling and glancing good-naturedly round the room. Gay voices rose every second above the roar of the general conversation like individual rills of water from the rush of a stream in spate. A laughing mouth, three youthful heads gathered together, while a fourth, distorted with laughter, uttered gasping protests; chins lifted and eyes narrowed between lashes with mirth; an azalea plant revealed as two persons drew back from the table to shout with laughter: such were the outward signs of a Good Party. And above them floated this invisible glittering cloud of success.

Suddenly Flora gave a slight start. Elfine had appeared at the door of the supper-room, accompanied by Richard Hawk-Monitor. They were glancing round the room as if in search of someone, and when Elfine caught sight of Flora's raised hand, in its pale-green glove, she smiled eagerly and said something over her shoulder to the young Hawk-Monitor, and they began to make their way between the tables to where Flora and Claud sat.

Flora's spirits, already excited by the pleasure of the ball, rose still higher. Richard must have proposed, and have been accepted. Nothing else could have made the two look so peculiarly radiant.

They came towards her, threading their way between the laughing groups, who looked up from their talk to smile at

Dick and to look curiously at Elfine; and then Elfine had paused at their table, and Claud had risen to his feet, and Elfine, reaching backwards for Richard's hand, drew him forward and said:

'Oh, Flora, I do so want you to meet Dick.'

Flora bowed and smiled, and said: 'How do you do? I have heard so much about you and I am so pleased to meet you'; but she found her hand taken into a friendly clasp and met the beam of a wind-reddened, open, boyish countenance. She noticed that he had perfect teeth, white as those of a young lion, and a little black moustache.

'I say, I'm awfully glad to meet you. Elf has told me all about you, too. I say, this is jolly, isn't it? Marvellous idea of the mater's, having the orgy here instead of in the family crematorium, what? I say, Miss Poste, it was awfully decent of you to bring Elfine. I simply can't thank you enough, you know. I mean, it's made all the difference in the world. We're engaged, as a matter of fact.'

'My dear! How charming! I am delighted! I congratulate you!' cried Flora, who was indeed overcome with relief and satisfaction.

'Charming,' murmured Claud, in the background.

'We're going to announce it at the end of the evening,' Richard went on. 'Good opportunity, what?'

Claud, sardonically wondering what the feelings of Mrs Hawk-Monitor would be when she heard the news, said that the occasion might have been made for the announcement of the event. Flora then introduced him to Richard, and there was some general conversation, made interesting by the aura of happiness which hovered over the betrothed pair and the smiling sympathy with which Claud and Flora listened to their talk.

CHAPTER 15

IT was now nearly twelve o'clock, and a general movement was made to return to the ballroom. The orchestra had been refreshed by some supper, and broke immediately into a jolly tune to which the 'Lancers' could be danced, and away pranced everybody, and danced until every cheek was crimson and the floor was scattered with fans, hairpins, shoe-buttons, and wilting flowers.

Claud was as light on his feet as the harlequin he somewhat resembled, and while Flora was springing round the room, just guided by the cool touch of his hands, she observed Elfine in Richard's arms, and saw with satisfaction how marvellously happy she looked and how beautiful. Flora glowed with content. Her aim was achieved. She felt as though she had shaken her fist in the face of Aunt Ada Doom. Elfine was rescued. Henceforth, her life would be one of exquisite, sunny, natural content. She would bear children and found a line of pleasant, ordinary English people who were blazing with poetry in their secret souls. All was as it should be.

And Flora, energetically prancing herself to a standstill as the Lancers ended, clapped her hands vigorously, half with the desire for an encore, but more for the joy she felt in her evening's work.

'How you do enjoy yourself, don't you, Florence Nightingale?' observed Claud.

'I do,' retorted Flora; 'and so do you.'

It was true; he did. But never without a pang of exquisite pain in his heart, and a conviction that he was a traitor.

In the pause that followed the music, Flora observed that Richard was leading Elfine to the staircase, and they went slowly up it, to where his mother sat on the balcony with a number of her old friends. Flora moved forward also, in case she should be needed, but before she could begin to mount the stairs Richard left his mother, over whom he had been bending in conversation, and, coming forward to the balcony rail, held up his hand for silence. Elfine stood beside him, but slightly in the background. Flora could not see the expression on the face of Mrs Hawk-Monitor, who was hidden by Richard's body, but she observed that the face of Joan Hawk-Monitor bore an expression which was a curious blend of dismay and interest and envy. ('But then, that shade of blue would do anything to anybody's face,' Flora comforted herself.)

'Ladies and gentlemen,' said Dick. 'It's been awfully jolly seeing you all here to-night. I'm awfully glad you could all come. I mean, I shall always be glad to remember you were all here on my twenty-first birthday. It makes it all so much jollier somehow ... I mean, I do like a cheery mob around me, what?'

He paused. There was laughter and some clapping. Flora held her breath. He must – he *must* announce the engagement! If he did not, she would know (whatever might happen afterwards) that her plot had failed.

But it was all right. He was speaking again. He was drawing Elfine forward to face the guests, and taking her hands in his.

'And this is a particularly jolly evening for me, because I've got something else to tell you all. I want to tell you that Miss Starkadder and I are engaged.'

There! It was out! A storm of clapping and excited comment broke forth, and people began streaming up the staircase to offer their congratulations. Flora, feeling quite weak after the nervous excitement of the past five minutes, turned to Claud, and said: 'There, that's over. Oh, Claud, but do you think we ought to go up and speak to Mrs Hawk-Monitor? I must confess that I would rather not.'

Claud, however, said decidedly that he thought it would be most incorrect if Flora did not do so, for she was there, after all, in the capacity of Elfine's chaperone, and the whole course of affairs had already been so irregular that anything Flora could do to give a colouring of convention to the situation would count in Elfine's favour.

So Flora, reluctantly agreeing, went up the staircase to tackle Mrs Hawk-Monitor.

She found the poor lady looking dazed. She was sitting in an alcove, receiving the thanks and congratulations upon the success of the ball from those guests who were already departing. Flora was relieved to notice that the healthy Joan was standing at some distance away, by the door, so she would not have to cope with *her*, as well as with Mamma H.-M.

Flora went forward with outstretched hand.

'Thank you so much . . . such a lovely party, and so nice of you to let us come.'

But Mrs Hawk-Monitor had risen, and was looking very gravely at her. She might be a vague woman and a darling, but she was not a fool. She took an eyeful of Flora, and knew that here was a young woman of good sense. Her heart longed for some reassurance in the midst of the dismay and doubt which possessed her. She said, almost pleadingly:

'Miss Poste, I will be frank with you. I cannot pretend that I am delighted at this engagement. Who is this young lady? I have only met her once before. I know next to nothing of her family.'

'She is a gentle, docile person,' said Flora, earnestly. 'She is only seventeen. I think she can be moulded into exactly what you would wish her to be. Dear Mrs Hawk-Monitor, pray do not be distressed. I am sure that you will learn to like Elfine. Do believe me when I say that she has excellent qualities. As for her family, if I may venture to offer you some advice, I should take steps at once to see that she sees next to nothing of them for the next few weeks. There will probably be strong opposition to the match.'

'Opposition? What imperti – '

She checked herself. She was amazed and at a loss. She had assumed that Elfine's family would be overjoyed at their offspring's luck.

'Indeed, yes. Mrs Starkadder, her grandmother, has always intended Elfine to marry her cousin, Urk. I am afraid there may be some opposition from him too. In fact, the sooner you can arrange for the marriage to take place the better it will be for Elfine.'

'Oh, dear! I had hoped for a year's engagement, at least. Dick is still so young.'

'The more reason why he should begin at once to be utterly happy,' smiled Flora. 'Indeed, Mrs Hawk-Monitor, I do really think it will be better if you can arrange for the wedding to take place in a month at the latest. Things at the farm are sure to be very unpleasant for Elfine until she leaves, and I am sure you do not want a lot of interference and discussion from the Starkadders, do you?'

'Such a dreadful name, too,' mused Mrs Hawk-Monitor.

At this moment, the arrival of Seth and Claud, dressed ready to depart, made it impossible to discuss the matter any further. Mrs Hawk-Monitor had only time to press Flora's hand, murmuring in a friendlier tone than she had yet used: 'I will think over what you say. Perhaps, after all, everything is for the best.'

So Flora went off in comparatively high spirits.

They found Elfine, looking like a white rose-peony, waiting for them at the door; Dick was with her, tenderly saying good night to her. Flora could see their car, with the chauffeur at the door, waiting for them at the foot of the steps, so after a pleasant farewell to Dick they got away at last.

Flora felt quite desolate after they had dropped Claud outside the Crown of Roses, where he was staying the night. She was rather sleepy and cross and suffering from a re-action after the evening's excitement. So she shut her eyes and slept more or less successfully until the car was within two miles or so from home. Then she woke with a little start. Voices had roused her. Seth was saying, in a tone which was distinctly tinged with gloating:

'Aye, th' old un'll have summat to say about this night's work.'

'Grandmamma can't stop me getting married!'

'Maybe not, but she'll have a dom good try.'

'She cannot do much in a month,' broke in Flora, coldly,

'and possibly Elfine will be staying with the Hawk-Monitors for most of the time. She must just avoid Aunt Ada while she is in the house, that's all. Heaven knows it ought not to be very difficult to do, considering that Aunt Ada never leaves her bedroom.'

Seth gave a low, gloating laugh. An animal quality throbbed in the sound like the network of veins below a rat's fur. The car was just drawing up at the gate leading into the yard, and Seth, leaning past Flora, pointed through the window with one thick finger at the farm-house.

Flora stared in the direction to which he pointed and saw, with a thrill of dismay, that the windows of the farm were ablaze with light.

CHAPTER 16

PERHAPS 'ablaze' is too strong a word. There was a distinct suggestion of corpse-lights and railway-station waiting-rooms about the lights which shone forth from the windows of Cold Comfort. But compared with the heavy, muffling darkness of the night in which the country-side was sunk, the lights looked looked positively rorty.

'Oh, my goodness!' said Flora.

'It's Grandmamma!' whispered Elfine, who had gone very white. 'She must have chosen this night, of all nights, to come downstairs, and have the family party.'

'Nonsense! You don't have parties at places like Cold Comfort,' said Flora, taking notes from her bag with which to pay the chauffeur. She got out of the car, stretching a little and inhaling the fresh, sweet night air, and put them into his hand.

'There. Thank you very much. Everything went off most satisfactorily. Good night.'

And the chauffeur, having thanked her respectfully for his tip, backed the car out of the yard, and away down the lane towards the road.

The headlights swept the hedges and touched the grass to livid green.

They heard him change into top, in the dead, eerie silence and darkness.

Then the friendly sound of the engine began to recede, until it was absorbed into the vast quiet of the night.

They turned and looked towards the house.

The lights in the windows had a leering, waiting look, like that on the faces of old pimps who sit in the cafés of Holborn Viaduct, plying their casual bartery. A thin wind snivelled among the rotting stacks of Cold Comfort, spreading itself in a sheet of flowing sound across the mossed tiles. Darkness whined with the soundless urge of growth in the hedges, but that did not help any.

'Ay, 'tes Grandmother,' said Seth, sombrely. 'She'm holding the Counting. Ay, 'tes her, all right.'

'What on earth,' said Flora, peevishly, beginning to pick her way across the yard, 'is the Counting, and why in the name of all that's inconvenient should it be held at half past one in the morning?'

''Tes the record of th' family that Grandmother holds ivery year. See – we'm violent folk, we Starkadders. Some on us pushes others down wells. Some on us dies in childerbirth. There's others as die o' drink or goes mad. There's a whole heap on us, too. 'Tes difficult to keep count on us. So once a year Grandmother she holds a gatherin', called the Counting, and she counts us all, to see how many on us 'as died in th' year.'

'Then she can count me out,' retorted Flora, raising her hand to knock at the kitchen door.

Then a thought struck her.

'Seth,' she whispered, 'had you any idea that your grandmother was going to hold this infernal Counting tonight?'

She saw the gleam of his teeth in the dimness.

'Reckon I had,' he drawled.

'Then you're a crashing bounder,' said Flora, vigorously, 'and I hope your water-voles die. Now, Elfine, brace up.

We are, I am afraid, for it. You had best not say a word. I will do the talking.'

And she knocked at the door.

The silence which swayed softly out from within to meet them was a tangible thing. It had plangency. It moulded and compelled. It imposed and awed.

It was broken by heavy footsteps. Someone was crossing the kitchen floor in hob-nailed boots. A hand fumbled with the bolts. Then the door was slowly opened, and Urk stood looking up at them, his face twisted into a Japanese Nō-mask of lust, fury, and grief. Flora could hear Elfine's terrified breathing behind her, in the darkness, and put out a comforting hand. It was clasped and held convulsively.

The great kitchen was full of people. They were all silent, and all painted over by the leaping firelight with a hellish red glow. Flora could distinguish Amos, Judith, Meriam, the hired girl; Adam, Ezra, and Harkaway; Caraway, Luke, and Mark, and several of the farm-hands. They were all grouped, in a rough semicircle, about someone who sat in a great high-backed chair by the fire. The dim gold lamplight and the restless firelight made Rembrandt shadows in the remoter corners of the kitchen, and threw the dwarf and giant shadows of the Starkadders across the ceiling.

A pungent scent came swooning out to meet the inrush of night air. It was sickly sweet, and strange to Flora. Then she saw that the heat of the fire had caused the long, pink buds of the sukebind to burst; the wreath which hung round the portrait of Fig Starkadder was covered with large flowers whose petals sprang back, like snarling fangs, to show the shameless heart that sent out full gusts of sweetness.

Everybody was staring at the door. The silence was terrific. It seemed the air must burst with its pressure, and the flickering movement of the light and the fireglow upon the faces of the Starkadders was so restlessly volatile that it emphasized the strange stillness of their bodies. Flora was trying to decide just what the kitchen looked like, and came to the conclusion it was the Chamber of Horrors at Madame Tussaud's.

'Well, well,' she said, amiably, stepping over the doorstep and drawing off her gloves, 'the gang *is* all here, isn't it? Is that Big Business I see there in the corner? Oh, I beg your pardon, it's Micah. I suppose there aren't any sandwiches?'

This cracked the social ice a bit. Signs of life were observed.

'There's food on the table,' said Judith, lifelessly, coming forward, with her burning eyes fixed upon Seth; 'but first, Robert Poste's child, you must greet your Aunt Ada Doom.'

And she took Flora's hand (Flora was very bucked that she had shed her clean gloves) and led her up to the figure which sat in the high-backed chair by the fire.

'Mother,' said Judith, 'this is Flora, Robert Poste's child. I have spoken to you of her.'

'How d'ye do, Aunt Ada?' said Flora, pleasantly, putting out her hand. But Aunt Ada made no effort to take it. She folded her own hands a little more closely upon a copy of the *Milk Producers' Weekly Bulletin and Cowkeepers' Guide*, which she held on her lap, and observed, in a low, toneless voice:

'I saw something nasty in the woodshed.'

Flora turned to Judith, with raised and inquiring eyebrows. A murmur came from the rest of the company, which was watching closely.

'''Tes one of her bad nights,' said Judith, whose gaze kept wandering piteously in the direction of Seth (he was wolfing beef in the corner). 'Mother,' she said, louder, 'don't you know me? It's Judith. I have brought Flora Poste to see you – Robert Poste's child.'

'Nay . . . I saw something nasty in the woodshed,' said Aunt Ada Doom, fretfully moving her great head from side to side. ' 'Twas a burnin' noonday . . . sixty-nine years ago. And me no bigger than a titty-wren. And I saw something na – '

'Well, perhaps she likes it better that way,' said Flora soothingly. She had been observing Aunt Ada's firm chin, clear eyes, tight little mouth, and close grip upon the *Milk Producers' Weekly Bulletin and Cowkeepers' Guide*, and she came to the conclusion that if Aunt Ada was mad, then she, Flora, was one of the Marx Brothers.

'Saw something nasty in the woodshed!!!' suddenly shrilled Aunt Ada, smiting Judith with the *Milk Producers' Weekly Bulletin and Cowkeepers' Guide*, 'something nasty! Take it away. You're all wicked and cruel. You want to go away and leave me alone in the woodshed. But you never shall. None of you. Never! There have always been Stark-adders at Cold Comfort. You must all stay here with me, all of you? Judith, Amos, Micah, Urk, Luke, Mark, Elfine, Caraway, Harkaway, Reuben, and Seth. Where's Seth? Where's my darling? Come – come here, Seth.'

Seth came pushing his way through the crowd of relations, with his mouth full of beef and bread. 'Here, grandma,' he crooned, soothingly. 'Here I am. I'll niver leave 'ee – niver.'

('Do not look at Seth, woman,' whispered Amos, terribly, in Judith's ear. 'You are always looking at him.')

'That's my good boy ... my mommet ... my pippet ...' the old woman murmured, patting Seth's head with the *Milk Producers' Weekly Bulletin and Cowkeepers' Guide*. 'Why, how grand he is to-night! What's this? What's all this?' And she jerked at Seth's dinner-jacket. 'What've you been doing, boy? Tell your granny.'

Flora could see, from the way in which Aunt Ada's remarkably shrewd eyes beneath their heavy lids were examining Seth's person, that she had rumbled their little outing. There was just time to save their faces before the deluge. So she took a deep breath and said loudly and clearly:

'He's been to Godmere, to Richard Hawk-Monitor's twenty-first birthday dance. So have I. So has Elfine. So has a friend of mine called Claud Hart-Harris, whom none of you know. And, what is more, Aunt Ada, Elfine and Richard Hawk-Monitor are engaged to be married, and *will* be married, too, in about a month from now.'

There came a terrible cry from the shadows near the sink. Everybody started violently and turned to stare in the direction whence it came. It was Urk – Urk lying face downward, in the beef sandwiches, with one hand pressed upon his heart in dreadful agony. The hired girl, Meriam, laid her rough hand upon his bowed head and timidly patted it, but he shook her off with a movement like a weasel in a trap.

'My little water-vole,' they heard him moan. 'My little water-vole.'

A babel broke out, in which Aunt Ada could dimly be discerned beating at everybody with the *Milk Producers' Weekly Bulletin and Cowkeepers' Guide*, and shrilly screaming: 'I saw it ... I saw it! I shall go mad ... I can't bear it ... There have always been Starkadders at Cold Comfort. I saw something nasty in the woodshed ... something nasty ... nasty ... nasty ...'

Seth took her hands and held them in his, kneeling before her and speaking wooingly to her, as though she were a sick child. Flora had dragged Elfine up on a table in a corner near the fireplace, out of the racket, and was pensively feeding the two of them on bread and butter. She had given up all hope of getting to bed that night. It was nearly half past two, and everybody seemed sitting pretty for the sunrise.

She observed several females unknown to her flitting dejectedly about in the gloom, replenishing plates with bread and butter and occasionally weeping in corners.

'Who's that?' she asked Elfine, pointing interestedly at one who had a perfectly flat bust and a face like a baby bird all goggle eyes and beaky nose. This one was weeping half inside a boot cupboard.

''Tes poor Rennet,' said Elfine, sleepily. 'Oh, Flora, I'm so happy, but I do wish we could go to bed, don't you?'

'Presently, yes. So that's poor Rennet, is it? Why (if it be not tactless to ask) are all her clothes sopping wet?'

'Oh! she jumped down the well, about eleven o'clock, Meriam, the hired girl, told me. Grandmamma kept on mocking at her because she's an old maid. She said Rennet couldn't even keep a tight hold on Mark Dolour when she *had* got him, and poor Rennet had hysterics, and then Grandma kept on saying things about – about flat bosoms and things, and then Rennet ran out and jumped down the well. And Grandma had an attack.'

'Serve her right, the old trout,' muttered Flora, yawning. 'Hey, what's up now?' For a renewed uproar had broken out in the midst of the crowd gathered round Aunt Ada.

By standing on the table and peering through the confusing flicker of the firelight and lamplight, Flora and Elfine could distinguish Amos, who was bending over Aunt Ada Doom's chair, and thundering at her. There was such an infernal clatter going on from Micah, Ezra, Reuben, Seth, Judith, Caraway, Harkaway, Susan, Letty, Prue, Adam, Jane, Phoebe, Mark, and Luke that it was difficult to make out what he was saying, but suddenly he raised his voice to a roar, and the others were silent:

'... So I mun go where th' Lord's work calls me and spread th' Lord's word abroad in strange places. Ah, 'tes terrible to have to go, but I mun do it. I been wrestlin' and prayin' and broodin' over it, and I know th' truth at last. I mun go abroad in one o' they Ford vans, preachin' all over th' countryside. Aye, like th' Apostles of old, I have heard my call, and I mun follow it.' He flung his arms wide, and stood with the firelight playing its scarlet fantasia upon his exalted face.

'No . . . No!' screamed Aunt Ada Doom, on a high note that cracked with her agony. 'I cannot bear it. There have always been Starkadders at Cold Comfort. You mustn't go ... none of you must go ... I shall go mad! I saw something nasty in the woodshed . . . Ah . . . ah . . .'

She struggled to her feet, supported by Seth and Judith, and struck weakly at Amos with the *Milk Producers' Weekly Bulletin and Cowkeepers' Guide* (which was looking a bit the worse for wear by this time). His great body flinched from the blow, but still he stood rigid, his eyes fixed triumphantly upon some far-off, ecstatic vision, the red light wavering and flickering across his face.

'I mun go ...' he repeated, in a strange, soft voice. 'This very night I mun go. I hear th' glad voices o' angels callin' me out over th' ploughed fields where th' liddle seedlings is

clappin' their hands in prayer; and besides, I arranged wi'
Agony Beetle's brother to pick me up in th' Lunnon milk-
van at half past three, so I've no time to lose. Aye, 'tes good-
bye to you all. Mother, I've broken yer chain at last, wi' th'
help of th' angels and the Lord's word. Wheer's my hat?'

Reuben silently handed it to his father (he had had it
ready for the last ten minutes).

Aunt Ada Doom sat huddled in her chair, breathing
feebly and fast, striking impotently at the air with the *Milk
Producers' Weekly Bulletin and Cowkeepers' Guide*. Her
eyes, slots of pain in her grey face, were turned on Amos.
They blazed with hate, like flaring candles that feel the
pressing dark all about them and flare the brighter for their
fear.

'Aye ...' she whispered. 'Aye ... so you go, and leave me
in the woodshed. There have always been Starkadders at
Cold Comfort ... but that means nothing to you. I shall go
mad ... I shall die here, alone, in the woodshed, with nasty
– things' – her voice thickened; she wrung her hands dis-
tractedly, as though to free them of some obscene spiritual
treacle – 'pressing on me ... alone ... alone ...'

Her voice trailed into silence. Her head sank into her
breast. Her face was drained of blood: grey, broken.

Amos moved with great, slow steps to the door. No one
moved. The hush which froze the room was broken only by
the idle rippling dance of the flames. Amos jerked open the
door, and there was the vast, indifferent face of the night
peering in.

'Amos!'

It was a screech from her heart-roots. It buried itself in
his plexus. But he never turned. He stepped blunderingly
out into the dark – and was gone.

Suddenly there was a wild cry from the corner in the
shadows by the sink. Urk came stumbling forward, dragging
the hired girl, Meriam, in his wake.

(Flora woke up Elfine, who had gone to sleep with her
head on her shoulder, and pointed out that some more fun
was just beginning. It was only a quarter past three.)

Urk was chalk-white. A trail of blood drooled down his chin. His eyes were pools of pain, in which his bruised thoughts darted and fed like tortured fish. He was laughing insanely, noiselessly. Meriam shrank back from him, livid with fear.

'Me and the water-voles ... we've failed,' he babbled in a low, toneless voice. 'We're beaten. We planned a nest for her up there by Ticklepenny's well, when the egg-plants was in bloom. And now she's given herself to him, the dirty stuck-up, lying – ' He choked, and had to fight for breath for a second. 'When she was an hour old, I made a mark on her feeding bottle, in water-vole's blood. She was mine, see? Mine! And I've lost her ... Oh, why did I iver think she were mine?'

He turned upon Meriam, who shrank back in terror.

'Come here – you. I'll take you instead. Aye, dirt as you are, I'll take you, and we'll sink into th' mud together. There have always been Starkadders at Cold Comfort, and now there'll be a Beetle too.'

'And not the first neither, as you'd know if you'd ever cleaned out the larder,' said a voice tartly. It was Mrs Beetle herself, who, hitherto unobserved by Flora, had been busily cutting bread and butter and replenishing the glasses of the farm-hands in a far corner of the long kitchen. She now came forward into the circle about the fire, and confronted Urk with her arms akimbo.

'Well ... 'oo's talking about dirt? 'Eaven knows, you should know something about it, in that coat and them trousers. Enough ter turn up one of yer precious water-voles, you are. A pity you don't spend a bit less time with yer old water-voles and a bit more with a soap and flannel.'

Here she received unexpected support from Mark Dolour who called in a feeling tone from the far end of the kitchen:

'Aye, that's right.'

'Don't you 'ave 'im, ducky, unless you feel like it,' advised Mrs Beetle, turning to Meriam. 'You're full young yet, and 'e won't see forty again.'

'I don't mind. I'll 'ave him, if un wants me,' said Meriam,

amiably, 'I can always make 'im wash a bit, if I feels like it.'

Urk gave a wild laugh. His hand fell on her shoulder, and he drew her to him and pressed a savage kiss full on her open mouth. Aunt Ada Doom, choking with rage, struck at them with the *Milk Producers' Weekly Bulletin and Cow-keepers' Guide*, but the blow missed. She fell back, gasping, exhausted.

'Come, my beauty – my handful of dirt. I mun carry thee up to Ticklepenny's and show 'ee to the water-voles.' Urk's face was working with passion.

'What! At this time o' night?' cried Mrs Beetle, scandalized.

Urk put one arm round Meriam's waist and heaved away, but could not budge her from the floor. He cursed aloud, and, kneeling down, placed his arms about her middle, and heaved again. She did not stir. Next he wrapped his arms about her shoulders, and below her knees. She declined upon him, and he, staggering beneath her, sank to the floor. Mrs Beetle made a sound resembling 't-t-t-t-t'.

Mark Dolour was heard to mutter that th' Fireman's Lift was as good a hold as any he knew.

Now Urk made Meriam stand in the middle of the floor, and with a low, passionful cry, ran to her.

'Come, my beauty.'

The sheer animal weight of the man bore her up into his clutching arms. Mark Dolour (who dearly loved a bit of sport) held open the door, and Urk and his burden rushed out into the dark and the earthy scents of the young spring night.

A silence fell.

The door remained open, idly swinging in a slow, cold wind which had risen.

As though frozen, the group within the kitchen waited for the distant crash which should tell them that Urk had fallen down.

Pretty soon it came; and Mark Dolour shut the door.

It was now four o'clock. Elfine had gone to sleep again.

So had all the farm-hands except Mark Dolour. The fire had sunk to a red, lascivious bed of coals, that waned, and then, on the other hand, waxed again in the slow wind which blew under the door.

Flora was desperately sleepy: she felt as though she were at one of Eugene O'Neill's plays; that kind that goes on for hours and hours and hours, until the R.S.P.C. Audiences batters the doors of the theatre in and insists on a tea interval.

There was no doubt that the fun was wearing a bit thin. Judith, huddled in a corner, was looking broodingly at Seth from under her raised hand. Reuben was brooding in another corner. The sukebind flowers were fading. Seth was studying a copy of *Photo Bits* which he had produced from the pocket of his evening jacket.

Only Aunt Ada Doom sat upright, her eyes fixed upon the distance. She was rigid. Her lips moved softly. Flora, from her refuge on the table, could make out what she was saying, and it sounded none too festive.

'Two of them ... gone. Elfine ... Amos ... and I'm alone in the woodshed now ... Who took them away? Who took them away? I must know ... I must know ... That chit. That brat. Robert Poste's child.'

The great bed of red coals, slowly settling into its last sleep towards extinction, threw a glare on her old face, and gave her the look of a carving in a Gothic cathedral. Rennet had crept forward until she was within a few feet of her great-aunt (for such was the relationship between Rennet and Ada Doom), and stood looking down at her with a mad glare in her pale eyes.

Suddenly, without turning round, Aunt Ada struck at her with the *Milk Producers' Weekly Bulletin and Cowkeepers' Guide*, and Rennet flew back to her corner.

A withered flower fell from the sukebind wreath into the coals.

It was half past four.

Suddenly, Flora felt a draught at her back. She looked round crossly, and found herself staring into the face of Reuben, who had opened the little concealed door behind the great bulge of the chimneypiece, which led out into the yard.

'Come on,' whispered Reuben, soundlessly. '"Tes time 'ee were in bed.'

Amazed and grateful, Flora silently woke Elfine, and with breathless caution they slid off the table and tiptoed across to the little door. Reuben drew them safely through it, and closed it noiselessly.

They stood outside in the yard, in a bitter wind, with the first streaks of cold light lying across the purple sky. The way to their beds lay clear before them.

'Reuben,' said Flora, too drunk with sleep to articulate clearly, but remembering her manners, 'you are an *utter* lamb. Why did you?'

'You got th' old devil out of th' way for me.'

'Oh ... *that*,' yawned Flora.

'Aye ... an' I doan't forget. Eh, th' farm'll be mine, now, surelie.'

'So it will,' said Flora amiably. 'Such fun for you.'

Suddenly a shocking row broke out in the kitchen behind them. The Starkadders were off again.

But Flora never knew what it was about. She was asleep where she stood. She walked up to her room like an automaton, just stayed awake long enough to undress, and then fell into bed like a log.

CHAPTER 17

THE next day was Sunday, so thank goodness everybody could stay in bed and get over the shocks of the night before. At least, that is what most families would have done. But the Starkadders were not like most families. Life burned in them with a fiercer edge, and by seven o'clock most of them were up and, to a certain extent, doing. Reuben, of course, had much to do because of Amos's sudden departure.

He now thought of himself as master of the farm, and a slow tide of satisfied earth-lust indolently ebbed and flowed in his veins as he began his daily task of counting the chickens' feathers.

Prue, Susan, Letty, Phoebe, and Jane had been escorted back to Howling by Adam, at half past five that morning, and he had returned in time to begin the milking. He was still bewildered by the fact of Elfine's betrothal. The sound of old wedding-bells danced between the tufts of hair in his withered ears, and catches of country rhymes sung before George the Fourth was born:

> 'Come rue, come snow,
> So maidies mun go'

he sang, over and over again to himself as he milked Feckless. He saw, yet did not see, that Aimless had lost another hoof.

The dawn widened into an exquisite spring day. Soft, wool-like puffs of sound came from the thrushes' throats in the trees. The uneasy year, tortured by its spring of adolescence, broke into bud-spots in hedge, copse, spinney, and byre.

Judith sat in the kitchen, looking out with leaden eyes across the disturbed expanse of the teeming country-side. Her face was grey. Rennet huddled by the fire, stirring some rather nasty jam she had suddenly thought she would make. She had decided to stay behind when the other female Starkadders had gone off with Adam; her flayed soul shrank, obliquely, from their unspoken pity.

So noon came, and passed. A rude meal was prepared by Adam, and eaten (some of it) by the rest in the great kitchen. Old Ada Doom kept to her room, whither she had been carried at six o'clock that morning, by Micah, Seth, Mark Dolour, Caraway, and Harkaway.

None dared go in to her. She sat alone, a huddled, vast ruin of flesh, staring unseeingly out between her wrinkled lids. Her fingers picked endlessly at the *Milk Producers' Weekly Bulletin and Cowkeepers' Guide*. She did not think or see. The sharp blue air of spring thundered silently on window-panes fogged by her slow, batrachian breath. Powerless waves of fury coursed over her inert body. Sometimes names burst out of her green lips: 'Amos ... Elfine ... Urk ...' Sometimes they just stayed inside.

No one had seen anything of Urk since he had gone galloping out into the night carrying Meriam, the hired girl. It was generally assumed that he had drowned her and then himself. Who cared, anyway?

As for Flora, she was still asleep at half past three in the afternoon, and would have slept on comfortably enough until tea-time, but that she was aroused by a knocking at her door and the excited voice of Mrs Beetle proclaiming that there was two gentlemen to see her.

'Have you got them there?' asked Flora, sleepily.

Mrs Beetle was much shocked. She said indeed not, they was in Miss Poste's parlour.

'Well ... who are they? I mean, did they tell you their names?'

'One's that Mr Mybug, miss, and the other's a gentleman 'oo says 'is name's Neck.'

'Oh, yes ... of course, how delightful. Ask them both to wait till I come. I won't be long,' and Flora began slowly to dress, for she would not make herself feel ill by bounding vigorously out of bed, even though she was delighted at the idea of seeing her dear Mr Neck again. As for Mr Mybug, he was a nuisance, but could be coped with easily enough.

She went downstairs at last, looking as fresh as a leaf, and as she entered her little parlour (wherein Mrs Beetle had kindled a fire) Mr Neck advanced to meet her, holding out both his hands and saying:

'Well, well, sweetheart. How's the girl?'

Flora greeted him with warmth. He had already had some conversation with Mr Mybug, who was looking rather sulky and miserable because he had hoped to find Flora alone and have a lovely long scene with her, apologizing for his behaviour last night, and talking a lot about himself. He became more sulky at first on hearing Mr Neck address Flora as sweetheart, but after listening to a little of their conversation, he decided that Mr Neck was the sort of Amusing Type that calls everybody sweetheart, and did not mind so much.

Flora instructed Mrs Beetle to bring them some tea, which soon came, and they sat very pleasantly in the sunlight which streamed through the window of the little green parlour, drinking their tea and conversing.

Flora felt sleepy and amiable. She had made up her mind that Mr Neck must not go without seeing Seth, and quietly told Mrs Beetle to send him to the parlour as soon as he could be found; but apart from this decision, she was not worrying about anything at all.

'Are you over here looking for English film stars, Mr Neck?' asked Mr Mybug, eating a little cake that Flora had wanted for herself.

'That's so. I want to find me another Clark Gable. Yeah, you wouldn't remember him, maybe. That's twenty years ago.'

'But I have seen him at a Sunday Film Club Repertory Show, in a film called "Mounting Passion",' said Mr Mybug eagerly. 'Do you know the work of the Sunday Film Club Repertory people at all?'

'I'll buy it,' said Mr Neck, who had taken a dislike to Mr Mybug. 'Well, I want a second Clark Gable, see? I want a big, husky stiff that smells of the great outdoors, with a golden voice. I want passion. I want red blood. I don't want no sissies, see? Sissies give me a pain in the neck, and they're beginning to give the great American public a pain in the neck, too.'

'Do you know the work of Limf?' asked Mr Mybug.

'Never heard of 'em,' said Mr Neck. 'Thank you, sweetheart' (to Flora, who was feeding him cake). 'You know, Mr Mybug, we gotta responsibility to the public. We gotta give them what they want, yet it's gotta be clean. Boy, that's difficult. I'll tell you it's difficult. I want a man who can give them what they want, yet give it them so's it don't leave a taste in their mouths.' He paused and drank tea. The sunshine, vivid as a Kleig light, revealed every wrinkle in his melancholy little monkeyish face and lit the fresh red carnation in his button-hole. For Mr Neck was a great dandy, who usually changed his button-hole twice a day.

'I want a man to fetch the women,' he went on. 'I want a new Gary Cooper (but, lessee, thass twenty years ago), only more ritzy. Someone who can look good in a tuxedo, and yet handle one of them old-world ploughs. (Say, I seen four ploughs since I been over this trip.) Well, who've I got? I got Teck Jones. Yeah, well, Teck's a good kid; he can ride all right, but he's got no body-urge. I got Valentine Orlo. Well, he looks like a wop. They won't stand for no more wops since poor Morelli went to the chair in '42. No, wops is off. Well, I got Peregrine Howard. He's a Britisher. No one can't say his first name right, so he's no good. There's Slake Fountain. Yeah, I'll say there is, too. We keep a gang of hoodlums on their toes at twenty a week each to sober him up every morning before he comes on the set. Then there's Jerry Badger, the sort of nice egg you'd like your kid sister to marry, but nothing to him. Nothing *at* all. Well, what do I get out of it? Nothing. I gotta find somebody, that's all.'

'Have you ever seen Alexandre Fin?' asked Mr Mybug. 'I saw him in Pepin's last film, "La Plume de Ma Tante", in Paris last January. Very amusing stuff. They all wore glass clothes, you know, and moved in time to a metronome.'

'Oh, yeah?' said Mr Neck. 'A frog, eh? Frogs is all under five feet. I want a big, husky fella; the kinda fella that would look good cuddling a kid. Is there another cup, sweetheart?'

Flora poured him some.

'Yeah,' he went on. 'I seen that film in Paris, too. It gave me a pain. Gave me a lot of new dope, though. What not to do, and all that. I've met Pepin, too. The poor egg's cuckoo.'

'He is much admired by the younger men,' said Mr Mybug, daringly, glancing at Flora for approval.

'That helps a whole heap,' said Mr Neck.

'Then your interest in the cinema, Mr Neck, is *entirely* commercial? I mean, you think nothing of its aesthetic possibilities?'

'I gotta responsibility. If your frog friend had to fill fifteen thousand dollars' worth of movie seats every day, he'd have to think of a better stunt than a lot of guys wearin' glass pants.'

He paused and reflected.

'Say, though, that's an idea. A guy buys a new tuxedo, see? Then he offends some ritzy old egg, see? A magician, or something, and this old egg puts a curse on him. Well, this egg (the guy in the tuxedo) goes off to a swell party, and when he comes in all the girls scream. That kind o' stuff. Well, he can't see his pants is turned into glass by this other old egg (the magician, see?), and he says: "Whattha hell", and all the rest of it. Yeah, that's an idea.'

While he was speaking, Seth had come silently, with his graceful, pantherish tread, to the door of the room; and now stood there, looking down inquiringly at Flora. She smiled across at him, motioning him to be silent. Mr Neck's back was towards the door, so that he could not see Seth, but when he saw Flora smile he turned half round, and looked across at the doorway to see at whom her gesture was directed.

And he saw Seth.

A silence fell. The young man stood in the warm light of the declining sun, his bare throat and boldly moulded features looking as though they were bathed in gold. His pose was easy and graceful. A superb self-confidence radiated from him, as it does from any healthy animal. He met Mr Neck's stare with an impudent stare of his own, his head lowered and slightly forward. He looked exactly what he was, the local sexually successful bounder. Millions of women were to realize, in the next five years, that Seth could be transported in fancy to a Welsh mining village, a shoddy North Country seaside town, a raw city in the plains of the Middle West, and still remain eternally and unchangeably the local irresistible bounder.

Is it any wonder that Mr Neck broke the silence by flinging up his hand and saying in a hoarse whisper: 'That's it, sweetheart! That's got it! Hold it!'

And Seth was so soaked in movie slang that he held it, for another second or so in silence.

Flora broke in by saying: 'Oh, Seth, there you are. I wanted Mr Neck to see you. Earl, this is my cousin, Seth Starkadder. He's very interested in the talkies. Mr Neck is a producer, Seth.'

Mr Neck, forgetful of everything else, was craning forward with his head slightly bent downwards, to hear Seth speak. And when that deep, warm drawl came – 'Pleased to meet you, Mr Neck' – Mr Neck looked up with an expression of such relief and delight that it was just as though he had clapped his hands.

'Well, well,' said Mr Neck, surveying Seth rather as though Seth were his dinner (as indeed he was to be for some years to come). 'How's the boy? So you're a fan, eh? You and me must get acquainted, huh? Maybe you'd thought of going in for the game yourself?'

Mr Mybug tilted comfortably back in his chair, choosing a little cake to eat, and prepared to enjoy the sight of Seth being roasted. But he had (as we know) backed the wrong horse.

Seth scowled and drew back. Mr Neck almost patted his face with rapture as he observed how Seth's every mood was reflected, like a child's, in his countenance.

'No . . . No, I'm not kidding,' he observed, amiably. 'I mean it. Would you like to go on the talkies?'

A great cry broke from Seth. Mr Mybug lost his balance and fell over backwards, choking with cake. No one noticed him. All eyes were on Seth. A glory lit his face. Slowly, lingeringly, the words broke from him:

'More than anything else in the world.'

'Well, ain't that dandy?' said Mr Neck, looking round proudly for agreement and support. 'He wants to be a movie star and I want to make him one. What do you know about that? Usually, it's just the other way about. Now, sweetheart, get your grip, and we'll be off. We're catching the Atlantic flier from Brighton at eight to-night. Say, though, what about your folks, huh? What about Momma? Will she need squaring?'

'I will tell you all about that, Earl. Seth, go and pack a bag with everything you need for the journey. Put on a big coat – you are going to fly, you know, and it may be cold at first.'

Seth obeyed Flora without a word, and when he had gone she explained his circumstances to Mr Neck.

'So it's all right if Grandma don't give it the razz, huh? Well, we must go out quiet, thass all. Tell Grandma not to fuss. We'll send her five grand out of the first picture he makes. Oh, boy' – and here he smote Mr Mybug, who was still choking over his little cake – 'I got him! I got him! Whaddya say his name is – Seth? Thassa sissy sort of a name, but it'll do. It's kinda different. Keep 'em guessing. Oh, boy, wait till I get him a tuxedo! Wait till I start his publicity. We must find a new angle. Lessee ... Maybe he'd better be shy. No ... poor Charley Ford ran that to death. Maybe he hates women ... yeah, thass it. He hates women and he hates the movies. Like hell he does. Oh, boy, that'll fetch 'em! It 'ud take more than anyone's grandma to stop me now.'

CHAPTER 18

WHEN Seth returned, wearing his best hat and his overcoat and carrying a suit-case, everybody moved towards the door. Mr Neck's car was waiting for him in the yard, and he hung on to Seth's arm every step of the way there as though he feared Seth would change his mind.

He need not have. Seth's face had the usual expression it bore of repose: an insolent complacency. Of course, he was going to be a film star. When once he had got over the first shock, he wanted to look as if the whole affair seemed perfectly natural to him. He was too conceited to show the fierce joy that surged deep within him. Yet there it surged, a tide of dark gold splendour, deep below the crust of his complacent acceptance.

Well, everything was bowling along swimmingly, and Flora was just patting the still-choking Mr Mybug on the back while they all stood round the door of the car saying good-bye, when the ominous sound of a window being pushed up was heard, and before they could all look up a voice floated out into the quiet air of the late afternoon. It was observing that it had seen something nasty in the woodshed.

Everybody looked up. Flora in some dismay.

Sure enough, it was Aunt Ada Doom. The window of her room, which was directly above the kitchen door, was open, and she was leaning heavily out, supporting herself upon her hands. A shape hovered in the dusty room behind her left shoulder, endeavouring to see over her vasty bulk. By the untidiness of its hair, it was Judith. Another shape hovered behind the right shoulder. Going by nothing but a woman's intuition, it was Rennet.

'Oh, mercy!' said Flora, hastily, in an undertone to Mr Neck, 'Hurry up and go!'

'What ... is that Grandma?' inquired Mr Neck. 'And who's the platinum blonde at the back? Come on, sweetheart' – he hustled Seth into the car – 'we've got to make that flier.'

'Seth ... Seth ... where are you going?' Judith's voice was a throbbing rod of terror and anguish.

'I saw something nasty in the woodshed!' screamed Aunt Ada Doom, flapping about her with something which Flora recognized as all that was left of the *Cowkeepers' Weekly Bulletin and Milk Producers' Guide.* 'My baby ... My darling. You mustn't leave me. I shall go mad. I can't bear it!'

'Can it!' muttered Mr Neck; but aloud he called

politely, waving his hand at Aunt Ada, 'Well, well, how's the girl?'

'Seth ... you mustn't go!' Judith implored, her voice a dry whine of terror. 'You can't leave your mother. There's the spring-onion harvest, too. 'Tes man's work ... You mustn't go.'

'I saw something in the woodshed!'

'Did it see you?' asked Mr Neck, tucking himself into the car beside Seth. The engine started, and the chauffeur began to back out of the yard.

'Gee, ma'am, I know it's raw,' shouted Mr Neck, craning out of the window of the car and peering up at Aunt Ada. 'I know it's tough. But, gee, that's life, girl. You're living now, sweetheart. All that woodshed line ... that was years ago. Young Woodley stuff. Aw, I respect a grandmother's feelings, sweetheart, but honest, I just can't give him up. He'll send you five grand out of his first film.'

'Good-bye,' said Seth to Flora, who returned his condescending smile with a friendly one of her own.

She watched the car drive away. It was going to Cloud Cuckoo Land; it was going to the Kingdom of Cockaigne; it was going to Hollywood. Seth would never have a chance, now, of becoming a nice, normal young man. He would become a world-famous, swollen mask.

When next she saw him, it was a year later and the mask smiled down at her in the drowsy darkness from a great silver screen: 'Seth Starkadder in "Small Town Sheik".' Already, as the car receded, he was as unreal as Achilles.

'Seth ... Seth ...'

The car turned the curve, and was gone.

Still the wailing voices of the women wound through the air like strung wires. It was hours before the stars would begin their idiot dance between the chimney-pots. There was nothing to do in between except wail.

Aunt Ada had now retreated from the window. Flora could hear Judith having hysterics. She went on quietly banging Mr Mybug, who was still choking, and saying, 'There ... there ... ' and wondering if she ought to go upstairs to her Aunt Ada's room and diffuse a spot of *The Higher Common Sense*.

But no. The hour for that was not yet.

She was roused from her reverie by Mr Mybug, who peevishly dodged away from her hand, exclaiming, between chokes: 'I'm quite all right now, thanks,' and went on choking in an irritating manner at some distance away.

Suddenly his chokes ceased. He was staring up at Aunt Ada's window, where Rennet had suddenly appeared and was peering palely out into the evening.

'Who's that?' asked Mr Mybug, in a low voice.

'Rennet Starkadder,' replied Flora.

'What a marvellous face,' said Mr Mybug, still staring. 'She has a brittle, hare-like quality . . . Don't you feel it?' He waved his fingers about. 'She has that untamed look you see sometimes in newly-born leverets. I wish Kopotkin could see her. He'd want to put her into plaster.'

Rennet was staring down at him, too. Flora could see it was quite a case. Oh, well, it would be quite a good thing if he carried Rennet off to Fitzroy Square and set a new fashion in hare-faced beauties . . . except that she, Flora, must make quite sure before they went that he would be kind to poor Rennet, and be a good husband to her. Probably he would be. Rennet was very domesticated. She would mend Mr Mybug's clothes (which nobody had ever done for him before, because, though all his girl friends could embroider beautifully, none of them ever dreamed of mending anything), and cook him lovely nourishing dinners, and fuss over him and simply adore him, and he would become so comfortable he would not know himself, and would be very grateful to her.

From these schemes she was aroused by Mr Mybug. He walked across the yard until he stood directly beneath the window, and called boldly up to Rennet:

'I say! Will you come for a walk with me?'

'What . . . now?' asked Rennet, timidly. Nobody had ever asked her to do such a thing before.

'Why not?' laughed Mr Mybug, looking boyishly up at

her, with his head flung back. Flora thought it *was* a pity he was rather fat.

'I must ask Cousin Judith,' said Rennet, glancing timidly over her shoulder into the darkened room. Then she withdrew into the shadows.

Mr Mybug was very pleased with himself. This was his idea of romance, Flora could see. She knew from experience that intellectuals thought the proper – nay, the only – way to fall in love with somebody was to do it the very instant you saw them. You met somebody, and thought they were 'A charming person. So gay and simple.' Then you walked home from a party with them (preferably across Hampstead Heath, about three in the morning) discussing whether you should sleep together or not. Sometimes you asked them to go to Italy with you. Sometimes they asked you to go to Italy (preferably to Portofino) with them. You held hands, and laughed, and kissed them and called them your 'true love'. You loved them for eight months, and then you met somebody else and began being gay and simple all over again, with small-hours' walk across Hampstead, Portofino invitation, and all.

It was very simple, gay, and natural, somehow.

Anyway, Flora was beginning to feel that things were happening a little too quickly at Cold Comfort Farm. She had not yet recovered from the Counting last night (was it only last night? – it seemed a month ago) and the departure of Amos; and already Seth had gone, and Mr Mybug was falling in love with Rennet, and doubtless planning to carry her off.

If things went on at this rate there would soon be nobody left at the farm at all.

She was extremely sleepy all of a sudden. She thought she would go and sit by the fire in her little green parlour and read until supper-time. So she told Mr Mybug she hoped he would have a pleasant walk, and added casually that Rennet had had a pretty septic life of it, on the whole, and hinted that she would probably appreciate a little gaiety and simplicity, in the Fitzroy Square manner.

Mr Mybug said he quite understood. He also attempted to take her hand, but she foiled him. Since seeing Rennet at the window he seemed to have a vague feeling that his one-sided affair with Flora was at an end, and that it was up to him to make some appropriate farewell remarks.

'We're friends, aren't we?' he asked.

'Certainly,' said Flora, pleasantly, nor did she trouble to inform him that she was not in the habit of thinking of persons whom she had known for five weeks as her friends.

'We might dine together in Town some time?'

'That would be delightful,' agreed Flora, thinking how nasty and boring it would be.

'There's a quality in you . . .' said Mr Mybug, staring at her and waving his fingers. 'Remote, somehow, and nymph-like . . . oddly unawakened. I should like to write a novel about you and call it *Virginal*.'

'Do, if it passes the time for you,' said Flora; 'and now I must really go and write some letters, I am afraid. Good-bye.'

On her way to her parlour she passed Rennet, coming downstairs, dressed to go out. She wondered how she had managed to obtain permission from Aunt Ada Doom to do so, but Rennet did not wait to be questioned. She darted past Flora with a stare of terror.

Flora was extremely glad to get back to her parlour and to sink into a comfortable little arm-chair covered in green tapestry, which stood by the fire. The refreshing Mrs Beetle was there, clearing away the tea-things.

'Miss Elfine sent you 'er best love, Miss Flora, and she's gone over to spend six weeks at Howchiker Hall. Mr Dick came for her at lunch-time to-day in 'is motor,' said Mrs Beetle. 'Nice-looking boy, ain't he?'

'Very,' said Flora. 'So she's gone, has she? Oh, well, that's splendid. Now the family will have time to settle down and get over the engagement. And where's Urk? Is it true he's drowned Meriam?'

Mrs Beetle snorted.

'It 'ud take more than 'im to drown 'er. No, 'e's as large

as life and twice as natural, down at mine, playin' with the kids.'

'What . . . the jazz-band? I mean, with Meriam's children?'

'Yes. Givin' 'em rides on 'is back and pretendin' 'e's a water-vole (nasty things). Oh, you *should* 'ave 'eard 'ow Agony created when I let on that our Meriam was goin' to marry one of them Starkadders! Create! I thought 'e'd 'ave to be picked off the ceiling.'

'So she really is going to marry him?' asked Flora, leaning languidly back in her chair and enjoying the gossip.

Mrs Beetle gave her a look.

'So I should 'ope, Miss Poste. I don't say as there's been Anything Wrong between them yet, but there ain't goin' to be, neither, until they're safely married. Agony stands firm by that.'

'And what does old Mrs Starkadder say to Urk marrying Meriam?'

'She said she saw something narsty, as usual. Well, if *I*'d 'ad sixpence for all the narsty things I've seen since I bin working at Cold Comfort I could buy the place up (not that I'd want to, come to that).'

'I suppose,' asked Flora idly, 'you haven't any idea of what she really *did* see?'

Mrs Beetle paused in the act of folding the tablecloth, and regarded Flora earnestly. But all she said, after the pause, was that she couldn't say, she was sure. So Flora pursued her inquiries no further.

'So I 'ear that there Seth's gone, too,' was Mrs Beetle's next remark. 'Coo! 'is mother won't 'alf take on!'

'Yes, he's gone to Hollywood to be a film star,' said Flora, sleepily.

Mrs Beetle said sooner 'im than 'er, and added that she wouldn't 'alf 'ave a lot to tell Agony when she got home.

'So Agony likes a spot of gossip, does he?'

'If it ain't spiteful, 'e does. 'E always creates at 'ome something awful when I've finished telling 'im anything spiteful. Oh, well, I must be off now and get Agony's supper. Good night, Miss Poste.'

Flora passed the rest of the evening quietly and pleasantly, and was in bed by ten. Her satisfaction with the way matters were progressing at the farm was completed by the arrival of a postcard for herself by the nine o'clock post.

It represented Canterbury Cathedral. The postmark was Canterbury. On the back was written:

Praise the Lord! This morning I preached the Lord's Word to thousands in the market-place. I am now going out to hire one o' they Ford vans. Tell Micah if he wants to drive it he must come with me out of charity. I mean, no wages. Praise the Lord! Send my flannel shirts. Fond love to all.

A. STARKADDER

CHAPTER 19

AFTER the departure of Seth, life at the farm settled down and became normal again (at least, as normal as it ever was), and Flora was quite glad to have a rest after the strenuous weeks during which she had drilled Elfine, and the series of shocks which had resulted in the whisking of Seth and Amos away from Cold Comfort.

The first of May brought a burst of summer weather. All the trees and hedges came into full leaf overnight; and from behind the latter, in the evenings, cries could be heard of: 'Nay, doan't 'ee, Jem', and 'Nay, niver do that, soul', from the village maidens who were being seduced.

***At the farm, life burgeoned and was quick. A thick, shameless cooing was laid down, stroke on stroke, through the warm air from the throats of the wood-pigeons until the very atmosphere seemed covered with a rich patina of love. The strident yellow note of the cockerel shot up into the sunshine and wavered there, ending in a little feather-tuft of notes. Big Business bellowed triumphantly in the great field. Daisies opened in sly lust to the sun-rays and rain-spears, and eft-flies, locked in a blind embrace, spun radiantly through the glutinous light to their ordained death. Mrs Beetle appeared in a cotton dress, well skewered up at the neck by a brooch with 'Carrie' engraved on it. Flora wore green linen and a shady hat.

The first rays of May fell into the room where Judith lay on her bed in silence; and were withered. The sordid flies, intent on their own selfish pleasure, buzzed in idiotic circles above her head with as much noise and as little meaning as life itself, and their sound drew a web of scarlet pain into her withdrawn darkness. She had veiled each of the two hundred photographs of Seth with a little black crêpe curtain. This done, what else did life hold? The flies buzzed in answer above the dirty water standing in the washbasin, in which floated a solitary black hair.

It, too, was like life – and as meaningless.

The old woman kept her room also, seated before the fire that danced palely in the thick, coarse sunlight, and muttering at intervals. Flares of hate lit her darkness. She sensed the insolence of summer heating on the window-panes and wooing away, with its promises, all the Starkadders from Cold Comfort. Where was Amos? The sunlight answered. Where was Elfine? The ring-doves crooned in reply. Where – last blow of agony – was Seth? She did not even know where he had gone or why. Mrs Beetle said he had gone on them there talkies. What was a talkie? Was Mrs Beetle mad? Were they all mad – all except you, who sat on here alone, in the old crumbling tower of your body? And Urk – a Starkadder – saying he was going to marry the paid slut, Meriam, and openly defying you when you forbade him, and jingling three and sixpence in his pocket which he had earned by selling water-vole skins to a furrier in Godmere . . .

This room was your citadel. Outside, the world you had built up so fiercely for twenty years was crumbling into fantastic ruin.

It was she, Robert Poste's child. The wrong done to him had come back to roost. 'Curses, like rookses, comes home

to rest in bosomses and barnses.' She had poured poison into
the ears of your family and sent them out into the world,
leaving you alone. They would all go: Judith, Micah, Ezra,
Harkaway, Caraway, Luke, and Mark, and Adam Lambsbreath. Then ... when they had all gone ... you would be
alone – at last – alone in the woodshed.

Flora was having quite a nice time.

It was now the second week in May and the weather was
still superb. Reuben was now looked upon by everybody as
the owner of Cold Comfort, and had at once (much to
Flora's pleasure) set about making improvements in it, and
had asked her if she would go into Godmere with him and
help him choose fertilizers and new grinders and what not.
Flora told him she did not know anything about grinders,
but that she would try anything once; so, accordingly, they
drove off together one Wednesday morning in the buggy,
armed with a copy of the *Internationally Progressive Far-
mers' Guide and Helpmeet*, which Flora had ordered from
London, where it was printed by some Russian friends of
hers living in West Kensington.

'Where did you get the money to buy all these lovely
grinders, Reuben?' asked Flora, as they sat at lunch in the
coffee-room of the Load of Beets, after a busy morning's
shopping.

'Stole un,' replied Reuben simply.

'Who from?' asked Flora, who was bored by having to
pretend to be shocked at things, and really wanted to
know.

'Grandmother.'

'Oh, I say, what a sound scheme. But how did you get
hold of it? I mean, did you have to get it out of her stock-
ing, or something?'

'Nay. I falsified th' chicken-book, and when we sold a
dozen eggs I writes down we sells two eggs, see? I been
doin' that for nigh five years. I had me eye on them grinders
for five years, so I plans it all out, see?'

'My dear, I think you're *masterly*,' said Flora. '*Quite*

195

masterly. If you only keep on as you've begun you will make the farm *too* prosperous.'

'Aye ... if th' old devil don't change his mind and come back,' said Reuben doubtfully. 'Happen he may think America's a long way off – too fur for an old 'un like him to go, eh?'

'Oh, I'm sure he won't,' said Flora decidedly. 'He seems to be – er – main set on the idea.' And she produced from her handbag, for the tenth time that morning, a postcard showing Liverpool Cathedral. It said:

Praise the Lord! I go to spread the Lord's Word among the heathen Americans, with the Rev. Elderberry Shiftglass, of Chicago. Praise the Lord! Tell Reuben he can have the old place. Send clean socks. Love to all except Micah.

A. STARKADDER

'Oh, yes, I am sure he means it,' repeated Flora. 'It's a pity he says "the old place" instead of "the farm", but if any question ever arises, we can always do a spot of forgery, and write "the farm" instead. I wouldn't worry, if I were you.'

So they finished their apple tart in leisurely comfort. Just as he was lifting the last spoonful to his lips, Reuben halted with it in the air and said, looking across at Flora:

'I don't suppose 'ee would marry me, Cousin Flora?'

Flora was much moved. She had grown to like Reuben in the last fortnight. He was worth whole sackfuls of the other male Starkadders. He was really very nice, and kind too, and ready to learn from anyone who would help him to improve the condition of the farm. He had never forgotten that it was she who suggested to Amos that he should go off on the preaching tour; a move which had resulted – after Reuben himself had worked on his father's feelings to take Flora's advice – in Reuben getting possession of the farm; and he was deeply grateful.

She put out her hand across the table. Wonderingly, Reuben took it in his and stared down at it, while the spoonful of apple tart wavered to and fro in his other hand.

'Oh, Reuben, that *is* nice of you. But I am afraid it would never do, you know. Think a moment. I am not at all the kind of person to make a good wife for a farmer.'

'I like yer pretty ways,' said Reuben gruffly.

'That's charming of you. I like yours, too. But, honestly, it wouldn't do. I think somebody like Mark Dolour's Nancy would be much nicer for you – and more useful, too.'

'She'm not fifteen yet.'

'All the better. In three years the farm will be doing really well, and you will have a really nice home to offer her.' Flora's heart faltered as she thought of what Aunt Ada Doom might have to say to such a marriage, but she was beginning to feel a way towards a plan for coping with that old incubus. In three years – who knows? – Aunt Ada might have left the farm!

Reuben reflected, still staring down at Flora's hand.

'Aye,' he said, slowly, at last, 'maybe I'd best have Mark Dolour's Nancy. My chickens have been keeping her dolls in feathers for their 'ats these two years. Reckon it's only right she should have th' chickens too in the end.'

And he released Flora's hand, and finished his spoonful of apple tart. He did not seem at all offended or hurt, and they drove home together afterwards in comfortable silence.

Elfine's visit to the Hawk-Monitors had been extended for a further week, and Flora had twice been over there to tea. Mrs Hawk-Monitor seemed quite won over to Elfine, much to Flora's relief, and described her to Flora as 'a dear little thing. Rather brainy, but quite a nice little thing.' Flora congratulated Elfine in private, and warned her not to talk quite so much about Marie Laurencin and Purcell. The end was achieved; there was no point in overdoing it.

The wedding was fixed for the fourteenth of June. Mrs Hawk-Monitor had decided that it should take place in the church at Howling, which was a beauty. She then stunned Flora by suggesting that the reception should be held at Cold Comfort: 'So much more convenient than coming all the way back here, don't you think?'

'Oh, I say,' said Flora, pulling herself together in response to an agonized glance from Elfine. 'I rather doubt if that would do, you know. I mean, old Mrs Starkadder is a bit of an invalid and what not. The – er – the noise might upset her.'

'She need not come down. A tray of cake can be taken up to her in her room. Yes, I think that would certainly be the best thing to do. Is there a *large* room at the farmhouse, Miss Poste?'

'Several,' said Flora, faintly, thinking about them.

'Splendid. Just the thing. I will write to old Mrs Starkadder to-night.' And Mrs Hawk-Monitor (who was rather wanting to shift some of the botheration of the wedding on to Elfine's family) vaguely but effectively changed the subject.

So there was a new horror on the horizon! Really (thought Flora, riding home in state in the giant Hawk-Monitor Renault) there was no end to her worries. She was beginning to think she would never get the farm tidied up in her life-time. No sooner did she get one person comfortably 'fixed up than somebody else began to tear up the turf about something, and she had to begin all over again.

It was true, though, that matters were better since Reuben had taken up the position of owner of the farm. Wages were paid regularly. Rooms were swept out occasionally; nay, they were even scrubbed. And though the bi-weekly inspection of the books by Aunt Ada Doom still went on, Reuben had started another set of books of his own, in which he put down the farm's real takings. The books which Aunt Ada saw twice a week were cooked liked Old Harry.

Aunt Ada had not been downstairs since the night of the Counting; and Micah, Ezra, and the other Starkadders had taken advantage of her temporary set-back. They had also been encouraged by the getaway of Seth, Elfine, and Amos. They realized that Aunt Ada, like the rest of us, was only human.

So they commanded Prue, Letty, Jane, Phoebe, and Susan, to say nothing of Rennet, to come up to Cold Comfort from the village and establish themselves and their possessions in some of the empty rooms of the farm-house as far away as possible from Aunt Ada's chamber.

And there they were, all living like fighting cocks; and wherever Flora went she seemed to stumble over hen-faced female Starkadders in cotton dresses. As for Mrs Beetle, she said all them old witches fair gave her the sick, and she was quite glad to get 'ome to Urk and Meriam and the water-voles.

So, on the whole, life at the farm-house was much pleasanter for the Starkadders than it had ever been before; and they had Flora to thank for it.

But Flora was not satisfied.

She was thinking, as she was borne homewards in the Hawk-Monitor chariot, how much yet remained to be done at Cold Comfort before she could really say that the farm-house was in a condition to satisfy the Abbé Fausse-Maigre.

There was the problem of Judith. There was old Adam. And there was Aunt Ada Doom herself, the greatest problem of all, and the hardest.

She decided that she must tackle Judith next. Judith had been lying in her room with the window shut quite long enough. Twice had Mrs Beetle asked if she could turn out the room; and twice Flora had been forced to reply that it was not yet convenient. But now (Flora decided) things had gone far enough; and she would beard Judith as soon as she got home.

The evening sunlight lay across the corridor in sharp tiger-bars as she approached Judith's room. The door was shut. It was like a forbidding hand, pressed soft and flat against the silence of the corridor. Flora tapped against it, and waited a few seconds for an answer. But there was only the indifferent silence. Oh, well ... she thought, and, turning the handle, walked in.

Judith was standing at the washstand, rinsing one of the two hundred little crêpe curtains which hung over the two hundred photographs of Seth.

***Her blank eyes burrowed through the fetid air between herself and her visitor. They were without content; hollow pools of meaninglessness. They were not eyes, but voids sunk between two jutting pent-houses of bone and two bloodless hummocks of cheek. They suspended two raw rods of grief before their own immobility, like frozen fountains in a bright wintry air; and on these rods the fluttering rags of a futile grief were hung.

'Oh, Cousin Judith, would you care to come up to Town with me to-morrow?' asked Flora pleasantly. 'I want to do some shopping, and I hope to lunch with a very charming Austrian – a Doctor Müdel from Vienna. Do come.'

Judith's laugh shocked even the careless flies that circled above her head into a momentary silence.

'I am a dead woman,' she said simply. Her hands lay piteously at her sides. 'Look ... the little curtain was dusty,' she murmured. 'I had to rinse the dust off it.'

Flora refrained from pointing out that if you rinsed something that was dusty you merely made it worse. She said patiently that she proposed to catch the ten-thirty to Town, and that she would expect Judith to be ready by nine o'clock.

'I think you will enjoy it, Cousin Judith, when you get there,' she urged her. 'You mustn't carry on like this, you know. It – er – it depresses us all no end. I mean, all this lovely weather and what not. It's a pity to waste it.'

'I myself am a waste,' said Judith stonily. 'I am a used husk ... a rind ... a skin. What use am I ... now he's gone?'

'Well, never mind that now,' said Flora soothingly. 'Just you make up your mind to be ready by nine o'clock to-morrow morning.'

And before she left her that evening, she managed to gain from Judith a vague half-promise that she would be ready as suggested. Judith did not seem to care what happened to her so long as she was not made to talk; and Flora took advantage of her lassitude to impose her fresh will upon her cousin's flaccid one.

After leaving Judith, she sent Adam down into Howling with the following wire:

Herr Doktor Adolf Müdel,
    National Institute Psycho-Analysis,
        Whitehall, S.W.
Interesting case for you can you lunch two of us Grimaldi's
one fifteen to-morrow Wednesday hows the baby love F. Poste.

And at nine o'clock that night, while she was sitting at the
open window of her little parlour inhaling the fragrance of
a may tree and writing to Charles, a telegram was delivered
to her (by Mark Dolour's very Nancy herself) which read:

But of course delighted baby has marked paranoiac tendencies
nurse assures me quite normal at eight months she knows much
more than I do perfect treasure looking forward seeing you what
weather eh ... Adolf.

CHAPTER 20

HER day with Judith in London was a complete success,
though there were, it is true, some minor disadvantages.
Judith's hair, for example, fell down every fifteen minutes
and had to be re-pinned by Flora. Then there were the
sympathetic and interested inquiries of fellow-travellers to be
fobbed off, who were naturally intrigued by hearing Judith
refer to herself at intervals as a Used Gourd and a Rind.

But when once their journey was over, Flora's worries
were over as well. Seated opposite Dr Müdel and Judith at
a quiet table near a window at Grimaldi's, she watched,
with a feeling of relief, Dr Müdel taking command of the
situation.

It was one of his disagreeable duties as a State psycho-
analyst to remove the affections of his patients from the
embarrassing objects upon which they were concentrated,
and focus them, instead, upon himself. It was true that they
did not remain focused there for long: as soon as he could,
he switched them on to something harmless, like chess or
gardening. But while they *were* focused upon himself, he had

rather a thin time of it and earned every penny of the eight hundred a year paid to him by a judicious Government.

And Flora, observing how soon Judith began to glow darkly and do the slumbering volcano act in Dr Müdel's direction, could not help admiring the practised skill with which he had effected the transference in the course of the commonplace conversation throughout lunch.

'She will be oll right now,' he murmured soothingly to Flora, in an undertone, when lunch was over, while Judith was gazing broodingly out of the window at the busy street below. 'I shall take her to the nursing home, and let her talk to me. There she will stay for six months, perhaps. Then I send her abroad for a little holiday. I make her interested in olt churches, I think. Yes, olt churches. There are so many in Europe, and it will take her the rest of her life to see them all. She has money, yes? You must have money in order to see all the olt churches you want. Well, that is oll right, then. Do not distress yourself. She will be quite happy. Oll that energy . . . it is a pity, yes. It oll turns *in* instead of *out*. Now I turn it out . . . on to the olt churches. Yes.'

Flora felt a little uneasy. It was not the first time she had seen a distraught patient grow calm beneath the will of the analyst, yet she had never grown used to the spectacle. Would Judith *really* be happier? She looked doubtfully at her cousin. Certainly Judith *looked* happier already. Her eyes followed every movement of Dr Müdel as he paid the bill for the lunch; Flora had never seen her look so animated and normal.

'I understand that you are going to stay with Dr Müdel for a while, Cousin Judith?' she said.

'He has asked me. He is very kind . . . There is a dark force in him,' returned Judith. 'It beats . . . like a black gong. I wonder you do not feel it.'

'Oh, well, we can't all strike lucky,' said Flora amiably. 'But really, Judith, I do think it would be quite a sound scheme if you went. You need a holiday, you know, after all the – er – fuss there's been at home lately. It will do you no end of good. Set you up and what not. And then after a

bit you might go abroad and see some of the sights of
Europe. Old churches, and all that. Don't worry about the
farm. Reuben will look after that for you, and send you a
fat piece out of the takings every month.'

'Amos ...' murmured Judith. She looked as though the
threads which bound her to her old life were snapping one
by one, yet still held her in a frail tenure.

'Oh, I wouldn't fuss about him,' said Flora easily. 'He's
gone off to America with the Reverend Elderberry Shiftglass by now, I shouldn't wonder. He'll let you know when
he's coming back. Don't you bother. You enjoy yourself
while you're young.'

And this was what Judith evidently decided to do, for she
drove off with Dr Müdel in his car looking quite content:
at least she looked illumined and transfigured and reft out
of herself and all the rest of it, and even when allowances
were made for her habit of multiplying every emotion she
felt by twice its own weight, she probably *was* feeling fairly
chirpy.

Before they said good-bye Flora arranged to send on to
the nursing home the five dirty red shawls and sundry
bundles of hairpins which seemed to make up the greater
part of Judith's wardrobe; and also a comfortable sum of
money which should pay for her pleasures during the next
six months. Dr Müdel could, of course, be trusted to see that
her funds were properly administered.

So that was all settled; and Flora watched the doctor's
car drive away with feelings of considerable satisfaction.

It was with a feeling of satisfaction, too, and with something strangely like affection, that she caught her first
glimpse of the farm-house on her return that night to Cold
Comfort.

It was a mild and lovely evening. The rays of the sun
looked heavy, as they frequently do towards the approach
of a summer sunset, and lay between the tunnels of green
leaves like long rods of gold. There were no clouds in the
blue sky, whose colour was beginning to deepen with the
advance of night, and the face of the whole country-side

was softened by the shadows which were slowly growing in the depths of the woods and hedgerows.

The farm-house itself no longer looked like a beast about to spring. (Not that it ever had, to her, for she was not in the habit of thinking that things looked exactly like other things which were as different from them in appearance as it was possible to be.) But it had looked dirty and miserable and depressing, and when Mr Mybug had once remarked that it looked like a beast about to spring, Flora had simply not had the heart to contradict him.

Now it looked dirty and miserable and depressing no longer. Its windows flung back the gold of the sunset. The yard was swept clean of straws and paper. Check curtains hung crisply at most of the windows, and someone (as a matter of fact it was Ezra, who had a secret yen for horti-culture) had been digging and trimming up the garden, and there were already rows of beans in red flower.

'I,' thought Flora simply, as she leant forward in the buggy and surveyed the scene, 'did all that with my little hatchet.' And a feeling of joy and content opened inside her like a flower.

But then she looked upwards at the closed, bland face of the window immediately above the kitchen door, and her face grew pensive again. Aunt Ada's room. Aunt Ada was still there, fighting her losing battle. Aunt Ada, the spirit of Cold Comfort, was hard pressed, but still undefeated. And could she, Flora, really congratulate herself upon her work at the farm, and flatter herself that the end of that work was in sight, while Aunt Ada Doom still brooded aloft in her tower?

'Yer supper's on the table, duck,' said Mrs Beetle, open-ing the gate to let Reuben lead Viper into the yard. 'Cold veal and salad. I'm off 'ome now. Oh, and there's a blam-onge. Pink.'

'Lovely,' said Flora, with a sigh of pleasure, as she climbed down from the buggy. 'Thank you, Mrs Beetle. Miss Judith won't be back to-night. She is going to stay in London for a while. Has everything been all right?'

'*She* took on something awful about Miss Judith going off 'smorning,' said Mrs Beetle, lowering her voice and glancing significantly upwards at the closed window. 'Said she *was* all alone in the woodshed now, and no mistake. She says she don't count Reuben. (She wouldn't, of course – 'im bein' the pick of the bunch.) Still, she keeps 'er appetite, I will say that for 'er. Three 'elpings of veal and two of suet roly for 'er dinner to-day. Can you beat it? Well, this won't buy the baby a new frock. Good night, Miss Flora. I'll be 'ere eight sharp to-morrow.'

And off she went.

Flora went into the kitchen, where a lamp already burned on the table. Its soft light fell into the hearts of a bunch of pink roses in a jam-jar. There was a letter from Charles propped against the jar, too, and the roses threw down a heavy, rounded shadow on to the envelope. It was so pretty that Flora lingered a moment, looking, before she opened her letter.

The serene weather held; and Flora and everybody were hoping that it would last until Elfine's wedding reception at the farm on the fourteenth of June, which was Midsummer Day.

The preparations for this reception were now Flora's chief care. She was anxious that the farm should not disgrace Reuben and his sister; so she went frankly to the former and told him that she must have money to buy decorations and a feast for the wedding guests. Reuben seemed pleased at the idea of holding the reception at the farm, and gave her thirty pounds with which to do her damnedst, but, he added, glancing meaningly up at the ceiling:

'What about the old 'un?'

'Leave her to me,' said Flora decidedly. 'I am thinking out a plan for coping with her, and in a few days I am going to try it out. I will see about decorations and food at once. Oh, and *need* we have all the pictures wreathed with that smelly sukebind? I am afraid it might have a bad effect on Meriam and Rennet. They're so easily upset.'

"'Tes no choice o' mine. 'Tes grandmother's choice. Do as you please, Cousin Flora. I niver wants to see a sprig of it again.'

So, armed with his permission, Flora began her preparations.

The days passed pleasantly. She had plenty to do, and even paid three visits to Town, for she was having a new dress made for the reception and it had to be fitted. Mrs Smiling was still abroad; she was not expected home until the day after the wedding, so 1 Mouse Place was shut up. Julia was in Cannes; Claud Hart-Harris at home in Chiswick, whither he repaired every summer, for a month, because he said he could at least be sure of meeting no one he knew there. But Flora could amuse herself; and dined and lunched in pleasant solitude.

In the intervals of fitting her dress and of superintending a simply colossal spring cleaning of the farm (the first it had received for a hundred years) Flora kept a weather eye upon the affair of Mr Mybug and Rennet. She thought it would be best, of course, if they got married; but she was well aware that marriage was not the intellectual's long suit, and she did not want Rennet landed with a shameful bundle.

Mr Mybug, however, did ask Rennet to marry him. He said that, by God, D. H. Lawrence was right when he had said there must be a dumb, dark, dull, bitter belly-tension between a man and a woman, and how else could this be achieved save in the long monotony of marriage? As for Rennet, she accepted him at once and was perfectly happy choosing saucepans. So that was all right; and they were to be married at a register office one week-end in Town and have a share in Elfine's reception on the fourteenth.

As the evenings grew longer towards Midsummer Day, Flora would sit alone in the little green parlour, where the scent of the may tree came in through the open window, reading in *The Higher Common Sense* the chapter on 'Preparing the Mind for the Twin Invasion by Prudence and Daring in Dealing with Substances not Included in the Outline'.

It would help her, she knew, to deal with Aunt Ada Doom. Those long words in German and in Latin were solemn and cragged as Egyptian monoliths; and when the reader peered more closely into the meaning of their syllables that rang like bells, backwards and backwards into Time, they were seen to be frosted with wisdom, cold and irrefutable. Before them, Passion, awed, slunk back to its lair; and divine Reason, and her sister, Love, locked in one another's arms, raised their twin heads to receive the wreath of Happiness.

Aunt Ada was most emphatically one of the Substances not Included in the Outline. As Flora read on, evening after evening, she was aware that a conviction was growing in her mind that this was one of the cases (the chapter warned the student that such might exist) in which she must meekly await the help of a flash of intuition. The chapter would help her to prepare her mind for the invasion, but it could do no more. She must await the moment.

And on an evening of more than common peace and beauty the moment came. She had put aside *The Higher Common Sense* for half an hour while she partook of her supper, and had opened *Mansfield Park* at random to refresh her spirits.

'It was over, however, at last; and the evening set in with more composure to Fanny . . .'

And suddenly – the flash! It was over indeed: her long indecision and her bewilderment about how to deal with Aunt Ada Doom. In a few seconds she had her plan clearly in her head, with every detail as distinct as though the scheme had already been carried through. Calmly she detached a leaf from her pocket-book and wrote the following telegram:

Hart-Harris,
    Chauncey Grove,
        Chiswick Mall.

Please send at once latest number vogue also prospectus hotel miramar paris and very important photographs fanny ward love Flora.

Then she summoned Mark Dolour's Nancy, who had come in to help with the spring cleaning, and sent her down to the post office in Howling with the telegram.

As Nancy ran off through the clear summer twilight, Flora reverently shut the covers of *The Higher Common Sense*. She needed it no longer. It could remain closed until the next time she encountered a Substance not Included in the Outline. And she retired to bed that night in the calm confidence that she had found the way to deal with Aunt Ada Doom.

There was now only a week to go before the wedding, so Flora hoped very much that Claud would send at once the papers for which she had asked. It would probably take time to deal with Aunt Ada, and no time must be wasted if her aim was to be achieved by the day of the wedding.

But Claud did not fail her. The papers arrived by air-mail at noon next day. They were dropped neatly into the great field by the air-postman, and were accompanied by a plaintive note from Claud asking her what in heck she was up to now? He said that except for the fact that she was larger, she reminded him of a mosquito.

Flora undid the parcel and made quite sure that all the things for which she had asked were there. She then re-coiled her hair and put on a fresh linen dress and (as it was luncheon time) directed Mrs Beetle to give to her the tray upon which was arranged Aunt Ada's lunch.

'Go on. You'll strain yourself,' said Mrs Beetle. 'It weighs about 'alf er 'undredweight.'

But Flora quietly took the tray and (under the awed eyes of Mark Dolour's Nancy, Reuben, Mrs Beetle and Sue, Phoebe, Jane and Letty) she arranged upon it the copy of *Vogue*, the prospectus of the Hotel Miramar in Paris, and the photographs of Fanny Ward.

'I am going to take her lunch up to Aunt Ada,' she announced. 'If I have not come down by three o'clock, Mrs Beetle, will you kindly bring up some lemonade. At half past four you may bring up tea and some of the currant cake Phoebe made last week. If I am not down by seven o'clock, please bring up a tray with supper for two, and we will have hot milk and biscuits at ten. Now, good-bye, all of you. I beg of you not to worry. All will be well.'

And slowly, before the fascinated gaze of the Starkadders and Mrs Beetle, Flora began to mount the stairs which led to Aunt Ada's chamber, bearing the tray of lunch steadily before her. They heard the light sound of her footsteps receding along the corridor; they paused, and the listeners heard, in the airy summer stillness of the house, her tap on the door and her clear voice saying: 'I have brought your lunch, Aunt Ada. May I come in? It is Flora.'

There was a silence. Then the door was heard to open, and Flora and the tray of lunch passed therein.

That was the last that anyone heard or saw of her for nearly nine hours.

At three o'clock, at half past four, and at seven o'clock Mrs Beetle took up the refreshments as she had been instructed. Each time she returned she found the empty plates and cups packed neatly outside the closed door. From within there came the steady rise and fall of voices; but though she listened for many minutes she could not distinguish a word; and this disappointing piece of information was all she had to carry back to the eagerly waiting group downstairs.

At seven o'clock Mr Mybug and Rennet joined the band of watchers, and after waiting until nearly eight o'clock for Flora to come downstairs, they decided that it would be best to begin without her, and made their supper of beef, beer, and pickled onions, pleasantly spiced by anxiety and speculation.

After supper they settled down once more to watch and wait. Mrs Beetle wondered a dozen times if she should not just run up with a few sandwiches and some cocoa at nine, in order to see whether there were any developments to be observed. But Reuben said no, she was not to; she had been told to take up hot milk at ten o'clock, and hot milk at ten she should take; he would not have Flora's instructions disobeyed by the tiniest detail. So she stayed where she was.

They all got very cosy, sitting round the open door in the lingering twilight; and presently Mrs Beetle made them all some barley water, flavoured with lemon, and they sat sipping it comfortably, for their throats were quite sore with talking and wondering what on earth Flora could be saying to Aunt Ada Doom, and recalling details of the farm's history for the past twenty years, and reminding each other what a nuisance old Fig Starkadder had always been, and wondering how Seth was getting on in Hollywood and whether he would run into Amos there, and saying how lovely Elfine's wedding was going to be, and wondering how Urk and Meriam would get on when they were married, and speculating as to what on earth Judith was doing in London, and, if so, why, and who with? It grew slowly dark and cooler outside, and the summer stars came out.

They were talking away so hard that they never heard the clock strike ten, and it was not until nearly a quarter past that Mrs Beetle suddenly made them all jump by leaping from her chair and saying loudly: 'There now! I fergot the milk! I'll ferget me own name next. I'll take it up at once.'

And she was just going over to the range to put wood on to the ashes, when a sound outside made them all start, and turn their heads in the direction of the dark doorway of the kitchen.

Someone was coming slowly downstairs, with light steps that dragged a little.

Reuben stood up and lit a match, which he held above his head. The light grew, and into it, through the dark doorway, walked Flora . . . at last.

She looked composed enough, but rather pale and sleepy, and a curl of her dark gold hair hung loose against her cheek.

'Hullo,' she said, pleasantly, 'you're all here, then? (Hullo, Mr Mybug, surely it's time you were in bed?) Can I have that milk now, please, Mrs Beetle? I'll drink it down here. You need not take any up to Aunt Ada. I've put her to bed. She's asleep.'

There was a gasp of wonder from everybody.

Flora sank into Reuben's empty chair, with a long yawn.

'We was feared for 'ee, soul,' said Letty, reprovingly, after a pause in which lamps were lit and the curtains drawn. Nobody liked to ask any questions, though they were all pop-eyed with curiosity. 'Duna-many times we near came up to fetch 'ee down again.'

'Too nice of you,' said Flora, languidly, with one eye on the preparation of the milk. 'But it was quite all right, really. Everything's settled now. You need not worry, Reuben; there will be no fuss at the wedding or anything. We can go right ahead with the food and the decorations. In fact, everything ought to be rather good, in one way and another.'

'Cousin Flora, no one but 'ee could have done it,' said Reuben simply. 'I – I suppose 'ee wouldn't tell us how 'twas done?'

'Well,' said Flora, diving into the milk, 'it's a long story, you know. We talked for hours. I can't possibly tell you all we said. It would take all night.' Here she repressed a vast yawn. 'You'll see, when the time comes. On the wedding day, I mean. You wait. It will be a surprise. A lovely surprise. I can't tell you now. It would spoil things. You just wait and see. It will be simply lovely. Surprise!'

Her voice had been growing sleepier and sleepier towards the end of her speech, and just as it finally dwindled into silence, Mrs Beetle darted forward and was just too late to catch the glass of milk as it fell from her hand. She was asleep.

'Like a tired child,' said Mr Mybug, who, like most of your brutal intellectuals, was as soft as a cheese underneath. 'Just like a little tired child,' and he was just reaching out in a dreamy, absent kind of way to stroke Flora's hair when Mrs Beetle gave a sharp dab at his hand, exclaiming:

'Paws off, Pompey!' which so much upset him that he marched off home, pursued by the wailing Rennet, without pausing to make any farewells.

Mrs Beetle then shoved Susan, Letty, Phoebe, Prue, and

Jane off to their own chambers, and with the assistance of Reuben roused Flora from her slumber.

She stood up, still very sleepily, and smiled at Reuben as she took her candle from his hand.

'Good night, Cousin Flora. 'Twere a good day for Cold Comfort when first 'ee came here,' he said, looking down at her.

'My dear soul, don't name it. It's been the most enormous diversion to me,' said Flora. 'Just you wait until the wedding day, though. That *is* going to be fun, if you like. Mrs Beetle, you know how I dislike making complaints, but the cutlets Mrs Starkadder and I had for supper were slightly underdone. We both noticed it. Mrs Starkadder's, indeed, was almost *raw*.'

'I'm sorry, I'm sure, Miss Poste,' said Mrs Beetle.

And then everybody went sleepily up to bed.

CHAPTER 21

MIDSUMMER DAY dawned with a thick grey haze in the air and a heavy dew on the meadows and trees.

Down among the little gardens of the still-sleeping cottages of Howling an idyllic procession might have been observed making its way from flower-bed to flower-bed, like ravaging bees. It was none other than the three members of Mrs Beetle's embryo jazz-band, shepherded by the patriarchal form of Agony Beetle himself.

They had been commissioned to pick the bunches of flowers which were to decorate the church and the refreshment-tables up at the farm. A lorry load of pink and white rose-peonies, from Covent Garden, had already been discharged at the gates of the farm; and even now, Mrs Beetle and Flora were crossing and re-crossing the yard with their arms full of sleeping flowers.

Flora noted the heat-haze with joy. It would be a day of heat; brilliant, blue, and radiant.

Adam Lambsbreath had been even earlier astir, making wreaths of wallflowers with which to garland the horns of Feckless, Pointless, Graceless, and Aimless. It was not until he actually came to affix the decorations that he observed that none of the cows had any horns left, and had been forced to fasten the wreaths round their necks and tails instead. This done, he led them forth to their morning pasture, singing a smutty wedding song he had learnt for the marriage of George IV.

As the day emerged from the heat-haze, and the sky grew blue and sunny, the farm buzzed with energy like a hive. Phoebe, Letty, Jane, and Susan were whisking syllabubs in the dairy; Micah carried the pails of ice, in which stood the champagne, down into the darkest and coolest corner of the cellar. Caraway and Harkaway were fixing the awning across from the gate of the yard to the door of the kitchen. Ezra was putting his rows of beans under a net to protect them from damage during the festivities. Mark and Luke were arranging the long trestle tables in the kitchen, while Mrs Beetle and Flora unpacked the silver and linen sent down in crates from a London store. Reuben was filling with water the dozens of jars and vases in which the flowers were to be arranged. Mark Dolour's Nancy was superintending the boiling of two dozen eggs for everybody's breakfast. And upstairs on her bed lay Flora's new dress, a wonder of frilled and quilted, ruffled and tucked, pinked and shirred green batiste, and her plain hat of white straw.

At half past eight everybody sat down to breakfast in the dairy, for the kitchen was being prepared for the reception, and could not be used for meals to-day.

'I'll just take up 'er breakfast,' said Mrs Beetle. 'She'll 'ave to 'ave it cold to-day. There's 'alf an 'am and a jar of pickled onions. I won't be a jiff.'

'Oh, I've just been in to see Aunt Ada,' said Flora, looking up from her breakfast. 'She doesn't want anything for breakfast except a Hell's Angel. Here, give me an egg. I'll mix it for her.' She rose and went over to the newly stocked store cupboard.

Mrs Beetle stared, while Flora tossed an egg, two ounces of brandy, a teaspoonful of cream and some chips of ice in a jam-jar, and everybody else was very interested, too

'There,' said Flora, giving Mrs Beetle the foaming jam-jar. 'You run along upstairs with that.'

So Mrs Beetle ran; but was heard to observe that it would take more than a mess like that to keep *her* stomach from rumbling before one o'clock. As for the other Starkadders, they were considerably intrigued by this dramatic change in Aunt Ada's diet.

'Is the old un gone off again?' asked Reuben anxiously. 'Will she come down and upset everything after all, do 'ee think, Cousin Flora?'

'Not on your sweet life,' said Flora. 'Everything will be all right. Remember, I told you there was going to be a surprise. Well, it's just beginning.'

And the Starkadders were satisfied.

Breakfast over, they all fell to work like demons, for the ceremony was at half past twelve and there was much to be done.

Agony Beetle and the jazz-band arrived with their arms full of nasturtiums, sweet-william, and cherry-pie; and were sent off on a second journey for more.

Reuben, obeying a request from Flora, pulled out from the cupboard in which it was usually kept the large carved chair in which Aunt Ada had sat on the night of the Counting; and Mark and Luke (who were so stupid that they could have been relied upon to lay a mine under the house without commenting upon it) were told to decorate it with wreaths of rose-peonies.

It was half past ten. The awning was up, looking immediately festive, as awnings always do. And in the kitchen the two long trestle tables were decorated and ready.

Flora had arranged two kinds of food for the two kinds of guests she was expecting. For the Starkadders and such of the local thorny peasantry as would attend there were syllabubs, ice-pudding, caviare sandwiches, crab patties, trifle, and champagne. For the County there was cider, cold home-cured ham, home-made bread, and salads made from local fruit. The table from which the County were to feed was rich with cottage flowers. The rosy efflorescence of the peonies floated above the table from which the peasantry would eat.

Wreaths of little flowers, like chains of little gems, hung from the rafters. Their reds, oranges, blues, and pinks glowed against the soft, sooty-black of the ceiling and walls. The air smelled sweet of cherry-pie and fruit salad. Outside the sun flamed in glory; and inside the kitchen there were these sweet smells and cool, delicious-looking food.

Flora took a last look round, and was utterly satisfied.

It was eleven o'clock.

She went upstairs to Aunt Ada's room, knocked at the door, and in response to a crisp: 'Come in, my dear,' entered and shut the door carefully behind her.

Phoebe, who was on her way to her room to put on her wedding array, nudged Susan.

'Did 'ee see that, soul? Ah! there's somethin' strange in the air to-day, love 'ee. And to think on it ... our Rennet is no more a maid! Last night, as ever was, un came to say good-bye to me before un took the twelve-thirty train from Godmere with un's husband-to-be.'

'Was un weepin', poor soul?' inquired Susan.

'Nay; but un said un would feel safer when once the words was said, and un's man could not get away. Well ... 'tes done now, Lord love 'ee. And they will be here for th' breakfast, man and wife, as ever was.'

A hush now fell upon the cool, flower-garlanded, sweet-smelling farm. The sun climbed royally towards his zenith, and the shadows grew shorter. In a dozen bedrooms the Starkadders struggled with their wedding garments. Flora came out of Aunt Ada's room exactly at half past eleven, and went along to her own room.

She was soon dressed. A bathe in cold water, ten minutes brushing of her hair and some business with her make-up boxes, and she emerged, serene, gay, and elegant, and ready for the pleasures of the day.

She went straight down into the kitchen, to reassure herself that everything was still as it should be; and arrived just in time to prevent Mr Mybug, who had arrived unexpectedly early, from picking a cherry off one of the cakes. Rennet was imploring him not to, and he was laughing like a boyish faun (or so *he* thought) and just about to pick at it when Flora sailed in.

'Mr *My*bug!' exclaimed Flora.

He jumped as though he had been stung and gave a boyish laugh.

'Ah, dear lady . . . there you are!'

'Yes. And so are you, I see,' said Flora. 'There is plenty for *everybody*, Mr Mybug. If you are hungry, Mrs Beetle will cut you some bread and butter. How are *you*, Mrs Mybug?' and Flora pressed Rennet's hand graciously, and congratulated her upon her striking toilette, which had been borrowed from one of Mr Mybug's girl friends who drank rather a lot in one way and another and kept a tame boxer in her studio for the sheer love of the thing.

The other Starkadders now began to come downstairs; and as the sound of the church clock coming across the sunny fields now warned them it was twelve, they thought it time to go down to the church.

After a last glance round the flowery kitchen, Flora floated out with one hand on Reuben's arm, and the others followed.

They found quite a big crowd already assembled outside the church, for the wedding had aroused much interest in neighbouring villages, as well as in Howling itself. The little church was crammed, and the only empty seats were those for the County and those in which the party from the farm now took their places.

On rising from her knees, Flora had leisure to study the decorations. They were really charming. Agony Beetle had done them, with the help of Mark Dolour. They had agreed with pleasing unanimity that only white flowers were suitable to Elfine's extreme youth and undoubted purity. So the pews were hung with chains of marguerites, and two tall lilies stood like archangelic trumpets at the end of each pew, lining the aisle. There were many jars filled with white pinks, and the altar steps where the bride would kneel were banked with snowy geraniums.

Flora repressed the unworthy reflection that it reminded her of a White Sale at Messrs Marshall & Snelgrove's, and turned her attention to Letty, Jane, Phoebe, Prue, and Susan, who had all begun to cry. Silently she fitted them all out with clean handkerchiefs from a store previously laid in for this very purpose.

Reuben, very nervous, stood at the door, waiting for Elfine. The sun blazed down outside, the organ wandered softly through a voluntary, and the crowd respectfully buzzed at the County as it came in, bursting with curiosity and wearing its direst hats. The hands on the clock tower jumped on, minute by minute, to the half-hour.

Flora took one cautious glance round the church before she settled down to wait in decorous quietude for the last few minutes.

The church seemed full of Starkadders. They were all there; and all there by her agency, except the four whom she had helped to escape.

There they all were. Enjoying themselves. Having a nice time. And having it in an ordinary human manner. Not having it because they were raping somebody, or beating somebody, or having religious mania or being doomed to silence by a gloomy, earthly pride, or loving the soil with the fierce desire of a lecher, or anything of that sort. No, they were just enjoying an ordinary human event, like any of the millions of ordinary people in the world.

Really, when she thought what they had all been like, only five months ago . . .

She bowed her head. She had accomplished a great work; and had much to be thankful for. And to-day would see her achievements crowned!

At last! The organ struck bravely into 'Here Comes the Bride!' and every head turned towards the door, and every eye fixed itself upon the large car which had just drawn up outside the church. A low murmur of interest went up.

And now the crowd was cheering. Something tall, white, and cool as a cloud detached itself from the car, and floated quickly along the path to the church door.

Here comes the bride! Here is Elfine, pale and serious and starry-eyed, as a bride should be, leaning upon the arm of Reuben. Here is Dick Hawk-Monitor, his pleasant red face betraying none of the nervousness he must feel. Here is Mrs Hawk-Monitor, looking vague in grey; and the healthy Joan Hawk-Monitor in pink organdie (a deplorable choice – quite deplorable, thought Flora, regretfully).

The procession reached the altar steps, and halted.

The music ceased. Into the hush that fell, the vicar's voice broke quickly yet gravely: 'Dearly beloved . . .'

It was not until she was standing in the vestry, smilingly watching the best man (Ralph Pent-Hartigan) kiss the bride, that Flora felt an unusual sensation in the palm of her right-hand glove. She looked down at it, and saw to her surprise and amusement that it was split right across.

She realized then that she had been extremely nervous lest anything should go wrong. But nothing had; and now she was extremely happy.

Susan, Letty, Phoebe, Prue, and Jane were still roaring away like town-bulls, and Flora had to tell them rather sharply not to make such a noise. Several persons had already asked them, in kindly concern, if they were in pain, or had had bad news.

'Of course,' Mr Mybug was explaining to Rennet, who was also crying because she had had only a nasty register-office wedding and no lovely dress or wreath – 'of course, this is all the sheerest barbarism. It's utterly pagan . . . and a bit obscene, too, if we only look below the ritual. That business of throwing the shoe, for instance – '

'Mr Mybug, we are all going up to the farm now. Of course you're coming too?' Flora had interrupted him, she felt, just at the right moment. He hastily promised Rennet another wedding, a proper one, if she would only stop crying, and rushed away with her under his arm after the rest of the party.

CHAPTER 22

IN fifteen minutes they were all going in at the farm gate, chattering and laughing and experiencing that curious exultation which always follows a wedding or a funeral.

And how gay and cheerful the farm looked, with the awning all bravely white and crimson in the sun, and the wreaths of flowers and the rosy clouds of peonies shining out of the darkness of the kitchen, through the open door. And, oh, look! Someone had put a rope of wallflowers and geraniums round the neck of Big Business, who was proudly stamping round the big field, and pausing to stare over the hedge at the wedding guests with his huge, soft eyes.

'What a charming idea. So original,' said Mrs Hawk-Monitor, thinking it was rather indelicate. 'And the cows, I see, are also wreathed. Quite an idea.'

Adam came forward; the desolate Atlantic pools that were his eyes were filmed with the ready tears of ninety years. He stopped in front of Elfine, who looked kindly down at him, and held out to her his cupped hands.

'A wedding present for 'ee, maidy,' he crooned (much to Flora's annoyance, who was afraid the ice would melt and the champagne be tepid). 'A gift for my own wild marsh-tigget.'

And he opened his hands, revealing a marsh-tigget's nest with four pink eggs in it.

'Oh, Adam . . . how sweet of you,' said Elfine, pressing his arm affectionately.

'Put it in thy bosom. 'Twill make 'ee bear four children,' advised Adam, and was proceeding to give further instruction when Flora broke up the meeting by sweeping Adam before her towards the kitchen, with the soothing assurance that Elfine would certainly do as he suggested when she had had something to eat.

She led the way into the room, followed by the bride and bridegroom, Mrs Hawk-Monitor and Joan, Ralph

Pent-Hartigan, Reuben, Micah, Mark, and Luke, Caraway, Harkaway, Ezra, Phoebe, Susan, Letty, Mr Mybug and Rennet, Jane, and, following somewhat in the rear, such minors as Mrs Beetle, Mark Dolour's Nancy, Agony and the jazz-band, Mark Dolour himself, and Urk and Meriam, to say nothing of Mrs Murther from the Condemn'd Man and a number of other worthies whom Reuben considered were entitled, by their connection with the farm, to come to the feast. These included the three farm-hands who worked directly under Mark Dolour, and old Adam himself.

As she crossed the threshold and passed from the hot sunshine into the cool room, Flora suddenly stepped aside, to let the guests have a clear view of the kitchen, and of somebody who rose from a chair wreathed in peonies, greeting them with a ringing cry:

'So here you all are! Welcome to Cold Comfort!'

And a handsome old lady, dressed from head to foot in the smartest flying kit of black leather, advanced to meet the astounded party. Her hands were stretched out in welcome.

A roar of amazement broke from Micah, who never did have any tact, anyway.

''Tes Aunt Ada! 'Tes Aunt Ada Doom!'

And the others, released from their first frozen shock of surprise, broke also into ejaculations of amazement:

'Why, so 'tes!'

''Tes terrible!'

''Tes flying in the face of Nature!'

'Aye . . . and in trousers, too! Do 'ee mark 'em, lovee?'

'The first time these twenty year . . .'

'She'm rising eighty.'

''Tes enough to kill her.'

'Dear me . . . how delightful . . . so unexpected. How do you do, Miss Doom . . . or should I say Mrs Starkadder? . . . so confusing.'

'Oh, *Grandmother*!'

''Tes the old un herself!'

'Well, you could knock me down with a warming-pan! Miracles will never cease!'

'Aye . . . fruit and flower, by their growth 'ee shall know 'em! That I should live to see this day!'

Aunt Ada stood in smiling silence while the roar of voices gradually subsided. She glanced once or twice at Flora, with raised eyebrows, and her friendly smile deepened into one of amusement.

At last she held up her hand. Silence immediately fell. She said:

'Well, good people, all this is very flattering, but if I am to spend any time with my granddaughter and the rest of you, we must hurry up and begin the wedding breakfast. I leave for Paris by air in less than an hour.'

On this, confusion broke forth again. The Starkadders were so flabbergasted, so knocked clean out of the perpendicular by the bosom-shattering stupendosity of the event, that nothing but a good deal of food could persuade them to shut their mouths.

So Flora and Ralph Pent-Hartigan (she was beginning to approve of that young man: he had the rudiments) caught up plates of crab patties and began to circulate among the guests, persuading everybody to begin to eat and keep up their strength.

Then Elfine, roused from her fascinated stare at her grandmother by a gentle touch from Flora, cut the wedding cake; and the feast officially began.

Soon everybody was enjoying themselves tremendously. The shattering surprise of Aunt Ada's appearance gave everybody something to talk about, and enhanced the delicious flavours of the food they ate. It would, of course, have been even more stimulating to the appetite if she had appeared in her usual clothes and with her usual manner, and tried to stop the wedding, and had been defied by the Starkadders in a body. That *would* have been worth seeing, if you like. However, one cannot have everything, and what there was, was good.

After she had moved around a little among the guests,

and said a few pleasant phrases to everyone, Aunt Ada sat down again in her flowery chair, and addressed herself to champagne and some caviare sandwiches.

Flora sat by her side, also eating caviare. She thought it best to watch over her handiwork up to the last minute. In only half an hour the aeroplane which was to take Aunt Ada to Paris would land in Ticklepenny's Field. But a lot of things could happen in half an hour. Apparently, Aunt Ada had thoroughly realized what a nasty time she had had for twenty years, and had now made up her mind to have a nice one. But you never knew.

So there Flora sat, watching her aunt, smiling occasionally at people from under the brim of her hat, and seeking an opening in the conversation with her aunt to introduce her rights; those mysterious rights Judith had mentioned in her first letter to Flora nearly six months ago.

Soon it came. Aunt Ada was in excellent spirits. She thanked Flora for the hundredth time for pointing out to her what a nice time was had by Miss Fanny Ward, who looked so much younger than she really was; and for telling her how luxurious was the Hôtel Miramar in Paris, and emphasizing what a pleasant life could be had in this world by a handsome, sensible old lady of good fortune, blessed with a sound constitution and a firm will.

'And I will remember, my dear,' she was saying, 'to preserve my personality, as you advise. You shall not find me plucking my eyebrows, nor dieting, nor doting on a boy of twenty-five. I am very grateful to you, my pippet. What pretty thing shall I send you from Paris?'

'A work-box, please. Mine is wearing out,' said Flora, promptly. 'But, Aunt Ada, there is something else you can do for me, too, if you will. What was the wrong that Amos did to my father, Robert Poste? And what are my "rights", of which Judith used to speak? I feel that I cannot let you go off on your tour without asking you.'

Aunt Ada's face grew grave. She glanced round the kitchen, and observed with satisfaction that everybody was eating much too hard and talking much too fast to take any notice of anyone else. She put her wrinkled hand over Flora's cool young one, and drew her towards her, until aunt and niece were both sheltered by the curving brim of Flora's hat. Then she began to speak in a quick murmur. She spoke for several moments. An observer would not have noted much change in Flora's attentive face. At last the murmur ceased. Flora lifted her head, and asked:

'And did the goat die?'

But at this very second Aunt Ada's attention was distracted by Elfine and Dick, who came up to her accompanied by Adam. Flora's question went unheard, and she did not care to repeat it in front of the others.

'Grandmother, Adam wants to come to live at Hautcouture Hall with us, and look after our cows,' said Elfine. 'May he? We should so like him to. He knows all about cows, you know.'

'By all means, my dear,' said Aunt Ada, graciously. 'But who will care for Feckless, Graceless, Pointless, and Aimless if he deserts them?'

A piercing cry broke from Adam. He flung himself forward. His gnarled hands were knotted in anguish.

'Nay, niver say that, Mrs Starkadder, ma'am. I'll take 'em wi' me, all four on 'em. There's room for us all at Howchiker Hall.'

'It sounds like the finale of the first act in a musical comedy,' observed Aunt Ada. 'Well, well, you may take them if you want to.'

'Bless 'ee. Now bless 'ee, Mrs Starkadder, ma'am,' crooned Adam, and hurried away to tell the cows to make ready for their journey that very afternoon.

'And did the goat die? And what about my rights?' asked Flora, a little louder this time. Dash it, the thing must be straightened out.

But it was no use. Mrs Hawk-Monitor chose that identical second to come up to Aunt Ada, murmuring that she was so sorry that Mrs Starkadder was going away at once, and that none of them would have an opportunity of seeing her during the summer, but that she must come to dinner the very moment she returned from her world-tour, and Aunt Ada said that *she* was so sorry, too, but would be delighted to.

So Flora's question was not answered.

And it was fated never to be answered. For the next interruption was the high, sinister drone of an aeroplane engine, so near that it could be heard even above the roar of conversation in the kitchen; and the youngest member of the jazz-band (who had gone out into Ezra's bean rows to be quietly sick from too many crab patties) came rushing in, his sickness forgotten, proclaiming that there was an aeroplane, an aeroplane, falling into Ticklepenny's Field.

Everybody at once charged out into the garden to look at it, except Mrs Hawk-Monitor, Flora, the bride and bridegroom, and Aunt Ada. In face of the bustle of buckling Aunt Ada into her kit, and exchanging embraces and messages and promises to write and to meet at Hautcouture Hall at Christmas, Flora could not put her question a third time. It would have been ill-bred. She must just relinquish her rights – whatever they might be – and be resigned never to know whether the goat died or not.

Everybody streamed out across the fields to see Aunt Ada off. The pilot (a dark, cross-looking young man) was presented, to his obvious repugnance, with a piece of wedding cake. They all stood round the machine laughing and talking, while Agony Beetle dashed somebody else's glass of champagne over the propeller, and Aunt Ada made her farewells.

Then she climbed into the cockpit and settled herself comfortably. She tucked her chin deeper into her helmet, and looked down with smiling benevolence on the assembled Starkadders. Flora, standing close to the machine, had her shoulder patted, and was thanked again, in a low voice, for the transformation she had achieved in her aunt's life.

Flora smiled prettily; but could not help feeling a bit disappointed about the goat and the rights.

The propeller began to revolve. The machine trembled.

'Three cheers for Aunt Ada!' cried Urk, flinging his voleskin cap into the air. They were just at the beginning of the third 'Hurrah!' when the machine took a run forward and rose from the ground.

It skimmed the hedge, and rose to the level of the elms and above them. The crowd had a last glimpse of Aunt Ada's confident face turned over her shoulder to smile. She waved; and, still waving, was carried from their sight into the heavens.

'Now let's go back and drink a good deal more,' suggested Ralph Pent-Hartigan, taking Flora's hand in a familiar but rather pleasing way. 'Dick and the *sposa* will be taking off in half an hour, you know. Their plane is timed for three-thirty.'

'Goodness . . . it's nothing but people going off in aeroplanes,' said Flora, rather crossly. 'I had best go and help Elfine change her dress.'

And so, while all the others flowed back into the kitchen and sank their fangs into what was left of the provender, she slipped upstairs to Elfine's room, and helped her to put on her blue going-away suit. Elfine was very happy and not at all tearful or nervous.

She embraced Flora warmly, thanked her a thousand times for her goodness, and promised solemnly never to forget all the good advice Flora had given her. The latter placed in her hands a copy of *The Higher Common Sense*, suitably inscribed, and they went downstairs together affectionately entwined.

The second aeroplane came down in the Big Field opposite the farm, punctual to the second. (Big Business had been led away by Micah a few moments previously – a suggestion from some of the blither spirits to the effect that it should be left there 'to see what he makes of the aeroplane' having been vetoed by Flora.)

The second departure was noisier than the first. The Starkadders were not used to drinking champagne. But they liked it all right. There was a great deal of cheering, and some tears from Susan, Prue, Letty, Phoebe and Jane, and Meriam, and some thunderings from Micah warning Dick to be good to his lily-flower.

Flora took advantage of the scrimmage to slip back to the kitchen and warn Mrs Beetle, who was sombrely beginning to tidy up, not to open any more champagne.

'Only in case of illness, Miss Poste,' promised Mrs Beetle.

When Flora got back to the field the aeroplane was just rising from the ground. She smiled up at Elfine's lovely little face framed by the black flying-cap, and Elfine blew her a tender kiss. The roar of the engine swelled to a triumphant thunder. They were gone.

'Well, *now* will you come back and drink a good deal more?' asked Ralph Pent-Hartigan, showing an inclination to put his arm round Flora's waist.

Flora dodged him, with her prettiest smile. She *was* so wishing that everybody would go home. The wedding breakfast seemed to have been going on for ever. Except that this was a cheerful occasion and the other had been a dismal one, it reminded her of the Counting...

('Oh,' she thought, 'and I shall never know what it was that Aunt Ada saw in the woodshed. How I wish I had asked her about that as well.')

In the kitchen the party was at last showing signs of breaking up. All the food was eaten. All the drink had gone long ago. The pretty ropes of flowers were fading in the heat. The floor was littered with crumpled paper napkins, cigarette stubs, crushed flowers, champagne corks, spilt water. The air seemed to sink under its burden of tobacco smoke and mingled smells. Only the rose-peonies were unharmed. The heat had made them open to their full extent, so that they showed their hearts of gold. Flora put her nose into one. It smelled sweet and cool.

She endeavoured to compose her spirits. She was conscious that for the last hour they had been agitated and melancholy. What could be the matter with her? She wished only to be alone.

It was with some difficulty that, in saying good-bye to everybody at the door of the kitchen, she maintained an air of cheerfulness. But she was comforted by the fact that everybody seemed to have had a perfectly lovely time. Everyone, especially Mrs Hawk-Monitor, congratulated her upon the organization of the wedding breakfast and the deliciousness of the food and the elegance of the decorations.

She received invitations to dine with the Hawk-Monitors next week, to visit Mr Mybug and Rennet at the studio (with sink) in which they proposed to live in Fitzroy Square. Urk and Meriam said that they would be honoured if Miss Poste would come to tea at 'Byewaies', the villa which Urk had bought out of his savings from the water-vole trade, and into which he and his bride would move next week.

Flora thanked them all smilingly, and promised to go to all of them.

One by one the guests departed, and the Starkadders, sleepy with champagne and the novelty of enjoying themselves in a normal manner, slipped away to their bedrooms to sleep it off. The figure of the last guest, Agony Beetle, disappeared over the curve of the hill on the path that led down to Howling, accompanied by the jazz-band. Quiet, which had been driven from the farm at six o'clock that morning, began timidly to creep out of shadowy corners and to take possession of it once more.

'Miss Poste. You look done up. Come for a run in the old bouncer?' said Ralph Pent-Hartigan, who was about to start up his eight-cylinder Volupté which stood in the yard.

Flora came down the two little steps leading from the kitchen door and crossed the yard to the car.

'I don't think I'll come for a run, thanks,' she said. 'But it would be very kind of you if you would take me down into the village. I want to telephone.'

He was delighted. He made her get in beside him at once, and soon they were spinning down the hill into Howling. The speed made a wind of grateful coolness that fanned their flushed cheeks.

'I suppose you wouldn't care to dine with me in Town

to-night? Marvellous evening. We might dance at the New River, if you like?'

'I would have loved it, but the fact is I've just made up my mind to leave the farm to-night. I shall have packing and things to do. I'm so sorry. Some other time it would be delightful.'

'Well . . . but . . . look here, couldn't I run you back?'

The car stopped outside the post office. Flora got out.

'Again, I'm so sorry,' she said, smiling into his disappointed young face, 'but I think my cousin is going to fetch me. I'm just going to see if he is at home. We made the arrangement months ago.'

Fortunately there was only a delay of a few minutes to the Hertfordshire exchange. Flora, waiting in the stuffy telephone box, was not in the mood to be sensible about delays. She had not even started to fume when the bell rang, sounding deafening in that narrow space.

She took off the receiver, and listened.

'Hullo,' said Charles's quiet, deep voice, seventy miles away. It was made tiny by distance, but not less musical.

She gave a little gasp.

'Oh . . . hullo, Charles. Is that you? This is Flora. Look here, are you doing anything to-night?'

'Not if you want me.'

'Well . . . could you be an absolute angel, and come and fetch me away from the farm to-night in Speed Cop the Second? We've had a wedding here to-day, and I've tidied everything up. I mean there's nothing left for me to do here. And I really am tired. I would like to be fetched . . . if you could . . .'

'*I'm coming*,' said the deep voice. 'What time may I be there? Is there a big field near the house?'

'Oh, yes, just outside. Can you be here by eight, do you think? It's nearly five o'clock now.'

'Of course. I'll be there at eight.'

There was a pause.

'Charles,' said Flora.

'Yes?'

228

'Charles ... I mean, it isn't putting you out or anything?'

Smiling, she hung up the receiver to the tiny distant sound of Charles's laughter.

CHAPTER 23

YOUNG Pent-Hartigan drove her back to the farm. She said good-bye to him and promised to dine with him very soon. Then he drove off; and with the retreating noise of his engine the last invader of the farm's quietude was gone. Quiet flowed back into the sunny empty rooms like the returning sea. The only sounds were the tiny ones of a summer's day that is drawing towards evening.

Flora went upstairs and changed from her party dress into a tweed suit in which she could fly without feeling cold. She brushed her hair and cooled her hands and forehead with eau-de-Cologne. Then she packed, and labelled her trunk for 1 Mouse Place. It would be sent off to-morrow. She took with her only the *Pensées, The Higher Common Sense,* and what Chaucer has summed up for all time as 'a bag of needments'.

It was six o'clock when she came slowly downstairs again. The kitchen was tidy and empty. All signs of the feast had been cleared away. Only the awning was left, its stripes of red and white glowing against the deep blue sky of early evening. The shadows of the bean rows were long across the garden, and their flowers were transparent red in the sunlight. All was cool, quiet, blessedly peaceful. Flora's supper was neatly laid, and of the Starkadders there was not a sign. She supposed that they must all be asleep upstairs or else gone a-mollocking off to Godmere. She hoped they would not come downstairs before she left. She loved them all dearly, but this evening she just did not want to see them any more.

She sat down, with a sigh, in a comfortable deep chair, and relaxed her limbs. She would sit here, she thought, until half past six; then she would eat her supper; and then go out into the Big Field and sit on the stile under the may-tree and wait for Charles.

Her dreamy musings were interrupted by the distant soft jangling of bells. She recognized the sound: it was made by the bells that (copying a heathen foreign fashion he had once seen demonstrated on the talkies) Adam had hung round the necks of Graceless, Pointless, Feckless, and Aimless.

Even as she listened a procession came into sight. It wound across the winding path which she could see, silhouetted against the blue sky and held as if in a frame by the open door, from where she sat.

It was Adam and the cows, on their way to Hautcouture Hall.

Adam went first, wearing his ancient hat and his age-green corduroys. The liddle mop was slung round his neck. His head was lifted to the sinking sun, whose strong rays turned him to gold. He was singing the bawdy song he had learned for the wedding of George IV.

Behind him came the cows in single file, still wreathed with their wedding garlands of wallflowers. They swung their heads in lowly content, and their bells chimed in time to Adam's singing.

Slowly they passed across the frame of the doorway. Then they were gone. Nothing could be seen save the green path, rising away into the empty blue of the evening sky. The dying sound of the bells came back to Flora, softly and more softly until it was lost in silence.

Smiling, Flora drew her chair to the table and ate her supper. She did not think of anything, except that in an hour she would see Charles, and tell him about everything she had done, and hear what he had to say about it all.

When she had finished her supper she wrote an affectionate little letter to Reuben, explaining that her work at the farm was now finished, and that she felt she would like to go back to Town. She promised to come down again very soon to see them all, and enclosed a pound note and her earnest thanks for Mrs Beetle.

She left the note open on the table, where everybody could read it, and not even a Starkadder could be alarmed by it or mysterious about it. Then she slipped on her coat, picked up her bag of needments, and sauntered out into the cool evening.

The Big Field was covered with long, fresh grass which threw millions of tiny lengthening shadows. There was not a breath of wind. It was the loveliest hour of the English year: seven o'clock on Midsummer Night.

Flora crossed the grass to the stile, the cool grass swishing against her ankles. She sat down on the step of the stile, leaning back comfortably against the gate part, and stared up into the black boughs of the may-tree. Beneath, they were in shadow. Above, they held their white flowers and green leaves up into the gold of the last sun-rays She could see the flowers and leaves dazzling against the pure sky.

The shadows grew slowly longer. A cold, fresh smell came up out of the grass and fell from the trees. The birds began their sleep song.

The sun had almost disappeared behind the black traceries of the may-hedge on the far side of the field. Such of his rays as struck through the branches were still, heavy, and of the softest gold.

The air cooled slowly. Flowers shut before Flora's very eyes, but gave out fragrance still. Now there were more shadows than light. The last blackbird that always flies chattering across a summer evening's quiet came dashing down the meadow and vanished in the may-hedge.

The country-side was falling asleep. Flora drew her coat round her, and looked up into the darkening vault of the sky. Then she glanced at her watch. It was five to eight. Her ears had caught a steady, recurrent murmur that might or might not have been the beating of her own blood.

In another moment the sound was the only one in the whole heaven. The aeroplane appeared over the top of the may-hedge, swooping downwards. The under-carriage touched the earth, and then it was taxi-ing comfortably to a standstill.

Flora had stood up as it came in sight. Now she went down the field towards it. The pilot was getting out of the cockpit, loosening his helmet, looking towards her. He came across the grass to meet her, swinging his helmet in his hand, his black hair ruffled by the way he had dragged off the cap.

It was purest happiness to see him. It was like meeting again a dearest friend whom one has loved for long years, and missed in silence. Flora went straight into his open arms, put her own round his neck, and kissed him with all her heart.

Presently Charles said:

'This is for ever, isn't it?'

And Flora whispered: 'For ever.'

It was nearly dark. The stars and moon were out, and the may-trees glimmering. Flora and Charles sighed at last, looked at one another and laughed, and Charles said:

'Look here, I think we ought to go home, you know, darling. Mary's waiting for us at Mouse Place. She got back a day earlier. What do you think? We can talk when we get there.'

'I don't mind,' said Flora, placidly. 'Charles, you do smell nice. Is it stuff you put on your hair, or what? Oh, it is nice to think what years we have got in which to find out things like that! Quite fifty years I should think, wouldn't you, Charles?'

Charles said he hoped so; and added that he did not put stuff on his hair. He also added inconsequently that he was glad he had been born.

They were both in rather a state of dither, but Charles finally pulled himself together, and began to jab purposefully at the interior of the aeroplane, while Flora hovered round telling him all about what she had done at Cold Comfort, and also about Mr Mybug; and Charles laughed, but he said Mr Mybug was a little tick and Flora ought to be more careful. He also said she was the Local Busybody, adding that he did not approve of people who interfered with other people's lives.

Flora heard this with delight.

'Shall I be allowed to interfere with yours?' she asked. Like all really strong-minded women, on whom everybody flops, she adored being bossed about. It was so restful.

'No,' said Charles. And he grinned at her disrespectfully, and she noticed how white and even his teeth were.

'Charles, you have got *heavenly* teeth.'

'Don't fuss,' said Charles. 'Now, are you ready, my dearest darling? Because I am, and so's Speed Cop. We'll be home in half an hour. Oh, Flora, I'm so unbearably happy. I can't believe it's true.' He snatched her roughly into his arms, and looked longingly down into her face. 'It *is* true, isn't it? Say "I love you".'

And Flora, unutterably moved, told him just how much she did.

They climbed into the aeroplane. The roar of the propeller rose into the exquisite stillness of the night. Soon they were rising above the elms, that were faintly silvered by the moon, and the country-side lay spread beneath them.

'Say it again.'

She saw Charles's lips move, as the farm dropped away beneath them, and guessed what he was saying.

He was fully occupied with keeping the machine clear of the topmost branches of the elms, and could not look at her, but she saw by his troubled profile that he feared (so fantastically beautiful was the night and this discovery of their love) that it might be some cruel mistake.

Flora put her warm lips close to his cap.

'I love you,' she said. He could not hear her very well, but he turned for a second, and, comforted, smiled into her eyes.

She glanced upwards for a second at the soft blue vault of the midsummer night sky. Not a cloud misted its solemn depths. To-morrow would be a beautiful day.

PENGUIN ESSENTIALS

EVA LUNA/ISABEL ALLENDE

'My name is Eva, which means "life", according to a book of names my mother consulted. I was born in the back room of a shadowy house, and grew up amidst ancient furniture, books in Latin, and human mummies, but none of those things made me melancholy, because I came into the world with a breath of the jungle in my memory.'

Isabel Allende tells the sweet and sinister story of an orphan who beguiles the world with her astonishing visions, triumphing over the worst of adversity and bringing light to a dark place.

'A heartfelt novel, powerful enough to make a dictator cry' *Evening Standard*

OUT OF AFRICA/KAREN BLIXEN

'I had a farm in Africa, at the foot of the Ngong Hills . . . Up in this high air you breathed easily . . . you woke up in the morning and thought: Here I am, where I ought to be.'

From the moment Karen Blixen arrived in Kenya in 1914 to manage a coffee plantation, her heart belonged to Africa. Drawn to the intense colours and ravishing landscapes, Blixen spent her happiest years on the farm, and her experiences and friendships with the people around her are vividly recalled in these memoirs.

Out of Africa is the story of a remarkable and unconventional woman, and of a way of life that has vanished for ever.

'A compelling story of passion and a movingly poetic tribute to a lost land' *The Times*

PENGUIN ESSENTIALS

A CLOCKWORK ORANGE/ANTHONY BURGESS

'What we were after was lashings of ultraviolence'

In this nightmare vision of youth in revolt, fifteen-year-old Alex and his friends set out on a diabolical orgy of robbery, rape, torture and murder. Alex is jailed for his teenage delinquency and the State tries to reform him – but at what cost?

Social prophecy? Black comedy? Study of freewill? *A Clockwork Orange* is all of these. It is also a dazzling experiment in language, as Burgess creates a new language – 'nadsat', the teenage slang of a not-too-distant future.

'A gruesomely witty cautionary tale' *Time*

BREAKFAST AT TIFFANY'S/TRUMAN CAPOTE

'What I've found does the most good is just to get into a taxi and go to Tiffany's. It calms me down right away, the quietness and the proud look of it; nothing very bad could happen to you there, not with those kind men in their nice suits...'

Meet Holly Golightly – a free spirited, lop-sided romantic girl about town. With her tousled blond hair and upturned nose, dark glasses and chic black dresses, Holly is a style sensation wherever she goes. Her apartment rocks to Martini-soaked parties and she plays hostess to millionaires and gangsters alike. Yet Holly never loses sight of her ultimate dream – to find a real life place like Tiffany's that makes her feel at home.

Full of sharp wit and exuberant, larger-than-life characters which vividly capture the restless, madcap era of 1940s New York, *Breakfast at Tiffany's* will make you fall in love, perhaps for the first time, with a book.

'The most romantic story ever written' Alex James, *Guardian*

PENGUIN ESSENTIALS

MY FAMILY AND OTHER ANIMALS/GERALD DURRELL

'What we all need,' said Larry, 'is sunshine…a country where we can *grow*.'

'Yes, dear, that would be nice,' agreed Mother, not really listening.

'I had a letter from George this morning – he says Corfu's wonderful. Why don't we pack up and go to Greece?'

'Very well, dear, if you like,' said Mother unguardedly.

Escaping the ills of the British climate, the Durrell family – acne-ridden Margo, gun-toting Leslie, bookworm Lawrence and budding naturalist Gerry, along with their long suffering mother and Roger the dog – take off for the island of Corfu. But the Durrells find that, reluctantly, they must share their various villas with a menagerie of local fauna – among them scorpions, geckos, toads, bats and butterflies.

Recounted with immense humour and charm *My Family and Other Animals* is a wonderful account of a rare, magical childhood.

'A bewitching book' *Sunday Times*

THE GREAT GATSBY/F. SCOTT FITZGERALD

'There was music from my neighbour's house through the summer nights. In his blue gardens men and girls came and went like moths among the whisperings and the champagne and the stars.'

Everybody who is anybody is seen at the glittering parties held in millionaire Jay Gatsby's mansion in West Egg, east of New York. The riotous throng congregates in his sumptuous garden, coolly debating Gatsby's origins and mysterious past. None of the frivolous socialites understands him and among various rumours is the conviction that 'he killed a man'. A detached onlooker, Gatsby is oblivious to the speculation he creates, but always seems to be watching and waiting, though no one knows what for.

As the tragic story unfolds, Gatsby's destructive dreams and passions are revealed, leading to disturbing consequences. A brilliant evocation of 1920s high society, *The Great Gatsby* peels away the layers of this glamorous world to display the coldness and cruelty at its heart.

'Not only a page-turner and a heartbreaker, it's one of the most quintessentially American novels ever written' *Time*

PENGUIN ESSENTIALS

ON THE ROAD/JACK KEROUAC

'What's your road, man? — holyboy road, madman road, rainbow road, guppy road, any road. It's an anywhere road for anybody anyhow.'

Sal Paradise, young and innocent, joins the slightly crazed Dean Moriarty on a breathless, exuberant ride back and forth across the United States. Their hedonistic search for release or fulfilment through drink, sex, drugs and jazz becomes an exploration of personal freedom, a test of the limits of the American Dream.

A brilliant blend of fiction and autobiography, Jack Kerouac's exhilarating novel defined the new 'Beat' generation and became the bible of the counter culture.

'Pop writing at its best. It changed the way I saw the world, making me yearn for fresh experience' Hanif Kureishi, *Independent on Sunday*

LADY CHATTERLEY'S LOVER/D.H. LAWRENCE

'Connie was aware, however, of a growing restlessness ... It thrilled inside her body, in her womb, somewhere, till she felt she must jump into water and swim to get away from it; a mad restlessness. It made her heart beat violently for no reason ...'

Lady Constance Chatterley is trapped in a loveless marriage to a man who is impotent. Oppressed by her dreary life, she is drawn to Mellors the gamekeeper. Breaking out against the constraints of society she yields to her instinctive desire for him and discovers the transforming power of physical love which leads them both towards fulfilment.

Banned for many years for its frank depiction of sex, *Lady Chatterley's Lover* was first published by Penguin in 1960 and was at the centre of a sensational obscenity trial at the Old Bailey. D. H. Lawrence himself called it 'the most improper novel in the world'.

'No one ever wrote better about the power struggles of sex and love' Doris Lessing

PENGUIN ESSENTIALS

STEPPENWOLF/HERMANN HESSE

'The unhappiness that I need and long for ... is of the kind that will let me suffer with eagerness and die with lust. That is the unhappiness, or happiness, that I am waiting for.'

Alienated from society, Harry Haller is the Steppenwolf, wild, strange and shy. His despair and desire for death draw him into an enchanted, Faustian underworld. Through a series of shadowy encounters – romantic, freakish and savage by turn – Haller begins to rediscover the lost dreams of his youth.

Adopted by the Sixties counterculture, *Steppenwolf* captured the mood of a disaffected generation that was beginning to question everything.

'The gripping and fascinating story of disease in a man's soul, and a savage indictment of bourgeois society' *New York Times*

LOLITA/VLADIMIR NABOKOV

'Lolita, light of my life, fire of my loins. My sin, my soul. Lo-lee-ta: the tip of my tongue taking a trip of three steps down the palate to tap, at three, on the teeth. Lo. Lee. Ta.'

Humbert Humbert is a middle-aged, frustrated college professor. In love with his landlady's twelve-year-old daughter Lolita, he'll do anything to possess her. Unable and unwilling to stop himself, he is prepared to commit any crime to get what he wants.

Is he in love or insane? A silver-tongued poet or a pervert? A tortured soul or a monster? Or is he all of these?

'You read Lolita sprawling limply in your chair, ravished, overcome, nodding scandalized assent' Martin Amis, *Observer*

PENGUIN ESSENTIALS

The Penguin Essentials are some of the twentieth-century's most important books. When they were first published they changed the way we thought about literature and about life. And they have remained vital reading ever since. These new, stylish editions remind readers that once upon a time each book in the Essentials series was the only book worth being seen with.

Eva Luna by Isabel Allende
Out of Africa by Karen Blixen
A Clockwork Orange by Anthony Burgess
Breakfast at Tiffany's by Truman Capote
My Family and Other Animals by Gerald Durrell
The Great Gatsby by F. Scott Fitzgerald
A Room with a View by E.M. Forster
Cold Comfort Farm by Stella Gibbons
Goodbye to All That by Robert Graves
Steppenwolf by Hermann Hesse
On the Road by Jack Kerouac
Lady Chatterley's Lover by D.H. Lawrence
Lolita by Vladimir Nabokov
Wide Sargasso Sea by Jean Rhys
Bonjour Tristesse by Françoise Sagan
Hell's Angels by Hunter S. Thompson
A Confederacy of Dunces by John Kennedy Toole
Cat's Cradle by Kurt Vonnegut
Brideshead Revisited by Evelyn Waugh

PENGUIN ESSENTIALS

BONJOUR TRISTESSE/FRANÇOISE SAGAN

'Late into the night we talked of love, of its complications. In my father's eyes they were imaginary. . . This conception of rapid, violent and passing love affairs appealed to my imagination. I was not at the age when fidelity is attractive. I knew very little about love.'

The French Riviera: home to the Beautiful People. And none are more beautiful than Cécile, a precocious seventeen-year-old, and her father Raymond, a vivacious libertine. Charming, decadent and irresponsible, the golden-skinned duo are dedicated to a life of free love, fast cars and hedonistic pleasures. But then, one long, hot summer Raymond decides to marry, and Cécile and her lover Cyril feel compelled to take a hand in his amours, with tragic consequences.

Bonjour Tristesse scandalized 1950s France with its portrayal of teenager *terrible* Cécile, a heroine who rejects conventional notions of love, marriage and responsibility to choose her own sexual freedom.

'A funny, thoroughly immoral and thoroughly French tale' *The Times*

A CONFEDERACY OF DUNCES/JOHN KENNEDY TOOLE

'This city is famous for its gamblers, prostitutes, exhibitionists, anti-Christs, alcoholics, sodomites, drug addicts, fetishists, onanists, pornographers, frauds, jades, litterbugs, and lesbians . . . don't make the mistake of bothering *me*.'

Ignatius J. Reilly: fat, flatulent, eloquent and almost unemployable. By the standards of ordinary folk he is pretty much unhinged, too. But is he bothered by this?

No. For this misanthropic crusader against an America fallen into vice and ignorance has a mission: to rescue a naked female philosopher in distress. And he has a pirate costume and hot-dog cart to do it with . . .

'A fine funny novel. This is the kind of book one wants to keep quoting from' Anthony Burgess